Secret SURRENDER

HARLOW SERIES BOOK TWO

KATERINA SIMMS

One

Sarah Overton sat on a fallen log along the edges of the Annual Harlow soiree, her hand lifted in a half-hearted wave at Emilia Bonacci. *Radiant Emilia.* She stood across the clearing with her fingers curved around the crook of Blaine Callaghan's arm. Her coffee-colored curls entwined about her dainty jasmine crown, her rose-pink fairy costume only adding to her overall angelic glow and her sweet, apologetic smile.

Sarah's stomach hardened. The immaculate woman made hating her impossible. Meanwhile, Blaine—Sarah's ex-fiancé—shone with pride, his emerald gaze permanently fixed on his new girlfriend.

Sarah turned away and opted to stare at the thicket of trees ahead. Sure, she wanted Blaine, a man she'd dated for three whole years, to be happy. But not *this* happy.

Crack!

A golf-ball sized rock smacked into the tree next to her head, ripping her mind away from her deep remorse.

"Oh man, you missed." Aaron Chadley's wobbly teenage voice had her twisting toward the bushes behind her. Presumably, he berated his brother. "Your aim sucks, Weasel."

As if being sidelined at this party wasn't humiliating enough, the music slowed and couples cuddled together. Sarah groaned, intent not to encourage the boy and his two equally annoying siblings with any kind of protest. What with Blaine and Emilia's earlier saccharine scene, the loved-up dancing couples now, and the ever-irritating Chadley brothers... maybe it was time to leave.

She'd taken in Mirabella Falls and its wooded perfection, the soiree's candy stands, costumed guests, and twinkling fairy lights. Enough people had seen her here that maybe tomorrow's town whispers about the state of her jilted and broken heart would simply not happen.

Any minute now, she'd get up and get on with her life. A quiet life. One she would have had if she'd never decided to fall in love.

Unlike all the other under thirty-year-olds in this town, she wasn't all that enamored with change or drama. She hated surprises, preferred stability. Heck, craved sameness and having control of what happened to her next.

Crack! Crack!

More rocks. *Fudging Chadleys!*

She dipped her chin to her overly long costume's crushed turquoise velvet.

Ignore them. Just ignore them.

Crack! Crack! Crack!

Right, well, since she was about to leave anyway...

She shot to her feet, the center of her chest all prickly and hot, her gaze darting over the crowd.

The Chadley parents were nowhere, their absence in itself enough to light her desire to drag those pesky little beasts out and return them to their handlers. Even if she did hate playing mom to other people's kids.

She stormed into the dense brush behind her, pine twigs snapping underfoot, determined to end the Chadley reign of terror, then go home *alone.* Just like she'd planned. A plan she would never stray from again.

The tangle of branches in her way wasn't enough to stop her, nor the mild scratches those branches left behind, her bare forearms lined in red welts. Despite the fairy dress and her long blond hair, the Chadleys were about to find out that she was far from Harlow's sweet and wilting flower. She could and would damn well defend herself.

She yanked her long hem, the heavy material dragging behind her, all while she grumbled under her breath. The warm Minnesotan night hugged her from every angle. The theme for this year's soiree was *A Midsummer Night's Dream*—perfect, given the spring season, late hour, and wooded location. But hell, Shakespearean costumes were *not* great for traipsing through forests.

And yes, she'd put others' happiness above her own, her lack of festive spirit largely her fault—not that she'd had much choice when it came to Blaine and Emilia—but the Chadley boys simply added to her current misery.

So much for doing the right thing. The *right thing* felt less fuzzy and warm, more stabby and excruciating, like a blunt knife to an already bruised and tortured heart.

She stopped in a clearing and peered about.

"Okay, fine." Her raised voice disappeared into the trees around her, but she listened for the expected sounds of the Chadleys' laughter and rustling leaves. "I tried. So if you get lost, I'm not taking the blame. You hear?"

She scanned her dark surroundings once more. The soiree lights faded in the distance, a warning not to wander too far.

Her shoulders rolled forward, and she blew out a hard breath. Time to head home. In a quick few minutes, she'd be in the parking lot, ready to drive away. Meanwhile, her long hem had caught on another gnarled branch, and her escape wouldn't happen until she wrangled herself free.

She swore under her breath and yanked hard. A ripping sound filled the air. *Great. Just great.* The snapping fabric propelled her forward, a motion that should have given her a quick introduction to the ground, except her face hit a different kind of unforgiving surface altogether.

Her forehead throbbed and she stumbled back, squinting up against the dull moonlight. A broad and stubbled jaw flashed in her vision. She craned her neck farther, attempting to inspect this man with an exceptionally long torso.

He loomed above her like a giant oak tree. Well, maybe not *that* tall, but his head did surpass hers by many inches. Maybe six foot six to her five nine, so two giants standing in the woods—kinda hilarious, really. Still, her mouth fell open in silent wonder. Not just at his height. No, but his rich, wavy, jet-black hair shrouding his brow in stark contrast to his startling, cobalt blue eyes.

His flat expression should have concerned her. She couldn't explain her general calm, but somehow, he gave no real sense of danger. The inconvenient flutter low in her belly though... that flutter that prompted her to splutter out something, *anything*, to break the silence...

"Forgot your costume?"

———————

Dean Holloway expected the usual mumbled apology people gave when they bumped into him, which happened a lot despite his height. *But this woman.* This woman with her classic beauty and startled gape, she simply let loose with a smart-ass question.

A slow grin tugged at his lips. What was wrong with her? She stood here alone with him. A man. Not just *any* man. One much larger than the average. One she'd never met. And in a location that kept her invisible to those at the party.

He pushed his smile down, not wanting to allow this strange woman a glimpse into his inner world. Her amber-green eyes glinted up at him, her pretty pout still parted; maybe he had scared her. Maybe she wasn't so irrational after all...

He knew what he looked like—a solid brick house dressed completely in black. His "look" downright paid his bills. The fact he lurked back here, in a dark forest... yeah, that probably didn't make him look any less intimidating to Miss American Peach, whose gaze darted behind him now, like she'd already wised up and sought her escape route.

Clever woman.

He put special effort into keeping a quiet presence. He couldn't blame her for not initially noticing him. He softened his scowl, the scowl he wore as a permanent mask. "Silly me."

Instilling fear meant people bothered him less, but for once, he didn't want to scare someone.

Strange.

His heart did a quick double-beat.

Strange again.

Still, he dismissed the reaction. Dismissed his desire to inspect her every detail, even though he'd already done a lot of that in the seconds before she quite literally bumped into him. He needed to get on with tonight's job, which meant he had to convince her not to run.

The last thing I need is this woman freaking out and telling everyone I'm here.

"I take it you're from out of town?" Her voice stayed relaxed, confident even, but her retreating steps belied her tone.

He pretended not to notice and gave an easy shrug, forcing his gaze *not* to pore over her ground-skimming fairy dress, the clingy turquoise velvet highlighting a trim figure underneath. Not exactly the most practical outfit for stomping through the woods.

His pulse hammered a little faster; his mind caught on how her impractical clothes had caused their collision and the brief knowledge of what her body felt like against his.

I know it's been too long, but shit, get your mind out of the gutter. I'm a man, not an animal.

"Someone at the grocery store mentioned a party." He focused on her eyes to forget about her body, the amber-green hue in no way a downgrade from anything lower. He could handle his attraction. Handle it like he handled everything else. With efficiency and control... "I thought I'd take a look while I'm in town."

Her posture eased, confirming he'd been right to mention a local spot like the grocery store. Familiarity did wonders for soothing most people's concerns.

See? Handling it.

"And let me guess." She lifted her chin, her thick row of lashes fluttering in her pause. "You missed the part where this was a costume party?"

He grinned, another effective way to cover a lie. Meanwhile, her cheeks flashed red, those dainty lashes beating heavier, like the animated wings of a dragonfly. Though her gaze veered to the side, he wanted to maintain a semblance of normalcy and refused to look anywhere but at her.

He pointed to a tiny red scratch across her thin collar bone. "You cut yourself. Let me help."

The lady blinked, and before she could protest, he pulled a handkerchief from his pocket and dabbed at the wound.

"Who the hell carries a handkerchief?"

His jaw clenched at how close he stood, so close her breath brushed at his hand and her citrusy-sweet scent enveloped him. A thick knot formed in his throat. She smelled like goddamn orange blossoms on a hot summer's day.

Her hand rose, her fingers wrapping around his wrist. She narrowed her eyes, hinting that he needed to answer her question.

The handkerchief. Right.

"You never know when you'll need one."

Like wiping away fingerprints after a job. Not that I'll admit that to you, lady.

He beamed at her, committing to the part of a friendly giant. Though he didn't move, her honey-blond hair fluttered in the night breeze, that hair still a mess from their earlier collision, the wisps flying in a halo about her head and lending to her wild air.

He'd been told many times that he had an endearing smile. Hopefully, that smile would work right about now, when he wanted to keep her talking long enough for her to decide he was no one worth mentioning to her friends.

The woman's fingers closed tighter at his wrist, the tinkle of jewelry drawing his attention to a chain bracelet jangling on her arm, the adornment fashioned with pointed gold leaves and probably how she'd cut herself.

He smiled wider. Useless dress. Useless jewelry. His useless thoughts of relieving her of both…

"Right." Her flat tone gave little away. "Did you see two boys pass through here?"

Her gaze shifted to her surroundings, momentarily pulling the heat off him.

He made a show of looking about. "No. Why?"

"They threw rocks at me. I came out here to find them."

An unexpected strain pulled at his brow, and he slammed his gaze back to her. "They threw rocks at you?"

Maybe he wasn't all that qualified to judge, but of all the bad he'd ever done, none of it had been for mere entertainment.

"Well, they tried." The muscles over the woman's face eased, and the blush returned to her cheeks, like she verged on a smile. Maybe his concern hadn't been all that expected. "But those Chadleys have always had terrible aim."

His shoulders dropped, and his next breath landed deeper within his lungs. He took his hand from her collarbone and eased back, her orange blossom scent still taunting him from a distance.

He nodded to her scratch. "You're not bleeding anymore, and those boys probably ran back to the party."

He eyed the light red mark over the bridge of her straight nose, a souvenir from her face connecting with his chest. Just like the Chadleys, he'd seen her approach from a mile off. He could have stopped her before she'd crashed into him. Why hadn't he?

His wayward gaze provided the answer, landing on her general lithe build, and then homing in on the tops of her small, pert breasts peeking out from her dress's low neckline. The smooth, honeyed skin there evoked thoughts of silk, and peaches and cream…

Orange blossoms? Silk? Peaches and cream?

Somehow, she'd highjacked his brain, leaving him with a yearning to lean down and kiss her; but damn, her narrowed stare said he'd be a fool to try.

Strength and beauty, with this one. And the strength always comes first.

The woman cleared her throat, only slightly dousing the heat that rushed his body.

"You can still join the party." She lifted her brows along with her posture, as if she noticed his staring and now toyed with him in showcasing the swell of her breasts.

A little witch in the best kind of way.

"Everyone's dressed like fairies, but with your height, no one would think twice if you said you were an ogre."

Two

THE MAN RELEASED A CHOPPY LAUGH, and Sarah jolted just as his eyelids flared in seeming shared surprise, as though her joke about him being an ogre caught him off guard. The laughter stopped and he pressed his lips into a hard, flat line.

Looking to fill the oppressive silence, she thrust out her hand, offering a hand shake that, in retrospect, she figured he wouldn't accept. *He's not a shaking hands sorta guy.*

"My name's Sarah. What's yours?" She took her hand back, the moment even more awkward.

His gaze darted over her face, brow now stiff, his smile long gone. "Dean."

She startled at his name, or more so his flat, monosyllabic delivery, the charming dimples on either side of his lips sadly gone.

The sounds of excited party chatter filtered into her focus. Nearby, the Mirabelle River babbled and the air held the river's damp scent. This guy and his controlled demeanor, he stuck out as a Harlow non-local. Then again, she couldn't say much different for herself.

Maybe I was switched at birth, and that's why I don't exactly fit in... maybe I'm not Harlow born and raised, after all.

Anyway, back to Dean, here. His accent held a different lilt too, none of that Minnesota heaviness on the *ah*, though the exact origins of his accent still escaped her.

As much as she'd lived in this small-town her entire life, as much as she too stuck out in her own way, Dean here gave her competition in the "not so quick to share secrets" department. Heck, most Harlowians tended to share their entire life's story within two minutes of meeting a stranger. Perhaps that's why she felt an uncanny affinity with this guy.

Frankly, the shared silence is nice for a change. Appearances being deceiving and all, maybe his caution doesn't need my suspicion…

"It was nice to meet you, Dean." She nodded a goodbye, deciding to give him the privacy he seemed to want. "Have a good night."

She turned her back and took her first steps away.

"Who are you supposed to be?" His baritone rumbled across the space, and she stopped mid-stride.

"I mean," he spoke quicker now, almost as if he didn't want her to leave. *Strange.* "Your costume. Who are you supposed to be?"

Her mouth wavered, his attempt at conversation holding her frozen. He pointed to her dress, his gaze sweeping over her again, tingles exploding throughout her body. A smoky heat swept in and subdued the tingles, a warm and sedate sensation taking over. *Strange again.*

She didn't know a thing about him, but the unexplainable sense of familiarity came once more. He reminded her a little of the male patrons at Maynard's, the bar her family owned and where she worked. Those patrons who sometimes confessed a rustiness when it came to talking to women. The ones she spared some extra compassion for because, if it weren't for being forced into running Maynard's so many years ago, she'd be a recluse by choice and exactly the same.

"Well." She took a few steps toward him, admitting that her engagement here wasn't merely an act of charity. She was lonelier than usual, and this man more intriguing than usual; and unlike most people around these parts, he didn't know her story or look at her with pity for being Harlow's jilted bride. "The theme this year is *A Midsummer Night's Dream.* So I dressed as Titania."

He quirked a brow, his shoulders easing some. "The Queen of Fairies?"

"You know the story?"

This man, with his rough, tough, standoffish demeanor, didn't come across as someone who cared about Shakespeare.

He shrugged, his handsome lips displaying what already seemed like a habitual mischievous curl at the corners. "Just what I remember from ninth-grade English, but this thing gave you away."

He lifted a hand and skimmed a finger over the star-spangled crown atop her head, infiltrating her space again, her pulse dancing at the radiant blue flicker in his eyes.

Her heartbeat gave a quick stumble and her breath paused, the spicy-warm scent of his cologne, combined with his unique masculine musk, crossing the short distance between them. Broken hearts and broken engagements be damned. The gentle dip of his chin brought him closer, the air shifting around her with a crackling electricity that made her attention dance everywhere but his eyes.

His wide shoulders took up an unabashed amount of space, and his muscles bulged there beneath his tight black t-shirt. He was sheer power, and having him so close brought a weakness to her limbs—not at all usual for a woman so rarely ruffled—his small moments of contact suggesting she might enjoy his touch in other ways.

She cleared her throat and took a half-step back, giving herself the gift of extra breathing room, even as his unwavering stare seemed to read her every thought.

A brand-new dimple sank beneath the light stubble of his cheek, a sign of amusement at her expense. A sign for her to deflect.

"So. Ah. Dean." She pulled her posture higher and hoped to God she didn't blush. "What brings a Boston man to Harlow?"

He jerked his chin back a little, as if her observation on his accent caught him offguard. She seemed to have that effect on him, which left her wondering just how much he underestimated her. Or maybe it was that her years of managing a bar had developed a sharp skill for reading people, which in itself had the ability to take them by surprise.

Well, except for when those powers of observation mattered most, like with her once-*fiancé*, for example…

She shut down that mood-dampening thought, preferring to focus on the zap of delight at witnessing this man's confusion. His physique gave off an air of pure masculine strength that made her feel small, that sensation, along with her ability to ruffle him right back, refreshingly exhilarating.

"I grew up in Boston." Dean's stare deepened, and her stomach compressed before he added. "I live in Los Angeles now, and I'm in Harlow for a work project."

Of course, Dean here didn't know that her little brother lived in Boston and had done so with their dad for the last ten years. Her heart ached a little every time she thought of Chip and the years they'd missed, though she'd visited a couple of times and had become familiar with the Massachusetts drawl.

Dean stepped closer, and she drew a quick breath, confused at how a simple dark look from him could disarm her. "And before you ask, no, I won't tell you what my work is."

Magnetic didn't sum him up. His quiet confidence put her own unaffected persona to shame. She should have enjoyed the unshakable prickle rushing over her skin, but no one she'd ever met held a matchstick to his strong presence. Not Blaine, not her father, not even the rowdy, raucous, salt-of-the-earth men she dealt with at work.

She slipped back, a nervous laugh escaping her lips. Since when did she do nervous laughs? "Why so secretive about your job?"

"I never said I was." His rough smile curled higher, revealing a row of perfect white teeth, the glint in his eyes hinting an awareness of his unfair advantage.

Unlike her, he was perfectly okay with whatever nerve-shattering tension buzzed between them, like he could handle being out of his element. His steady shift to close the small gap she'd created confirmed that fact. "I'm just having a hard time thinking about work right now."

She shuffled back again, and the glint in his eyes intensified, as though he knew something she didn't. Another step back revealed what that "thing" was. Her heel hit the trunk of a tree. She glanced up at the silver maple looming above her, her heart rattling against her ribcage, while her downward glance revealed the spread in Dean's grin.

He had her sandwiched between himself and the tree. His arching posture suggested he could kiss her if he wanted to. Her mind raced over her sudden lack of control. Was this what she wanted, too? Given her position, did she have a choice?

She snapped her attention to her right where she had room enough to run and never look back if she wished, but her legs held firm, refusing to move. Her focus collided with those deep cobalt eyes again, the hulking man before her shaking his head ever so slowly.

"Only if you want me to, Sarah."

The statement posed a dangerously sexy challenge, and one she might enjoy all too much. His gaze dropped lower to her lips, denoting the "want" she debated over. Did she want this man, with all his heat and intensity, to kiss her?

Her broken engagement and the potential for town gossip might have put her off men forever, but this particular man—a total stranger to her and anyone she knew—seemed like her one exception. He wouldn't be in town long. He couldn't rat her out to anyone here. And he might just be the distraction she needed.

She found herself nodding, a shaky, sharp sort of movement, before she spoke a raspy, "I want you to."

That stare, she didn't think it could get more intense, but the slight narrowing of his eyes proved her wrong. An immense amount of his focus honed solely on her while he lifted his large hand and pressed it into the tree beside her head.

The action inched him ever closer, but he still didn't touch her. "You're scared of me."

Her world stilled, though her mouth wavered, her failing attempt to deny. His hard features settled, and a sincere and gorgeous man stepped to the forefront. "I'm not here to hurt you."

A rough huskiness scrubbed all pride from his tone. More than anything in this moment, she wanted to believe him, but she'd heard those sentiments before. Hurt came in so many forms. Did she trust this man not to harm her on a physical level? Despite his size, yes, instinct said she could. But anything on an emotional level…

Don't overthink this. I deserve the escape. To just have fun. He'll leave Harlow soon enough.

She found herself nodding, her body burning with an urge for that fiery simmer of a forbidden first kiss. As if he'd read the yearning in her eyes, he leaned in, and her eyes slammed shut. The first smooth and decisive brush of his lips stilled her blood as well as her breath, his soft exploration quick to escalate to an all-engulfing kiss.

His hard pressure matched her growing desire, and she rose to his unspoken challenge, wrapping her arms around his shoulders and drawing him in. The tension in her body thawed in his embrace, her lips answering his in one hot and melting glide. He pressed his large and solid body into her, mirroring her hunger.

No one had ever ravished her like this. So insistent. So unreservedly passionate. His touch was a dark spell twisting low in her core, one that released an enthralling kind of magic. Everything about him, from his hypnotic scent to his overwhelming physicality, held her captive while obliterating all her cares.

She wanted more. More heat. More oblivion. But he broke the kiss and stared at her in a prolonged and painful silence.

"Shit!" He ground the expletive out, his now wide gaze snapping to a point over her shoulder.

She jolted. His abrupt change. His stiff posture. What had happened?

He turned away, his attention skittering about the clearing, his focus eventually landing on her again.

"I'm sorry." His expression fell slack, weak and apologetic, but then he did something truly unexplainable and bolted away.

Three

"Fuck, they're gone!"

Dean growled at the cramped and overflowing parking lot. Well, cramped and overflowing except for the one car that mattered most.

A rush of blood roared in his ears, drowning out the happy party sounds behind him, his crushing frustration taking center focus. The girl and her boyfriend, the two people he'd come to the soiree to find, *were gone.*

Ten years of hard work obliterated, and all it took was one beautiful woman. *Sarah.* One quick moment of distraction.

Fucking moron!

To forget why he'd hidden in those bushes in the first place—like something out of a cheap slapstick comedy movie—*oafish knuckle-dragger gets distracted by a hot lady...* Never had he messed up so epically. Never had he lost a target. The syndicate would have his skin for this. *And for what? A kiss.*

One kiss and his life was over.

Literally over.

Luciano Conti would want him dead.

He clamped his eyes shut and ran a hand through his hair, his mind flicking through a list of scenarios. His targets would likely go to one of two places. Her house or her boyfriend's. The best-case scenario would be if they went back to hers. At least then he'd have a chance of salvaging this mission.

The girl lived in a small cottage on the outer edges of town, and he'd left her hot-headed husband, his client, behind to keep watch. The guy had strict orders to call if the situation changed. Then again, even if the couple *did* go there, Dean didn't hold much hope. Her husband, Anthony Stucco, wasn't capable of staying out of trouble.

In the two days' drive to Harlow, Anthony hadn't shut up about wanting revenge, while Dean merely wanted to collect the money Anthony's wife supposedly had and go home.

He blew out a heavy breath and paced the parking lot's empty patch of gravel, aware he'd be shit out of luck if the couple went back to the boyfriend's house. His earlier reconnaissance revealed that Harlow was a small but tight-knit community, distributed in sparse patches across a wide geographical landscape.

He couldn't exactly plunge himself into the thick of this party and start asking questions about the woman and her boyfriend. The timing was off. The people here would notice he didn't fit in and get suspicious. Hell, he didn't even have a costume on. The boyfriend's house would be near impossible to locate at this late hour if Dean couldn't ask questions, especially without a starting point, like, say, the guy's damn name.

Anthony would not be reuniting with his money, at least not tonight. Even if that money *was* millions of dollars in embezzled funds he'd stolen from his wife's family and she'd rightfully "stolen" back.

What a bullshit mission.

Dean's best bet now was to lie low until the couple resurfaced. Perhaps another day or two, and maybe then he could return home, albeit later than he'd hoped.

He pried his phone from his jeans pocket and inspected the time, along with the gut-wrenching news Anthony hadn't called.

This mission was dragging on. Five weeks. Five weeks since Anthony's wife, Emilia, had gone missing. Dean had tracked her down clear across the country, though hadn't counted on her finding another man so fast. Then again, having met Anthony more than once over the years, maybe he should have.

Good for her. Bad for me.

Tonight's mission hadn't allowed for a new boyfriend. For a second location. Just a woman alone and unprotected in her rickety little cottage.

Fifteen minutes in this parking lot now. Still no call from Anthony. That meant the couple had probably gone to the boyfriend's house, and Dean would have to call Anthony and admit he'd fucked up.

If Anthony wasn't wilder than an angry honey badger before, the piece of shit will turn fully rabid over this.

Dean swore and pinched the bridge of his nose, defeat dragging heavily within his stomach, making him slam his eyes shut against the reality of his situation.

Ten years and this job dominated his existence, sucked the juice right out of his life, leaving nothing but hollow bones. Somehow, a few months of financial desperation had morphed into a decade of miserable servitude. But that was working for the syndicate. No one left. At least not alive. Though he hadn't known that when he'd first joined.

But just like Luciano Conti, Dean could be stubborn too. So, despite the rules and risks, he'd always planned to leave, just... not like this. Not so suddenly. Not at the hands of complete and rapid failure.

Then again, what did he care? Did he care about leaving with a glowing report card and a one-hundred percent success rate? Did he want to take the heat for what was a flawed mission from the beginning?

No. No. And fuck no.

That said, in a perfect world, he'd have time to make assurances. He'd implement an escape where no one would find him. There'd be no threats and no chase downs for leaving.

But then... Sarah.

Beautiful. Alluring. Bloody distracting. Sarah...

She'd crashed into his life. *Literally.* Royally screwed him over with her long-winded conversation about screwball teenage boys and Shakespearean plays. She'd made him forget who he was. Where he was. A miracle, since nothing and nobody let him forget he was a dirtbag lowlife with a dubious job and an ugly past, his future even less promising.

I'm a dead man walking.

"Fuck. Fuck. Fuck. Fuck. Fuck!" He kicked the dry gravel, the night spring air licking at his rage.

Not only had he blanked on why he'd come to the soiree in the first place, he'd gone so far as to tell the woman his hometown and which state he lived in.

Fuck!

He should have known the second he saw her. He should have stuck to just making to leave. And she had tried to leave. Why had he called her back? Why? And why, of all dumb-ass things to do, had he kissed her?

"Ahh… are you okay?"

He spun around at the steady female voice, his blood seeming to pause in his veins because Sarah stood about five paces away, her arms crossed, and a pissed frown dragging at her perfect features.

Four

DEAN HAD no idea how long Sarah had been standing there watching him lose his shit, but he knew one thing for certain. He needed her to leave. Leave now.

"Everything's just fine." He paused, inadvertently licking his top lip, and he swore he could still taste her mouth on his.

Not again, asshole. Don't get distracted again.

He veered his gaze from her and out to the parking lot, her crossed arms bringing too much attention to her chest. "Go back to the party."

"Are you sure you're fine?" He returned his attention to her blond hair cascading over one shoulder, her come-hither eyes narrowed like she didn't believe his statement about being fine. "I could have sworn you shouted the word 'fuck' on repeat while abusing the ground with your foot."

Her expletive had him pausing once more, the scent of her orange blossom perfume still punctuating the air. In his world, curse words, fairy costumes, and flowery perfume didn't mix.

He crammed any desire to show hospitality and instead clung to displaying annoyance. "It's not ladylike to swear."

She spat out a loud laugh and eyeballed him the entire time. "If you haven't noticed, we're not in Buckingham Palace here, and I'm not a lady. Besides, I was paraphrasing you. My cussing doesn't count."

He might have rolled his eyes, except her stage hysterics led to her bending forward slightly, bringing his attention back to her low neckline.

She stayed quiet for a moment, her green eyes slowly darkening. "So, plan on telling me why you ran?"

He scrubbed a hand over the scruff of his neck, holding back a desire to respond with, "Not really," only to give a more polite, "I had someone I needed to talk to but missed them, no big deal. Like I said, go back to the party."

"Oh, yeah? You're just going to tell me to go back to the party?" Her flaxen brows rose into high arches, like the physical vexed version of a certain restaurant chain's logo. She uncrossed her arms and stormed over, poking a bony finger hard into his chest, even this small and angry touch sending ripples through his body. "In what world is it okay to storm off on someone after unceremoniously detaching yourself from their face?"

His mouth trembled at yet another of this woman's smart-ass replies, but he forced himself to bury his smirk and settle for blowing out a slow, hard breath.

Sure, he'd kissed her. That kiss had been damn fun too. But one kiss didn't mean he owed her anything.

"You ask a lot of questions," he offered in a flat tone, sending the message that he wouldn't let her set all the rules here. "It's kind of rude."

"Excuse me?" Her eyes blazed, pupils wide, brows crammed together. "I was angry when you ran off, but then I figured something might be wrong, so I came out here to check you were okay. Obviously, there's nothing wrong with you. Well, nothing besides being a jerk who lacks basic manners."

She leaned back a little, shrugging like she was pleased with her dig at him.

"Okay. Fine." He paused to bite back a need to argue further. Maybe an apology would get her to leave. "I'm sorry."

"Nope." She jutted her chin out and shook her head. "Nope. One sorry isn't going to cut it. You put a lot of effort back there to insist you weren't out to hurt me, and then you ran. Way to dent a woman's ego."

He ground his teeth together, a dull ache spreading through his jaw. She had a point. She had been decent to him, trusted him, and he'd let her down. And even after all these years, after all that had happened to him and who he'd become… Sometimes. *Sometimes*, his moral code won out.

"Look, I don't have a good explanation for you, okay? Not one that won't require a lie." He eyed the ground and did his best to sound sincere. "So, can you accept that I'm genuinely sorry for the confusion back there? Then we can forget anything happened and get on with our night."

Her shoulders dropped, her eyes a little glassed over with disbelief or disappointment. The slight breeze lifted her golden hair so that the finer strands caught in the moonlight, and an ethereal dance played out around her head.

"I wish I could." The barely audible whisper fell from her lips, and she turned away, presumably toward her car, before she pitched a grin from over her shoulder and called out one last farewell. "Have a nice trip back to hell."

Her all-too-casual tone washed over him, and once again, he stood stock-still, while she rummaged through her purse, her head tilted down.

Should he laugh at her final dig, or succumb to the pang of guilt eating him up? He couldn't decide. Though her slumped posture revealed more disappointment than she let on.

His thoughts harked back to the moment he'd first spotted her. To the unguarded look she'd worn. Not too dissimilar to his mother's expression when she'd made him morning pancakes as a kid—a performance of domestic bliss to paper over his father's drunken behavior from the night before. The broken knickknacks. The yelling. Her bruises. That stunned and pale look….

He understood that look on a personal level, too. The show of someone whose life had drifted in the opposite direction to their plans. A look that revealed simultaneous hope amongst abject hopelessness.

He shouldn't have cared about her despondency, but he did. He didn't like this ending. Didn't like letting her go or letting her believe he'd lied.

Discord burrowed its way into the depths of his stomach, a discord that said it would linger if he let her drive away.

Dammit. Fine. I'll fix it.

He raced after her, his footfall loud enough on the gravel that she spun around, and her amber gaze caught his.

"Wait. I ruined your night." He paused, still not totally sure why it mattered to him that her mood lifted. "You don't have to leave."

"Don't flatter yourself. My night was ruined before I met you." She jangled her keys in his face and stepped back, continuing on her way in a swirl of turquoise material. "I'm going home to kick myself over ever coming here."

Even as she walked away, or maybe *because* she walked away, a vise wrapped around his heart, deepening his struggle to let her go.

Her night was ruined and so was his mission. As much as he could try to salvage things with work, he didn't truly want to. So maybe tonight's failure didn't have to be a total loss. Maybe he could turn this around.

There are worse ways to ruin my life.

"Take me with you." His muscles sagged as the words escaped his mouth, surprising even him.

Somehow this woman made his body work separate from his brain, but then, did he always have to be in complete control?

She turned, her sandy brows knitting together, and she gawped at him for the longest time. "You're not serious."

She tilted her head sideways, giving him an off-center stare, suggesting she maybe saw that he *was* serious.

That seriousness should have bugged him, but didn't. If she said yes, if she took him with her, he'd ditch tonight's mission and break with the syndicate altogether. Let this woman decide his fate. A rushed escape, sure. And even if he didn't plan to stick with this woman in any long-term way, she would provide his initial excuse to leave. His shot of courage.

The syndicate had always been a soulless endeavor, not much more than an illegal means of making rich men richer. This one poor life decision had been allowed to linger for far too long.

Or maybe I was just too chickenshit to leave…

He strolled over to her and tilted her chin up, a little lost on why this stunning woman had been absurd enough to ever look his way. Still, her motivations for looking weren't his concern. All he cared about was how he wanted this woman like he wanted his next breath. "We're both not having any fun here, but maybe our night doesn't have to end so badly after all."

"You really think I'm about to let you, a total stranger, into my car?" The skin at her eyes constricted into a scowl.

He did his best to hide any hurt at her rebuff. "You already let me kiss you."

She scoffed. "Yeah, and that turned out just great."

Despite her words, she didn't move. She merely blinked up at him as if a small part of her wanted him to convince her.

He pressed his palm to her face and used his touch to give her a moment to warm to his proposal of a second chance. Heaven knew and he knew, like most things in life, she was too good for him. So maybe he was being an unfettered jerk, but just once, he wanted to steal one of those good things. Even if just for one night.

"That kiss was *great.*" Color spread over her cheeks, and he stroked his thumb over her soft skin, a silent prayer playing through his mind that she'd come around. But prayers aside, he wouldn't leave her decision to fate alone, so he dropped a feather-light kiss to her lips, a reminder of what they'd already shared. His promise of what would come if she agreed. "My leaving had nothing to do with my interest in you, Sarah."

Her eyes drifted shut, as though the sound of her name got to her. "And I'm supposed to just drive us back to my place so we can… so we can…"

A breath fell from her, and she flung her eyes open, failing to finish the sentence.

"Yes." His answer came on a husky tone, and he leaned in, kissing the corner of her mouth, that kiss stealing his ability to determine who did the seducing here.

Despite her tough act, her gaze softened. "Who *are* you?"

The vise around his heart tightened again, her doubt feeding his desperation. "I told you."

"No." She shook her head. "You told me your name, but I don't know who you are. How can I trust you? This"—she pulled back a little, only to stop like she had second thoughts—"this is a terrible idea."

"No one in Harlow knows me, and I leave town tomorrow." He pulled her closer, and she let him. His heartbeat soared, this woman a rare and spirited find. "We want each other. I'm not about to rat you out to your neighbors. I won't ask anything beyond tonight. That makes this plan perfect."

Her cheeks went a shade darker, while her gaze darted over his face. Her generally stiff stance seemed less about fear and more about being all too used to holding herself accountable.

"I'd wager most single women around here don't get many chances to break away from maintaining their squeaky-clean image." He leaned in farther, set on assuring her there'd be no consequences. "What have you got to lose, Sarah?"

He dropped a final kiss to her lips, vowing he would abandon his need to convince her from here on out. Yes, he wanted her, but he'd already put forth his case and wouldn't bully her into a decision.

Her direct stare held him a beat longer before she blinked away her hyperfocus and lifted her hand, splaying her fingers over his chest in a demand for his full attention. "Get in the car."

Five

Sarah pushed the front door to her house open and turned to speak to Dean. He loomed behind her, the fire in his eyes swallowing her words while seconds passed with nothing but the quiet night as her buffer. He leaned in, his arms quick to enfold her, and his lips crashed down on hers, his unabated intensity suggesting he'd held onto his desire to kiss her the entire drive over.

To be fair, her body felt on fire that entire time too. Now that his tongue swept hers in hot, delicious strokes, she got the sense that earlier burning was a small spark compared to the inferno coming her way.

He walked her backwards into her house, a loud bang sounding as he kicked her front door closed. She didn't have time to think too much on the door kicking, his kiss devouring her soft moans while his hands worked up her waist and onto her shoulders, tugging down the straps of her dress.

The heavy material pooled at her feet and she chuckled. "Not wasting any time, are you?"

"We don't have time to waste." He hoisted her into his arms and she wrapped her legs around his waist. "Bedroom?"

She reached out an arm and pointed to a closed door behind her. Cool air brushed her near bare skin, his wide footsteps taking her across the floorboards to her bedroom door, where he pinned her against the cold wood panel.

For the first time since they'd crossed her threshold, he slowed— slow in that he cupped her face with his hands and drove home a deeper kiss, one that sent a prickling sort of shimmery sensation over her skin—his hands soon sweeping down the sides of her body and stealing her breath with his caress.

She'd come out of a long-term relationship, wasn't at all inexperienced when it came to sex, and while the actual "sex" part of this hookup hadn't even started, none of *that* felt like *this*. So thrilling. So all-encompassing.

He ground against her, excitement impossible to miss as his lips found a new place at the side of her neck. She closed her eyes and whispered a languid and breathy, "Oh, God help me."

He ground into her again, the pressure against her sex bringing forth another moan. "You'll have to settle for my help tonight, honey."

She flung her eyes open and eyeballed his dead-serious expression before laughter burst past her lips and shattered the heavy moment. His dire scowl faded, and his lips pulled into a wide and boyish grin, where before, nothing about him had read as sweet or endearing.

And those eyes. Those eyes held a glint like nothing she'd seen in him up until now. He'd held such a pent-up air, she hadn't considered him capable of unbridled joy, but he outright shone now, like if she peered any closer she'd see galaxies of stars inhabiting his irises.

The desperate energy between them shifted to something less obvious, something deeper, more personal. So she leaned in and instigated the next kiss, taking time to savor this moment and man, a stranger who could embody anything her mind decided for him.

Even then, she preferred to unravel whatever mystery lived here. She slid her hands under his t-shirt, feeling the soft lap of fire on her palms, a man hot with need, the side of his ribcage unforgivingly firm.

The door handle's light click had her sinking her weight into him. While he took her the short distance to her bed, she crept his shirt higher and over his head.

Cotton sheets crumpled beneath her, the metal crown from the soiree falling off her head and somewhere above her. She arched up, expecting his weight to cover her next, but that didn't happen. Instead, he knelt beside her, their gazes entangling for a moment before his attention slid down her body in slow appreciation. "You're perfect."

Heat rushed her face, and she flicked her gaze down to the breathtaking view of his broad shoulders and lightly tanned skin, lower to his chest and the light sprinkling of hair that trailed down to defined abs, then lower still to where that hair disappeared beneath the waistline of his black jeans.

She snapped her attention back to him watching her and the reminder of his statement on her "perfection", conceding he was far more qualified for the title.

"So are you."

His expression slacked, like her open praise surprised him, or maybe that a man with such a cagey presence didn't get all that many compliments. Either way, his strong stare didn't leave her, and he crawled over, his body covering hers.

She lost herself to another of his kisses, to the sensation of his skin on hers, and his weight pressing her into the bed. She wanted more. Wanted to obliterate the need growing within her. To, as he'd said, use what little time they had. So, she slid her hands down to his belt, only for him to press his palm over hers. "No. Not yet."

She pulled her lips away and frowned at him, his thumbs stroking her hairline on either side of her face while he held a grave expression.

"We both know where this is going, but I'll get there much quicker than you. So"—he leaned in again and slipped a hand under her back, unhooking her bra—"you first."

The top half of her underwear disappeared somewhere on the bed, his lips soon meeting the dip at her throat and traveling lower. First along her collarbone, his breath warming her skin, then to her breast, where his tongue met her nipple in a barely perceptible, soft brush.

She drew a sharp breath and arched into him, begging him to hurry, while he took his sweet time. His large hand engulfed her other breast, and she pressed into him some more, each soft kiss and gentle scrape of his teeth melting her cares.

She needed to forget the chain of disaster that had brought this man to her bedroom. Boy, did he deliver, his mouth traversing lower to her belly, his hands lower still—his fingers hooking to the sides of her panties and then stripping her bare.

His gaze caught her in a silent question, though even through her expanding need, she whispered, "You don't have to—"

"I want to." His expression didn't change, no smile, not even a frown, just simple acceptance. "You want me to."

She pressed her lips together and nodded, not used to giving over *any* control, somehow willing to just for this moment. He was right. She *did* want this. Wanted to lose herself. To experience someone else taking over... *if only for this short time.*

So, she watched as his hand swept to her knee, pushing her open.

He watched her too, watched her *there*, completely exposed, before his rapt attention snapped to hers. Her body responded with instant heat, melting her muscles into surrendering some more. He seemed to notice and crept lower, so that his lips made fast contact with her inner thigh.

She arched at the rousing sensation, each kiss traveling higher until he met the juncture of her sex, his kiss soon shifting to an unabashed brush of his tongue, his long fingers meeting with the center of her tummy.

He held her still and held her gaze, demanding she feel every changing touch he unleashed upon her body—soft and hard, fast and unhurried—the stroke of his thumb at her bud bringing her to a climbing pant. Something about his quiet approach suggested that he derived pleasure from her pleasure, that he gauged her reaction and adjusted his touch until she clawed at the bedsheets and rewarded his patience with her fast unraveling.

He used his elbows to pin her open, a subtle gesture for her to relax and surrender some more—surrender an alien concept to her, but one she tried, anyway.

One look at this beautiful stranger sent an electrified prickle through her body. All that power, and muscle, and a good dose of mystery. He clearly wouldn't give up until she followed where he led.

One moan after another wrenched free of her throat, his equal parts challenge and restraint allowing room for her to *feel*—to express the pleasure she often held close. She would not see him after tonight. What did she have to lose from exploring? Nothing. Absolutely nothing.

So, she begged for more, when she *never* begged for anything—and the more she gave in, the more he gave, too. As though he knew. As though he saw that she wasn't the type to yield, while for once, she could be more herself than she'd ever been.

She focused on what he did to her. The pressure of his touch. A pressure that grew until she groaned from the overpowering assault on her senses; all the while, he held her open and vulnerable, undoing her with every caress until a shuddering climax took her over.

Excitement swept the air from her lungs, forcing her to gasp for her next breaths, the soft clinking of his belt reminding her that he wasn't done. He was hard and ready, and he slid on a condom before quickly entering her in one long and confident stroke.

She arched and savored the tension and the heat, the undeniable connection, despite his newness to her. His cobalt stare refused to let her go—so intense, so direct—his hands clasping at her outer thighs, while he wrapped her legs around his waist. "You have amazing legs."

She opened her mouth to offer some self-critical reply, but he thrust into her again, burying himself deep and stealing her words. The feel of him, the explosion of each passionate thrust igniting her every sensitive nerve, rushed her second climax out to the open.

He answered her arousal with increased speed, capturing each of her moans with his mouth and releasing a few of his own satisfied sounds. With each passing second, his thrusts grew harder and wilder, her fingers digging instinctively into the heat of his shoulders before he swelled within her.

Eventually, the fever cooled, and he released her legs from his waist. Though he remained inside her, his elbows pressed into the mattress on either side of her head, and he bent to kiss her again. "I guess this is where I'm supposed to leave?"

The upward curve to his lips held an air of hope. He didn't want to leave.

She pressed her hands to his face and pulled him in for another kiss, only releasing him long enough to say, "Oh no, our night's only just starting."

Six

"I CAN'T BELIEVE something like this could happen in Harlow."

Sarah blinked and shook her head at Ally Egan's voice, that voice drowning out the fevered chatter at Maynard's Tavern and the jangle of thoughts clouding her mind. Ally, four years younger than Sarah, cradled a droplet-covered glass of lemonade between her palms, her elbows digging into the bar, while her lowered pale blue gaze half-hid under her flop of short ice-blond hair.

"Ally, tragedy doesn't always strike based on where you live." Sarah cleared her throat, the hard ball of friction in there not shifting. Or maybe that ball consisted of guilt, more than anything that could be easily moved.

Two days since the soiree and her hot night with Dean. He'd left her house early afternoon the next day, and she hadn't even gotten his full name, much less heard from him since—not that she wanted any other ending.

Still, while she'd spent her post-soiree morning sharing a shower with a tall, hot, mystery man, Blaine's world literally went up in flames. So of course, as per local tradition whenever anything dramatic happened, much of Harlow converged on Maynard's tonight to unload their shock and gossip.

"I just feel bad for Emilia." Ally shook her head, still not lifting her gaze from the bar counter. "That her deranged and estranged husband could storm into town, gun in hand and hell-bent on hurting her. I mean, he traveled all the way from LA, despite being on the run from police. What sort of entitled ass sets his wife's house on fire?"

A *deranged* one, obviously. And that same entitled ass had also come demanding Emilia return the millions *he'd* stolen from her family in the first place…

Deranged. Entitled. What a savage mix.

Sarah frowned down at her hands and the tall glass she polished. "I didn't even know Emilia was married."

How had she let go of her relationship with Blaine without knowing *that* piece of information?

Why does it matter? He didn't love me. At least, he didn't love me enough to stay.

And now Blaine lay in a hospital faraway in Minneapolis, all because the would-be hero had quite literally been caught in the crossfire between Emilia and her husband. As in, he'd taken a bullet to the chest, his chance of survival still unknown.

Ally's eyes welled with tears, and her shoulders trembled. "There wasn't any love between Emilia and her husband. She told me about Anthony just yesterday. She found him terrifying and had already filed for divorce. This is all so unfair. That horrible people can mess with the lives of everyone around them."

Yes, unfair. And Emilia also had injuries, since Anthony's attack had started on her before moving to Blaine. Only, Emilia somehow got hold of a knife, and Anthony's life ended soon after.

So much chaos. So much violence. So much blood and carnage. To some extent, Ally was right, this *did* sound like something from a much bigger city, not a perpetually boring town like Harlow.

Sarah lowered the glass in her hand and grabbed another, her confusion deepening. "Why would she marry someone so evil to begin with?"

Ally pressed her lips together in the face version of a shrug. "She married young and under pressure from her family. Anthony was the one who broke Blaine and Emilia up ten years before they met again in Harlow."

That's right. Blaine had explained that he'd known Emilia during his brief time in LA as a teenager, that it was never his choice to leave her. Because of that history, Sarah had conceded his happiness would never be with her. After three years together, she'd stepped back, not wanting to play second fiddle to his memories of another woman.

I chose to end things, and still, it hurts.

Then again, she couldn't say all parties were happier for her sacrifice after all.

Ally snatched a nearby napkin and dabbed at her eyes. "I'm sorry. I don't mean to blubber. I'm just worried about Blaine. It's so weird, you know? Not having him at Oak Tree to chew me out over every little thing."

Never one comfortable around displays of emotion, Sarah kept her attention low, though she did understand Ally's despair. Blaine was Harlow's only carpenter. Ally was his sales assistant. She kept his store running while he built furniture and carried out house repairs and renovations around town.

Ally and Blaine loved to bicker in the way two firm friends sometimes did. She'd also gotten close to Emilia, whilst being Sarah's friend too. An island of neutrality if ever there was one.

Sarah winked at Ally, her action meant to lighten the mood while muting her own sense of foreboding. "Sheriff Marlin said Blaine might return to the shop in a few weeks, and then you'll be back here telling me how much he's annoying you."

Ally's laugh hitched between sobs. "You handle difficult stuff like this so well. I don't know how you do it. You were engaged to Blaine, and you're holding it together. Meanwhile, I'm just his employee, and look at me, I'm a complete mess."

Sarah paused her polishing, Ally's comment a hard blow to her chest. She didn't handle tragedy any better than Ally. She was just more experienced at hiding her pain.

Blaine was more than her ex-fiancé. He was her closest friend, perhaps her only friend, aside from Ally. Pieces of her had fragmented in ending their relationship. That breakup had taught her that some love never died; it merely changed. So if she couldn't love Blaine as her partner, then she would love him as something else, though the weeks following the breakup hadn't afforded time to define what exactly.

There'd been the breakup. Her taking time to be alone. Him jumping into his shiny new relationship with Emilia. Then this new tragedy…

Screw this. He's not mine anymore. It's not my place to help him, remember? Even if I want to.

"Ally." Her stomach roiled under a new surge of remorse, her blissful night with Dean coming back to haunt her. "You're allowed to be more upset than I am. You're more than an employee to Blaine. You're honorary family."

Ally's lips pulled into a small smile before she finally took a first sip of her drink. "When do you think we'll be able to visit him?"

"Not sure." She nodded at a patron to her left, acknowledging their wave for another round. "If you like, I'll call the hospital tomorrow and let you know how he's doing."

Ally eased back in her seat, and the lift in her posture indicated a lift in her mood.

Sarah jutted her chin toward Ally's drink. "And those are on the house tonight too, okay?"

New and genuine laughter broke from Ally, her eyes taking on a sparkle that subdued a fraction of Sarah's guilt. "You run Maynard's like a well-oiled army. What's with you giving away free stuff?"

Sarah squinted at her friend, her words a jest but still a reminder of Sarah's reputation as the town's stoic face of misfortune. "I could always revoke that offer."

She slid her hand across the bar toward Ally's drink. Ally pulled her glass closer, half hugging it to her chest. "No, but seriously, I'm glad you're looking out for me."

Sarah laughed and took her hand back.

"But"—Ally's eyes lost some glint—"I'm a little embarrassed to admit I'm scared to go home. I know that sounds crazy, but I feel like someone might break into my house too. You know, like if it could happen to Emilia and Blaine, then maybe it could happen to us too?"

"Ally, you live with your parents, and as far as I know, you aren't on the run from a possessive husband." She slid a newly poured beer over to the patron from earlier, fixing Ally with a resolute stare. "Look, you have nothing to worry about. This was an isolated event, a personal vendetta, though you can stick around Maynard's as long as you like. As long as you don't mind me running around throughout the night."

Ally's gaze brightened, the strain in her cheeks releasing in seeming gratitude. "Thanks for keeping me company."

Sarah smiled and she collected two plates sitting on the pass, plates that had been out longer than she preferred. She was meant to be managing the venue while assisting the bar staff, not serving meals. Though part of managing the venue meant noticing when one of her wait staff went missing. In this case, Jenna.

Sarah marched through the break in the bar, calling to Ally as she strode toward an elderly couple a few tables away. "I'll serve out these meals and be right back."

Through her darkening mood, she kept her expression light, darting her attention about in search of Jenna, likely doing something not in harmony with her job description.

Sarah plastered on a wide smile and lowered the plates to the elderly couple's table. From their dressier clothes and unfamiliar faces, they stuck out as tourists, more and more of whom converged on Harlow during the warmer months. "How are you two finding Harlow?"

The woman's gray eyes exuded joy, like every other visitor who tended to come to Harlow in search of a pleasant taste of small-town country life, without experiencing the pit-falls of actually living in one. "Oh, Harlow is so beautiful. The lovely farms and open pastures, the little stores and cafes. Just darling. You must love living here."

"Sure do." Sarah kept a cheery tone, masking her subtle lie. She didn't hate living in Harlow exactly, but some things weren't as rosy or voluntary as they appeared from the outside. For example, where a person lived or just how much they wished to share with those who lived within close proximity. "If you have any questions about the area, or things to do around here, come speak with me at the bar, all right?"

Two wrinkly smiles grew before her, and she gave the couple a confident nod goodbye. She turned back for the bar, her low-rise heels clicking on the battered wooden floors as she spotted Jenna amongst a small group of college-aged holiday makers.

Sarah sent forth a heated glare, and the thirty-year-old waitress with long brunette hair and large, brown eyes, shot from her seat on a holiday maker's lap. With all the extra tourists from the soiree and town fair, plus the local folk converging on Maynard's to gossip over Blaine's near-death experience, Jenna picked a terrible night to slack off.

Sarah slid behind the bar and served more drinks, half-listening as Ally recounted the stress of managing Oak Tree Furniture without Blaine, only for the woman's words to dry suddenly, followed by a breathy, "Oh. My. God."

Sarah lifted her focus to a wide-eyed Ally proclaiming, "That has to be the most delicious man ever to set foot in Harlow."

Sarah twisted around and followed Ally's line of sight, instantly regretting she hadn't let go of the bar's beer tap the moment her attention snagged on a set of cobalt blue eyes.

A deluge of icy cold beer spilled over her fingers and instant sickness filled her belly. She let go of the tap and eased the glass in her hand to the rubber mat below.

Her *no-strings-attached* sex had just turned up at her workplace and strolled toward her and the bar, his all too casual, lopsided, and dimpled smile holding an air of recognition. As in, he didn't care about letting the world know they'd met before.

Dean.

Seven

"My heart just did a legit double-beat."

Sarah ripped her attention from Dean, still approaching, to Ally and her hazy stare on him. "I never understood how a person would call anyone anything as sappy as 'dreamy', but I get it now. That guy *is* dreamy, like, he can't possibly be real."

"Look at me." Sarah ground her words through gritted teeth, her *no-strings-attached* sex drawing closer and at her workplace of all places. "Don't even think about talking to that guy. Do you understand?"

He'd promised to leave. He'd promised not to be a problem. And here he was all the same.

Ally's brows bunched with a sudden frown. "Why the heck not? Did you see the way he winked at me when he first pushed through the door? Like I said, dreamy!"

Sarah growled. As naïve as Ally could be, on this front, Sarah had been no better. "I'm sure he has one of those winks for every woman who crosses his path."

Among other things…

Ally leaned back and pitched a skeptical scowl. "And how would you know?"

Sarah gave a casual shrug, mostly because Dean could see her and she didn't want him to take any hint that she might be talking about him as encouragement. "I'm good at reading people, remember? And... I might have seen him around."

Ally peered up at Sarah through a row of thick black lashes, her cropped locks kissing her jawline. "I would have heard something the second a man that sexy showed up in town."

Sarah sank back on her heels and ripped the nearest washcloth off the counter, attempting to look too busy to talk before Dean reached her.

Like most people in this town, Ally lived a sheltered existence, and her younger age and upbeat personality didn't help. Her foolhardiness often aligned better with a sixteen-year-old girl than a twenty-three-year-old woman. Honestly, Sarah loved that about her friend—that Ally was a dreamer, while she was a stark realist—and still, the two extremes had their pit falls.

Ally's innocent flirtations with danger came with consequences. She cared for love and romance, and a guy like Dean would stomp all over her starry-eyed heart. He would leave nothing but a trail of shattered pieces. And Sarah couldn't stay quiet while that happened.

She leaned over the bar, addressing Ally while glaring at Dean, who thankfully took a seat some distance away. "Listen, I met the guy at the soiree, all right? You didn't see him because he didn't make a point of mingling. Believe me. I know his type, and he's nothing but trouble."

Liar. Terrible, terrible liar!

Ally's eyes glinted and her smile grew. "Trouble, huh? Sounds perfect."

"Ally..."

"What?" Ally slid from her seat. "Why do you get to meet him, and I don't?"

Sarah rubbed the heel of her palm between her brows. "Oh. Trust me, I'm starting to wish I hadn't."

Ally turned toward the man in question, her hand resting on the bar as though she'd humor this conversation at least a little longer. "From the looks of him, I don't think so."

Sarah pressed her hand over Ally's. "I know he *looks* perfect, but he's not. Please, I don't want you to get hurt here."

"Who says I'll let him?" Ally's eyes glittered. A wicked sort of glitter that came from not really knowing what she was about to do. "Besides, how much could you possibly know from one meeting?"

Sarah snorted a short laugh, all while rolling her eyes to the heavens. If there was anyone useful up there, they certainly weren't listening or helping her now. "It was a very long meeting."

Ally snatched her hand back and started to walk away. "Well, I'm not leaving him to sit there by himself, anyway. Someone around here has to show that man a bit of Minnesota nice."

"Ally…" Sarah clawed her fingers into the bar's glossy woodgrain, but clawing at the bar was about as useless as her warning.

She turned her attention to Dean and his smug grin fixed her way. What was he doing here, and what did he want? She shook her head. Another useless warning, as she ignored the fiery sensation taking up space in her chest.

Ally took the empty seat beside Dean. Sarah couldn't watch, so she decided to disappear into the kitchen behind the bar for her overdue dinner break.

The kitchen's swinging double doors clanged in her wake, that familiar din filling her with gratitude for the sudden distance between herself and what would otherwise have been an awkward exchange. Besides, Ally was old enough to absorb the consequences of her silly decisions, and Sarah refused to give Dean the satisfaction of thinking she was jealous.

He could do whatever he liked. So could Ally. All Sarah wanted to know was why he hadn't left town like he'd promised, when she could count on never seeing him again.

As great as their night was, in the wake of what had happened to Blaine and Emilia, plus Sarah's complete lack of desire to be attached to anyone in any way, she really didn't want to complicate her life any further.

"You want a steak dinner or fish and chips?" Gordon's loud voice traveled from his usual spot before the industrial stove, the chef's full face glowing bright pink from the steam raising from a giant stock pot.

"I'm not hungry." She ripped at her apron strings, slapping the garment onto a steel bench beside the giant walk-in freezer, its soft buzzing filling her ears.

Sure, she could relate to Ally wanting a little adventure. She'd succumbed to Dean herself, after all, but Ally didn't handle disappointment like she did. Besides, maybe she owed Ally the truth about her night with Dean before the woman got too enraptured.

Gordon put his spoon down beside the stove, his squint seeming to inspect every frown line on Sarah's forehead. "What's your problem?"

"Nothing." She stalked toward a nearby shelf and swiped a large bottle of tequila, refusing to give him any direct attention. "I'm just not hungry."

She turned to Gordon when she didn't get one of his expected smart-ass replies back. His large, well-built torso hunched over another steel bench, and he stared through the pass leading into the bar. "Who's Ally talking to?"

Sarah glanced through the small gap, and her heart did an involuntary thump at Ally laughing with a ruggedly handsome Dean. "Whoever Ally flirts with is apparently none of our business."

She hated herself for sounding so sarcastic, and yet, she couldn't stop. "It's busy tonight; why have you stopped cooking?"

"You're not the only one who's allowed a break, Missy." Gordon crossed his arms and leaned back so he stood upright, his narrowed glare sweeping over her. "Besides, whatever's happening out there is way more interesting than watching soup boil."

Sarah squeezed her eyes shut, about to announce she was leaving, just as soon as she poured herself one sanity-saving drink. But before she could open her eyes again, a memory of Dean held her captive.

They were at the soiree, pale moonlight spilling over his face, his thick black hair brushing her forehead as he drew in to kiss her.

Holy smokes…

It was impossible to think about that, without thinking about what happened after. That she'd allowed herself to let loose with him and loved every minute of it.

Still, she should never have taken him home. Should never have let him get that far.

To make love to her. To allow herself to get so carried away when he did.

Then again, could she blame herself? She hadn't known he'd be back to haunt her with his unwelcome presence, on top of flirting with her best friend.

"Wow." Gordon's overloud voice had her throwing her eyes open in time to catch his wide-eyed astonishment. "Did you see that? Ally just slipped that guy her number."

Oh for fuck's sake!

Her belly clenched, and she drew nearer to the pass, taking the entire tequila bottle with her. Ally leaned her shoulder into Dean, her lips dangerously close to his ear. Meanwhile, whatever she said brought a smile to his face, his reply in turn making her throw her head back in a boisterous, enthusiastic laugh.

Gordon eyeballed Sarah. "See the size of that guy? I bet he eats sweet little girls like Ally for breakfast."

Sarah clung to the tequila bottle's cold neck. She hated gossiping. Ironic since her work at the bar meant townsfolk often came to her with theirs and everyone else's problems.

"Ally's no little girl." Her gruff voice surprised even her, and she stomped toward the back exit before she or Gordon could say anything more.

She huddled on the back step, the serene night ahead of her as she cracked the bottle lid open. She didn't normally drink but too much had happened. With Blaine. With Dean. Her entire life, really... Tonight, she needed an escape.

Eight

TEQUILA SOON BURNED down Sarah's throat, the initial scorch subsiding to a radiating warmth in her chest, though not enough to kill the raking anxiety that Dean might stay in Harlow after all. Maybe he planned to work his way through one girl after another, with her being his first victim.

Great. Just great.

Just her luck, he'd probably make friends with the less upstanding guys around, share the gory details of his exploits, including his night with her. She didn't care much about denying her needs, but she'd been with no one but Blaine for three years, and people in town would talk and speculate.

If Dean blabbed, her reputation as Harlow's guarded and practical-minded woman would be shot to shreds. It wasn't even that everyone would know that she, Sarah Overton, had sex. It was more about *who* she'd had sex with.

Everyone would take one look at a rough and tough-looking guy like Dean, especially if he stuck around long enough to be known as an overzealous sleazeball, and question her choices. Even more so if she'd picked the crude *sleazeball* so soon after breaking up with Harlow's golden guy, Blaine.

Hell, I'm such a reckless idiot.

The next swig of tequila didn't burn as much, but once again, it didn't obscure her disappointment either. Maybe she got too far ahead of herself. Maybe things would be okay, and Dean would at least keep their night together secret. Honestly, even after she got him home, he hadn't given her any creeper vibes.

Her heavy sigh disappeared against the racket of cicadas and the sweeping wind over the grass field ahead, and she resolved to only worry about what she could control.

She peeled herself away from the icy metal door behind her and slid back inside the kitchen, all while Gordon did his best to look busy. She tucked the tequila bottle inside the giant freezer and vowed to leave money for it in the register at night's end. The chilled bottle would come home with her after closing.

By the time she returned to her spot behind the bar, Ally was gone and Dean sat alone. The restaurant noises were still loud behind him.

"Where'd Ally go?" She made sure to keep her tone rigid as she spoke, not wanting him to think a repeat of their night together would ever happen.

If her harsh delivery bothered him, he didn't show it, only giving her an easy shrug in response. "Home, I guess."

She pressed both hands to the bar before him, brought her face close to his; still, his woodsy, spicy scent from the other night rushed at her, making her heart beat faster, a surge of hormones and memories delaying her response. "What are you doing here?"

He sipped at his half-finished beer, the motion all too casual for her liking, and still somehow alluring. "This is a bar, isn't it? I'm having a drink."

"You know what I mean." The strain in her voice only made her hate him more. "You said you were leaving town."

He shrugged again and looked away. "I changed my mind."

She paused, her earlier hypothesis about him lying seeming more and more likely. "Did you come here to find me, or are you just looking for your next victim?"

His expression stayed calm, though his stare narrowed a little on her, making her heart thump. "I had no idea you worked here. You never told me, remember?"

That was true. He'd asked questions the other night, though she thought she'd dodged them discreetly enough. Then again, he didn't address her question just now about finding his next "victim", so maybe he didn't deserve any sympathy after all.

She jutted her chin at him. "When are you leaving Harlow?"

"I don't know." He took another slow sip, his lips, along with her knowledge of what they could do, distracting as they pulled away from the glass and formed a slow smile. "I like Harlow. It's a good place."

The muscles around his eyes took on a harder edge, like he didn't appreciate her interrogation. Well, tough. Even if he did still make her insides flutter and her temperature shoot up about a thousand degrees, she liked that he expressed a little of the same discomfort his surprise reunion gave her.

"If I'd known you wouldn't leave, I would never have..." She snapped her mouth shut, unable to finish that sentence.

Never have what? Ignored my whacked-out family history? Made such a careless decision?

"Had sex with me?" Dean twisted in his seat and pinned her with a glare. "Go on, Sarah. You can say it."

But she didn't say a thing, and a heavy and awkward silence hung between them, his startling blue eyes bringing an involuntary tingle to her skin. "If you haven't noticed, you don't own this town, and my life doesn't revolve around you. Not that it's any of your business, but things have changed with work, unpredictable things, and I've decided to stay a while longer."

"Fine." She snapped to a stiff and straight position, crossing her arms. "Then keep away from my bar, got it? And don't chat up my friends, either. Ally Egan is off-limits to you, okay? Also, I don't want you telling anyone else about our night. You being here wasn't what I signed up for."

His challenging stare lingered, drawing out a painful silence, drawing her attention to the light stubble along his jaw and his annoyingly kissable lips curling into a proud smirk. "I don't know why you're so irked."

Her body thrummed at the memory of his rough whiskers, how they'd abraded her skin, against her thigh as he'd—

"You lied." Her accusation shot from her mouth, albeit as a hollow whisper, more wounded than critical.

His smile dropped, the skin around his eyes relaxed, as though her tone got to him. "I never lied. Like I said, circumstances changed."

"What changed?"

He didn't answer and merely kept staring at her, that stare seeming to say, "I don't have to tell you."

Again, a wave of anger burned through her chest. He had a point. Whether she liked it or not, they were reasonable adults, and he was entitled to stay in Harlow. Heck, even her attempt to ban him from the bar didn't hold much weight.

And still, she wanted to win. Didn't want to give him the benefit of the doubt, as much as being willfully unpleasant wouldn't make this situation any less hellish.

"Do me a favor then." She eased back, attempting to seem okay with finding a compromise.

He lifted his shoulders a little, hinting he might be open to whatever she suggested. "What is it?"

She ran a hand over the bar, removing non-existent dust simply so she wouldn't have to look at him as she voiced her next request. "Just keep your word about staying away from Ally, please."

"And what if Ally doesn't want to stay away from me?"

She focused on him taking another swig of beer, his cocky smirk around the glass making it seem as if he liked the idea of getting hold of Ally or simply liked toying with Sarah. Either option stoked the fire beneath her ribcage.

"This isn't a joke." Her shoulders stiffened, and she made no attempt to hide her anger. "If you touch Ally, I will downright break your fingers. Got it?"

He choked out a small laugh and pressed the back of his hand to his lips. Granted, he weighed more than twice as much as her, which made her threat ridiculous. Heck, she never resorted to threats… but this man… he had a way of inspiring the worst in her.

Perhaps she could just roll with the unhinged ranting and see where that took her…

"This town is my home, these are my people, and I can make your life miserable, got it?" She swept her ponytail away from her shoulder and then crossed her arms with a mocking sort of shrug. "So, like I said, take your pick out of any other willing woman, but leave Ally alone. She's too nice for a guy like you."

Nine

DEAN LOWERED his beer to the counter, not sure he wanted to hear any more of what Sarah had to say. "First you jump my bones, and now you tell me your friend is too good for me? If that's the case, what does that make you?"

Confusing, and now apparently mean. I thought I'd read her better.

Granted, he didn't fear her threat to "break his fingers", but the brutal barb about Ally being too good for him… That harsh statement left a reverberating tension between them, and now she clamped her mouth shut, her unreadable stare bouncing around his face.

He was used to having cruelty lobbed at him in the shape of more subversive digs—attempts to ruin his life with untrue claims, attempts to dismantle his happiness one piece at a time, cowardly attempts committed behind his back… But not like this. Not so brazen or direct.

She gawped at him, her cheeks slack, and her skin pale. "Sorry. I'm so sorry. That just kinda fell out."

He leaned in closer and inspected her, his movements slow with the intent to unnerve.

"Really?" He kept his tone low and steady. "So, you didn't mean a single word?"

Her gaze flicked to the side, a hint she'd meant at least some of it.

A sigh pushed past his lips, and he sat back, pitching forth a flat stare. "Right, and is it safe to assume you're usually this rude to people you're not sleeping with?"

Her slack mouth drew closed and formed a hard and twisted line, her glare lasting only a moment before her focus flicked about her, like she worried someone might have heard. "Okay, fine, I deserved that. And no, I'm not usually so rude."

He sank back a little, nodding through the mutual quiet. He partly wished to add to her discomfort, partly wanted to watch her, to figure her out. Apologies didn't come all that easily to this woman. Because he was getting to know her and, therefore, hadn't fully decided what he thought, he didn't feel all that inclined to make her apology easy.

He captured his beer and took another sip, maintaining an unaffected air. "What makes you Ally's gatekeeper? Shouldn't she be allowed to decide who and what she wants?"

Her gaze, luminescent against the dark bar atmosphere, narrowed on him, momentarily hard until a softer light seeped in. "She's a small-town girl who thinks spending time with you will be a bit of harmless fun. But before the week's done, she'll be infatuated, and then she'll be in love. I'm guessing you're not interested in any of that, much less the wedding and three babies she'll be planning for you in no time."

His stomach jolted with a wayward laugh, but he clamped his lips together and buried his amusement. "Sure, I don't want any of that."

Lies. He wanted *all* of that. Not necessarily with Ally, and especially not since marriage and kids were for people other than him, people not forced to live on society's fringes.

Despite her crossed arms, her shoulders crept higher. "You mess with my friends, you mess with me. One of the things everyone around here loves about Ally is she's the bubbly one. I'm sure I'm not the only one who doesn't want her to lose that or to see her brokenhearted. My earlier insult was a meaner way of saying you seem like someone well-traveled, while Ally isn't. The odds here aren't even."

He raised a brow, masking any unconvinced displeasure. "You sound so certain I'd go out of my way to hurt her."

He could understand how his staying in Harlow might leave Sarah with doubts about his honesty. He also got the feeling his presence wasn't her only issue. Her analytical stare measured his every move, as though she searched for any old reason not to trust him. So of course, he gave her nothing and waited for her to fill the stretching silence.

"I don't know you well enough to say." She shrugged, giving a weak performance of being unperturbed. "I made a promise to look out for her when my brother left town. He and Ally were close."

She stepped away a moment and grabbed a paper ticket from the bar's farther end, a ticket presumably with a long drinks order since she proceeded to work the taps in front of him.

Meanwhile, he twisted his glass, dragging out a deliberate pause. "So, your concerns about me and Ally are based on nothing more than a promise to your brother?"

"Yes." Her gaze didn't meet his.

He continued staring at his glass. "Is that all?"

"That's all."

Her answer came too fast, and he smirked.

"The way I see it"—he peered across at her stacking filled drinks onto a black tray—"if your brother cared, he'd be here looking out for Ally himself. That, or take her with him."

Maybe why I haven't left Harlow, even though Anthony Stucco being dead means I have no reason to stay. No reason, except Sarah.

He drew a sharp breath, refusing to think too hard on his motivations beyond following his gut instinct to stay a while longer. He was taking an educated guess that the syndicate wouldn't want to implicate themselves by looking for him in this town—the very place Anthony's crimes had taken place. He liked this town. Liked the woman standing before him. Whether that "like" was a wise idea remained to be seen.

She disappeared to the opposite corner again, this time carrying the drinks tray, a server quick to take that tray out to the tables. When she returned, all she offered was a mumbled, "Things aren't that simple."

"Oh, yeah?"

"Yeah." She wiped down her work area, frowning at him in the process. "Chip's always had a thing for Ally, but Ally in all her flightiness never cottoned on."

"So, what you're saying is"—he made a show of staring at the contents of his glass—"Ally doesn't like Chip, but I still have a chance?"

He lifted his gaze, hitting her with a full smile; one she countered with an even narrower glare.

"You're full of yourself, you know that?"

He bit back another laugh. Goading her was too much fun. "I'm stating a fact. I'm fresh meat around here, yes? So, of course I'm going to get some attention. Meanwhile, you're not at all jealous your friend might be interested in the same man you were with just the other night. Have I got that straight?"

Tension bunched her lips at the center, her head tilting to one side and nudging the end of her glossy ponytail off her shoulder. "Give me your phone."

She held out a hand, opening and closing her fingers in a gesture for him to hand it over.

He pressed his hand over his jeans pocket, part of him unwilling to rule out her vaulting over the bar to get his phone. "Why would I do that?"

She shrugged, her own smirk making an appearance. "I just figured since it's okay for you to make your way through my friends, I should be able to do the same with yours." She raised a brow, her fingers still doing their grasping motion. "So, hand your phone over. I have calls to make."

An unmissable heat took over his chest, his teeth grinding together and painfully so. He didn't want to imagine any man, especially anyone he knew, daring to look at Sarah, much less sleeping with her. Sure, it was far too soon to get possessive, but the little witch did a fine job of shining a light on his own jealousy.

He stared down at his beer, working hard to maintain his posture, despite the deflated sensation winding through his body. "This is a small town, and I assume every woman here is your friend. That doesn't leave me much choice, does it?"

He let out a caustic laugh, his choices limited in so many ways beyond women. Lack of choice was the theme for his life. And for some reason, with Sarah before him now, he didn't want some other choice.

I lied when I said my decisions didn't revolve around her.

His first taste of freedom in years had come from her. He wanted more of that. More freedom. *More her.* Maybe Luciano would track him down; no doubt he'd at least try, but Dean had a backup plan and refused to spend his life running from a literal mob of lowlife criminals.

He sat taller, deciding to punish Sarah for toying with him. "So if not Ally—or, I'm assuming, any of your friends—are you offering yourself again as a compromise?"

He stared directly into her eyes, daring her to look away, but she held up her end of the dare. "Nice try. You know I'm not about to sleep with you to spare someone else."

"Then what about sleeping with me simply because we had a damn good time?"

She barked out a laugh, turning to collect a few empty glasses from the bar, a number of patrons having cleared out. "Once again, no."

"I seem to recall you saying the exact opposite of 'no' the other night. Over and over, if I remember correctly."

She swung around and glared at him, though even that glare wasn't enough to douse his memory of having her. How she *had* asked, her ragged breaths mingling with his as she purred and pleaded beneath him.

"You know what I mean." She returned to her glass collecting.

Actually, he didn't know what she meant because, in his world, meeting someone he connected with was rare. Meeting someone he wanted to see again, as much as he did Sarah, outright never happened.

Except, we're not exactly getting along right now, are we?

He gulped down the last of his drink and stood, yet another golden opportunity shutting its door in his face. "I'm done here."

"Not yet." She stopped in front of him, the beauty in her stare sending warmth through his body in spite of his lack of optimism and her serious expression. "You haven't promised to keep away from Ally, and if your only offer is to bribe a second round at my place, that's not good enough."

"Looks like you've got no choice but to trust me." He pulled some cash from his pocket and placed it on the counter.

Her hand shot out, almost habitually to collect the money, her fingers touching his in the process. The lingering contact had his stomach gripping, her close proximity bringing the light dusting of freckles over her nose into focus. Freckles mostly only visible to someone close enough to kiss her. Something he'd done over and over not all that long ago.

Her gaze slid to where their hands met, that gaze bouncing back up to his under a quick shiver. *She felt something too.* Except the haze in her eyes cleared all too fast, sharpening into icy daggers as she snatched her hand back and surveyed the room. "These people know me, and I have to work here. Keep that in mind if you ever find yourself at Maynard's again."

Ten

WORD ON THE STREET IS, *Luciano is pissed. He's looking for you.*

Dean crammed his phone, along with the text from Ramos, into his jeans pocket and continued to wait at the counter of Harlow's only grocery store. Five days had passed since the soiree, and he was done living at the local motel. He'd lined up a rental home, and now, the store's jovial owners, Maureen and Frank Cooper, had agreed to receive some moving boxes on his behalf.

"Your delivery's out back." Maureen smiled from opposite the counter, her affable personality and sparkling blue eyes a nice change from the hard-edged characters he was used to. "I take it you got your new house sorted?"

"Thank you, and yes." He pointed to a doorway behind the counter, assuming that was where his boxes waited. "If it's all right by you, I'll come round and lift those boxes out myself."

Maureen turned and waved for him to follow. "Perfect. My back's not all that good anymore, and I don't mind the idea of watching those muscles of yours getting down to work."

She looked over her shoulder and gave him a cheeky wink, even though she outranked him by about thirty years. Still, he laughed, age having apparently not dimmed her enthusiasm for harmless flirting.

"Frank told me you're taking the Rudger's place, is that true?" She pushed aside a clear plastic curtain leading to a cold and dark storeroom with a musty-cool smell.

He bobbed down and lifted the first of four giant cardboard boxes. "Yep. The place is only a few years old, and as you can see, I don't have all that much stuff. So, I'll have room to spare."

Maureen led him down the rows of chest-height shelves that looked about twenty years old and out toward the street-facing exit. "Betcha didn't have all that much space back where you're from."

He shook his head, being careful not to trip as he stepped across the threshold and onto the sidewalk where a spring midday sun beat down on his face. "Just a pokey old apartment."

"I guess that's one advantage to moving to the sticks, yah?" She trailed behind him, probably because she didn't know which car on the main street was his. "The Rudger's is one lovely double-story brick. Large rooms, big yard, and Compton Drive is close to town. You did well."

That he had, and at a third of the price of his apartment, which only convinced him further he should have ditched LA long ago.

"What do you plan to do with yourself in Harlow?" Maureen's question caught him just as he bent to place the box on the ground.

He straightened, digging through his pocket for his keys. "I have a bit of money to tide me over for a while and figured I'd do odd jobs until I line up something more permanent."

In all his years working for Luciano, he'd never spent more than he needed. He didn't expect that to change now that he'd moved, either.

"Betcha get lots of offers." Maureen beamed a mischievous smile. "But I'll put the word out and pin a flyer up on the store's notice board about you looking for work, okay?"

"Thanks. I'd appreciate that." He popped the trunk of his black Cherokee.

The last time he'd come to the store, Maureen had rattled off a list of local single women she figured he should go out with. The woman wasn't half subtle, but she was well meaning enough, and he'd take her help to find work over finding him a woman.

Or maybe I've just stupidly figured I've found the one I want...

Yes, stupid, because his last encounter with Sarah had gone *so* well, and she'd been undeniably happy to see him again…

He shoved his moving box into his car's trunk. Too late now. He'd committed to Harlow and wasn't about give in so easily. Not to Luciano. Not to Sarah. Three lines of scribbled and jagged penmanship peered up at him from on top of the box, yet another omen about not giving up.

Adrian Ramos. The one person who hadn't given up on Dean. Not when everyone else ran in all directions away from him. The one person to believe in his innocence when everyone had branded him a deadbeat sergeant. Dean trusted Adrian with his life. Enough to have him collect these few belongings before news of the Stucco disaster reached the syndicate, and they started watching his apartment.

"Word is"—Maureen's voice pulled him from the black memory— "you've already found your way to Maynard's."

"Word travels fast." He slammed the trunk closed, perhaps to distract from the heaviness in his tone, set to get on with what was starting to feel like a fruitless task.

Maureen laughed and guided him back to the store. "Harlow is the worst place in America to keep a secret, don't cha know? Ally Egan has taken a real liking to you, too. She's another singleton you should consider."

"Maureen…" He tried not to growl the warning.

"Oh. Okay. Okay." She waved a hand at him, her eyes still bright. "I'll stop."

They walked in easy silence, his thoughts falling on Maureen's comment about Harlow being a bad place to keep a secret. Well, he'd spent his entire adult life keeping and uncovering secrets, become an expert on that very thing, and he didn't welcome anyone here figuring his out.

Even with Anthony Stucco's death hitting national headlines, Dean had always been careful not to link himself with the syndicate's dealings. He would have his clean break, or take the whole damn operation down with him.

Back in the storeroom, he picked up the second box, the service bell sounding with a high-pitched *ding* across the store.

Maureen looked over her shoulder. "I'll go see who's at the counter."

The older woman hobbled away, her years of back issues apparent in her stride.

"Hey, Maureen." A woman's voice cut through to the storeroom and a light tingle traversed up his spine, that clear and direct tone unmistakable. "The heat's really climbing outside. Could I get a refill on my water bottle?"

Dean struggled to hide a deadly-as-sin smirk as he ventured through the plastic curtain and out into the store, a moving box in hand. Sarah's calm gaze darkened.

"Hello, Sarah." He kept his voice bright, even though the tense look on her face brought a dull pain to his chest.

"Hi," she mumbled, quick to divert her attention to Maureen.

"Oh, how wonderful." Maureen directed a cheery grin at Sarah and then him, before swiping a see-through blue water bottle from Sarah's hand. "You two have met."

Sarah shook her head. "Not really. Just—"

"Oh, yeah, we've met." He made a show of looking her over in her fuchsia-pink running shorts and white tank top, her brows pinching together, suggesting that if she got anymore pissed at him her brows might snap and fall off completely. "Sarah was quick to welcome me to Harlow."

He broadened his grin, perhaps his attempt at testing his theory about her brows, even though right now the memory of her "welcome" took up fast real estate in his brain.

Maureen slipped past him and into the storeroom with Sarah's bottle in her hand, the sound of running water overlapping her next words. "Sarah here is the manager over at Maynard's, don't cha know? She's a natural at making our newcomers feel welcome."

He held Sarah's glare, and his lip wobbled, even as he chimed in with another golden opportunity to take a dig at her. "Her personal approach *is* impressive."

He bit the insides of his cheeks and curled his fingers hard around the corners of the box in his hands, trying hard not to drop it while he fought for composure. If she insisted on the frosty greeting, much less denying she even knew him, then she'd get ten times the frostiness she gave.

Her face turned red, and she leaned over the counter toward him. Maybe her brows wouldn't fall off after all. Maybe her head would outright explode.

"Stop it." She hissed through gritted teeth.

He shrugged and whispered back, "I don't know what you're talking about."

She turned to look over her shoulder, as if worried someone else might have entered the store and would hear what she had to say. "First your intrusion at the bar, and now this? Why are you trying to ruin my life?"

"No one noticed anything at Maynard's and same goes for here." He kept his whispered tone, at least giving her that. "I'd be happy to call a truce if you'd just stop being so unfriendly."

His gaze dipped from her hypnotizing amber eyes, to her defined collarbone, and down to the soft line of cleavage peeking from her low neck-line. He'd never enjoyed looking at a woman this much. Even if she was set on being perpetually pissed at him. She was majestic and magnificent, in spite of having sweated it out in the midday heat.

"My eyes are up here." She pointed to her face before jutting her chin toward the box in front of him. "So, you're staying now?"

He didn't need to answer for the strain on her face to grow, which only served to open a hollow in his stomach, leaving him somewhat gutted and deflated.

She really can't stand living in the same town as me, can she?

He stared down at his box with yet more of Ramos's writing scribbled atop it, unable understand why his staying annoyed her so much.

"I don't know how you do it, Sarah." Maureen burst back into the conversation, the clutter of plastic strips smacking in her wake. She slid the water bottle across the counter to Sarah, while addressing Dean. "Running full-pelt in this sweltering heat. It must take her close to an hour to cross the distance between her place and town. She runs most days too, you know. Always been Harlow's sporty lil' miss."

"Yeah, well…" Sarah's voice turned gruff, her glare flicking back to Dean. "Running keeps my stress levels down."

She swiped the water bottle from Maureen's hands and turned for the exit. Maureen gave Dean a heartened smile. "Poor girl's had a rough life."

Sarah stopped in her tracks, her ponytail swishing as she swung around, her unguarded and wide-eyed stare hitting Maureen. "Could you not—"

"Your hard work shows," Dean cut in.

The sudden ashen tone to Sarah's skin, her frozen stance—Maureen had clearly struck a sore spot—and he wanted to stop any potential further pain for Sarah, while halting the chance of an argument breaking out. Besides, he had no desire to pry into anything she didn't want to talk about, especially since he knew all about "rough lives".

Then again, he wasn't a total saint either, so he added, "I like running too. Maybe you'll invite me along one day?"

Her lips pursed and her habitual glare—at least where he was concerned—returned, before she slowly mouthed the word, "No."

Box still in hand, he lifted his elbow and turned his head to his arm, giving a fake cough. Fake because he wanted to cover his laugh.

Maureen wandered over, ending his coughing fit with a squeeze of his bicep. "Dean's hard work shows too, see? What do you say, Sarah?"

Sarah merely growled and turned on her heel. "I'm late for work."

Maureen squeezed Dean's bicep again before giving it a prolonged stroke, her gray eyes twinkling up at him with zero qualms about copping another feel. "Sarah's ex-fiancé was the one injured in that shooting the other day. She let him go so he could be with Miss Emilia. Before that, well, let's just say she's not always been so gruff."

Eleven

THE NEXT DAY, Sarah ran her usual route back from town, her water bottle strapped to the runner's belt around her waist, and her headphones plugged in. She rounded a corner into Compton Drive and let her usual exercise-induced daydreams take over. Sweet nothings filled her brain. Well, nothing but her running playlist and her feet pounding the pavement in time with the music. All until something hard nudged her shoulder, and she jolted, nearly tripping over.

"Hey! What gives?" She ripped her headphones out and glared to her left, almost tripping once again at the giant schmuck smiling beside her.

She stopped, instantly regretting the choice once it filtered through to her that the schmuck in question was Dean.

I should keep running. Just keep running!

So, she jammed her headphones back in and picked up pace again.

Except her music wasn't enough to drown out his heavy footfall on the sidewalk behind her or the muffled sound of him calling, "Mind if I join you?"

His longer stride made catching up to her easy, and she gritted her teeth, ignoring him. Not only did he have a frustrating habit of popping up just to bother her, but now he wanted to intrude on the one activity that brought her peace?

She peered down at his black sneakers and dark blue running shorts. He'd seen her running yesterday and planned on this ambush today. "Do I have a choice? You're already joining me." She pulled one headphone out to the heightened sound of his hard breaths.

"You always have a choice."

She stopped running and planted her hands on her hips, trying to hold herself perfectly upright despite her own panting. "So you're not following me, then?"

He stopped too and shrugged. "Fine, I did follow you, but only today. Those other times we met you came across me."

She scoffed, ignoring the rush of blood that came with realizing he'd plotted to meet her, much less how she didn't completely hate the idea. "So, it's my fault you hover in the same places I frequent?"

One corner of his lip quirked, and his shoulders relaxed some. "I'm not *hovering*. You approached me back at the bar. And at the grocery store, I was there first, remember? And let's also not forget you're the one who merrily face-planted into me at the soiree."

She drummed her fingers on her hip and struggled for purchase over her argument.

He said he was leaving, and then he didn't. He also never promised to leave Ally alone…

Exactly. Besides all that, she had her own mess to deal with, her parent's disastrous marriage setting the tone for her own broken engagement, and the oh-so-justified vow to stay single forever… "So, there's nothing behind those suggestive looks you keep giving me?"

His dangerously full lips spread wider into another suggestive look. One that made her want to sigh with the memory of just how sexy this man could be, whilst wanting to resume her run just so she could leave him in her dust.

"I never said that. There's definitely something behind those."

Her heart squeezed. "What about all your double meanings? Like yesterday when you told Maureen about my *personal approach* to welcoming you?"

His chest trembled a little, like he held onto a genuine laugh, but then he stepped a little closer, and for a moment there, she lost her breath. "Sure, those too. But I'm more than happy to stop *suggesting* and outright tell you what I want."

"Oh, no. No. No. No." She turned on her heel, his proximity and honesty too much and maybe a touch too tempting.

He lied. He lied. And even if he didn't, he will, or he'll do something to hurt me...

Her muscles ached, therefore making her steps rigid. Doubt tugged her in the opposite direction, her mind still caught on him, even as she ran away.

She'd promised herself *one night* with this man. That's it. Anything more would inadvertently plunge her into what she'd promised she'd do anything to avoid. Another relationship. Or at least, another chance at being humiliated. At having her heart broken.

What's wrong with being alone? I like being alone. Why is loneliness something everyone in this town always wants to fix?

A heavy hand grabbed her arm and spun her around. Dean's stare scanned her face, his lids narrowed, and his brow flexed in an analytical scowl. "You weren't so abrasive with me that first night, and I know you're not like this with everyone else in Harlow. What's changed?"

"I'm not—" The burgeoning lie died on her tongue. In truth, he was at least a little bit right.

"You're different." His voice hushed, somehow lending an uncanny intimacy to what was a roadside talk in broad daylight. "Colder."

She moved to shake him off, but his hand didn't budge. "I don't know what you mean."

Good one, play dumb. He won't see right through that.

His expression softened by another degree, and he drew in even closer, the scent of clean skin and woodsy spice melting something deep within her. "Is my staying really that much of a problem for you?"

"I just..." She released an exasperated sigh and allowed the strain in her stiff shoulders to go.

As if he sensed her willingness to explain, he took his hand off her, giving her the distance she needed.

"You didn't do anything wrong." She blinked down at her hands. Even his interrupting her run wasn't reason enough to drop her manners. Something he correctly pointed out she did a lot around him. "I know I'm being unfair, but having been in Harlow for all of five minutes, I'm sure you've heard my plate's full without having you looming over my shoulder."

He took a drawn breath, his broad chest becoming a whole lot broader. "You mean the stuff with your ex?"

She scoffed, even though she was a little thrown that he already knew about Blaine. A car zoomed past, the dinged light blue one that belonged to Mrs. Byrne, who lived just down the road from Sarah.

She wondered whether this encounter would gain top billing in the Harlow rumor mill by evening. "If by 'stuff' you mean my ex-*fiancé* leaving me for someone else and then getting himself shot—then yeah, that would be one reason."

Two lines scored the space between his brows, forming a frown. "Can't be easy being on the outside of that."

She pulled away, jamming one headphone back into her ear, having expected him to give her hell about her misfortune, and somewhat disappointed that he didn't. "I should keep running."

"You regret sleeping with me."

Though she already had her back to him, his direct tone had her stopping in her tracks. His statement ignored her one about wanting to leave. Still, it cut to the core of something she hadn't yet decided on.

Do I regret sleeping with him?

Her body warmed at the memory of the night. That he didn't make a secret of wanting her again. That she wanted him too. But again, she didn't know.

Taking Dean home with her had been one of her wildest decisions and felt like one of her most pointless. Had she been longing for a distraction? Yes, and he'd given her one. At least before her plan for distraction got shot to literal pieces. Would she gain much from inviting Dean back into her life? *No, just the opposite.*

Once was enough. More than that would inch her closer to disaster.

She turned back to him and released an audible sigh. "I'm not having a heart-to-heart with you about my ex, okay?"

"Then what will you have a heart-to-heart with me over?" The lines between his brow smoothed out, and his eyes seemed to take on new light, as though even with the weight of his question, he sought to lighten her mood.

She turned away again. Maybe he did mean well, but she didn't owe it to him to reciprocate. "Let it go, Dean."

"Then at least tell me you don't regret what we did."

She paused, growling under her breath, though maybe out of denial that he seemed to genuinely care whether she regretted her choice. "That's blackmail."

So why aren't I leaving already?

"Sarah." His attention skimmed over her face before latching on to her gaze, his unwavering stare hinting that he saw her dilemma over leaving, or perhaps having to ease his doubts over her regrets... or both... "That night at the soiree. You've never done anything like that before, have you?"

Instant cold hit her core. His stare, of course, noticing so much more than she gave him credit for. Because that would be just her luck. And even that knowledge didn't stop her from trying to deny everything yet again. "That's not. I—"

"Your hands shook the entire drive over." He took a giant step closer and crowded her space, though for a big guy, he had an ability to make his voice impossibly small. Somehow his gentle tone soothed and hurt her all at once. "I know what I saw. And as always, even as you say one thing, your body says something else altogether."

He lifted his hand and brushed a strand of hair from her barely covered shoulder. Her cheeks burned, and she fought not to look away. He'd noticed her nerves. And his comment about her body... what else had he noticed that night... or for that matter, every other interaction since?

His hand stayed on her shoulder now, searing her with the heat of his palm in collusion with the sultry weather around her. His touch once again awakened senses she shouldn't have wanted roused.

His thumb stroked the dent just above her collarbone, slow and far too tantalizing circles that pulled a sigh from her, changing her breath to something shallow, soft, and compliant.

"I had a bad night, and you were there." The huskiness in her broken whisper didn't fit with the unaffected confidence she sought to show. "Don't read too much into it."

She wanted to pull away, but her legs still refused to move. Maybe this was what he meant about her body betraying her.

A distinct weakness ran through her muscles, as if those same muscles hadn't been strong enough to jog her halfway across town just minutes ago. As if there hadn't been a time when those muscles had put her on a plane to Florida and on course to work with the world's top coaches…

And what was with this overly bewitching man and his ability to see through her lame excuses?

For years, she'd fooled everyone. Or at least trained them into playing ignorant. She'd done well to avoid all signs of vulnerability. The people of Harlow knew to assume she was in control. That she was fine. Just fine. And she *was* fine.

She could take care of herself. *Had* taken care of herself for as long as she could remember and wouldn't fall short now. Certainly not over a man.

He nodded, as if he saw something in her. Her doubts. Her defenses. Her ever-present need not to let her mother's curse repeat with her. And of course, he had something to say on the matter. "I don't regret one moment of that night."

She spluttered a laugh, one that caught within the tightness of her throat. "Yeah, well, lucky you. Your first night in a new town, and you convinced a woman to take you home. You hit the jackpot there, buddy."

She fought an urge to give him a congratulatory clap on the arm and resume her running.

"I did hit the jackpot." A small smile broke from his lips, the slackened muscles around his eyes denoting a man offering a compliment when he could have belittled her instead.

His kind expression caused a pain beneath her lower ribs. She dropped her gaze to his right hand opening and closing, as though he wanted to touch her again but held back. Part of her wished he would. A greater part saw the foolishness in that desire.

Silence dragged long enough now that his smile faded, and his gaze fixed to what was probably her own worried frown. His attention on her lips made her feel like a moth pulled to a flame. She wanted to draw closer, but still, she knew better than to do that.

"You're beautiful and I'm amazed you let me get that close." He paused, pressing his lips together as though he second-guessed what he said. "That's all I meant."

Everything within her stilled. What was she doing here, except perhaps willfully bringing about her demise? She choked out her next words. "Are you saying I shouldn't have?"

"No." He shook his head. "You just don't seem like the sort of girl who'd—"

"Oh. Wow." She held up her hand, signaling for him to please not finish that sentence. "Firstly, I'm not a girl…"

Her heart pounded. Their night together was meant to be just her letting off a little steam, but that night opened up a litany of possibilities she didn't want to face. What he'd been about to say confirmed another of her fears. That the person everyone thought her to be was one big, fat illusion.

Dean clenched his hands into fists at his side, his jaw momentarily clamping shut. "Look, I'm sorry. I'm not a huge talker, okay? Especially when it comes to women."

As if to unintentionally prove his point, he paused and another inordinately long silence drew out. "All I mean is, there's nothing wrong with what we did, and I get the impression you're not the type to let anyone get close—much less a stranger. I understand that our night together might have cost you something." His gaze flicked up, catching hers. "So maybe cut yourself some slack, and while you're at it, cut me some too. And maybe… if you're up to it… give me a chance to get to know you."

Twelve

"I'm going to need more convincing."

The unfiltered sarcasm slipped from Sarah's mouth. Dean's candid offer—a seemingly genuine expression of interest in her beyond the physical—twigged something. Something she wasn't sure she should explore.

"Before you bumped into me, I saw how absorbed you were in your own world—or should I say, problems." His eyes seemed to darken a shade, as though he refused to let her wriggle out of this exchange so easily. "You looked sad, Sarah."

She tore her attention from him and onto the empty street with its few houses and golden long grass as far as the eye could see. "I wasn't—"

"And for a moment there, when we left together, you weren't." His stare zeroed in on hers, resolute, as though his future truly hung on getting her to agree with his interpretation of events. "In our own twisted way, we got along and you know it."

Her heart pumped a little harder. His opening up to her did feel good. Too damn good. But she'd been fooled by good before. "We got along, that's all, and only because I thought you'd never show your face in town again."

His gaze hardened and he dipped his chin, his lowered stare an unmissable warning.

"No, no, no." She waved a finger at him. She wasn't finished. "And then when you *did* show your face again, you tried to hook up with Ally."

He rocked back and shot out a dry laugh, ripping his attention from her and up to the heavens. "You're still thinking about that, huh?"

She gave a forced shrug. "No, not really. You're free to do whatever you want. I'm just letting you know my eyes and ears are fully functional, and I'm not as naive as you seem to think."

He crossed his arms, which only made not checking out his biceps near impossible, so she focused on his flat stare instead. "Right."

His flat tone wasn't any better, so she added, "Look, I picked you that night because I wasn't interested in anything complicated—but here you are, complicating things all the same."

She waited a beat and got nothing from him, so shook her head and spun away.

"I'm not here to *complicate things*." His sharp tone followed her as she stormed down the road, the earth crunching beneath each of his hurried steps.

"But you want more." She refused to look at him and continued her escape. "It was only supposed to be one night, Dean. One night."

For the longest time, he didn't speak. Just power-walked alongside her, his movements rigid in her peripheral vision. His silence provided enough of an answer, and she mumbled what she hoped would be their final words on the matter. "Exactly."

His breaths panted beside her, and she wondered whether the exertion of keeping up wore him down, or perhaps something else. Her rejection. His seeming desperation to convince her he was more than bad news…

"Let me change your mind."

She barked out a laugh.

Did this guy ever quit? Any minute now she'd pick up speed and leave him in her literal dust. For someone who claimed to be not much of a talker, and even though she'd gotten that impression early on, he found far too many words around her.

His hand landed on her shoulder, gesturing for her to stop, to turn and speak to him directly. She shook him off, though even that didn't dissuade him. "Listen, you were happy that night. So was I. What's so complicated about that?"

A dull ache spread though her jaw, one that came from unknowingly clenching her teeth together. She used that clenching to her advantage and said nothing at all.

But even as she took another step, he stepped in front of her, blocking her path with his body, her feet nearly skidding on the rocky earth to keep from yet another collision with his chest. "Not yet. I want to ask one more question."

She huffed out a hard breath, making her annoyance known. "Fine. Ask."

His expression remained still and altogether non-threatening, though a bit too serious for someone who seemed to enjoy pestering her. "Are you attracted to me?"

Her brows strained together, and her weight shifted involuntarily back. "Sure, we established that the other night, but if you haven't noticed, our little moment in the sun is over."

The tension around his eyes eased, a subtle light seeming to spark at the back of his irises, as though he acknowledged only part of what she'd said. The part about her being attracted to him.

His strong hand grasped her elbow, and he pulled her in. Before she could follow what was happening, his lips hovered close to hers. And his body. Oh, his body brought about all the wrong memories. Or maybe they were the right ones, just at the wrong time. All that firm strength, the solid plane of his chest leading down to his defined abs, his bare arms rubbing hers…

Everything about him set her on fire, and nothing about him reminded her of any man she'd ever touched. He obliterated them all. *Even Blaine.* And just like their night together, his scorching presence stole every one of her thoughts and cares.

His lips crashed over hers, further scattering her thoughts. She did not care. She simply did not care about anything except how much she wanted him and everything he offered in this moment. He had a vise-like grip that, for the first time in her entire life, made her feel like she could let go a little. He made her heart beat faster, and her eyes slammed shut in the wake of her lax moan.

His hands cupped the back of her head, and he groaned right along with her, satisfied and exacting—that hard embrace dragging her under, like a kraken drowning prey beneath a turbulent sea.

Her mouth took on a life of its own and begged him not to stop because he felt so damn good. Too good. The biggest problem here? Hard and demanding she could deal with. The gradual softening of his lips—his slow, melting, all-too-tender caress—not so much.

And then there were her own reactions. The heat pooling between her legs, a yearning for more than one hot night with him, her muscles sagging and giving into him, expressing a desire that he should never let her go.

Cold reality zipped through her, dispersing the muddied senses that had allowed her to reciprocate his kiss like an infatuated teenager. Out here in the middle of an albeit mostly quiet road.

What the hell is wrong with me?

Breathless and painfully weak, she pushed him away. "Don't do that ever again. Especially not out here."

Her jagged tone reverberated through the air, and she looked about, thankful no one had driven past and that they stood between houses with large yards.

"Tell me you didn't feel something." Dean's cheeks hollowed, but his stare refused to let her be, his piercing blue eyes shredding her defenses.

"Just stop. Just stop, okay?" She slapped her hand to her forehead and backed away, her voice tight but raised. "Why do you keep assuming I have to do anything you tell me? Who are you anyway?"

His cheeks paled and he lowered his brow, as if he didn't like her questioning who he was. Not that she cared, or at least, she shouldn't have. And still, his stare burned into her, drawing out long seconds before he spoke again. "You want to pretend nothing happened?"

She gave a tight nod, glad he'd scaled his tone down compared to hers. "That's exactly what I want."

"You kissed me back. You felt something. And you *still* want to pretend?" His gaze flicked over her, stirring that low heat within her once again.

Clearly, her body had other ideas. Regardless, she crossed her arms and refused to budge. Her non-reply was designed to say she wouldn't repeat herself.

He nodded as if he heard the sentiment loud and clear and turned back to where he'd come from—toward the Rudger's house, presumedly where he now lived since the family had moved interstate not that long ago.

Her arms hung loose at her sides, and her shoulders sagged right along with them. The sweet and dragging call of chickadees echoed back and forth from a nearby silver maple, that dulcet call a jarring contrast to the unexpected disappointment she experienced now.

His leaving was the exact reaction she wanted, but her voice lashed free of her all the same. "What do you want from me?"

He half-turned and peered over, his chin dipped and his forehead creased. "Maybe you could start by not acting like being with me was one big, moronic mistake."

His words hit her square in the chest, a palpable force she wanted to stumble from. "Fine. Being with you wasn't a mistake. Does that make you happy?"

"No." His frown deepened, and he looked seriously pissed. "Maybe you could cut the sarcasm, too."

She fought her natural urge to defend herself, the man's powers of observation cutting, as a sliver of lightness traveled up her chest, into her throat, and stopped to tug at the corners of her lips. "Okay... I'll try."

She pressed her lips together to keep from saying anything else because, goddamnit, this man had a way of getting more from her than she intended to give. Though as much as she did enjoy sarcasm, she didn't enjoy hurting anyone. And really, Dean hadn't done much to deserve her attitude.

Well, nothing but be the temptation I really don't need...

"And..." He turned his body all the way forward and took a few steps toward her. "I'd be happier if you'd be open to us at least being friendly with each other. It'd be nice to say, 'Hi', without my ego taking a bruising every time."

Just a little proud of her verbal jabs and that they got to him, she hid the sprouting of a smile. "If you can *try* to stay away from Ally, I can try to *think* about getting along with you."

Dimples graced his cheeks, and she continued to suppress a mirroring smile.

"You have a deal." He drew nearer, and she crossed her arms and offered a playful shrug. "As the woman in this exchange, aren't I supposed to be the starry-eyed one looking for more than a one-night stand?"

At least, that's what so many novels and movies seemed to say…

He raised a brow, lips twisted together like he held back a laugh.

Right. She'd already failed to curb her sarcasm.

She held up both hands, then turned to continue her run, which turned into a quick walk since she allowed room for him to join her. "Sorry, I'll cut it out, and while we're making deals, maybe you can stop trying to trip me up in front of others? Oh, and promise you won't tell anyone about our night together?"

"I never planned to." His relaxed tone held an unmistakable sincerity.

She peered over at him, and her pitch lifted. "That easy?"

He'd given her hell at Maynard's, and then again at the general store. She hadn't expected him to agree so freely.

He shrugged, like their whole cat-and-mouse game never happened. "Sure, why not?"

"I just thought you'd… I don't know…" She frowned ahead, for some reason struggling to admit the next bit. "I figured you'd try to score points with the guys in town. I'm amazed everyone hasn't already heard."

"Do I look like someone who cares all that much about fitting in?"

His comment prompted her to actually *look* at him, and his grin expanded, those cobalt eyes glittering above. His sheer size and generally unperturbed demeanor more than supported his point. She gave a small laugh in agreement and then stared ahead, keeping the silence as they walked.

If only for a while, maybe she could ignore the voice telling her that, "Lonely was best." Dean here hadn't betrayed her. Not yet, anyway. No point punishing him for other people's shortfalls. So, she'd wait and see what he did with what little trust she gave him. Until then, she'd make sure he stayed clearly within the limits of this relationship, and only because he was set on staying in town.

"Friendship, nothing more. Okay?"

She peered back up to his frown, but he nodded all the same, out toward the long and dusty road ahead. "Sure. Now how about we pick up the pace? I wasn't lying when I said I like a run."

She quickened her steps, glad for the instant shot of adrenaline, all while not so confident the vow of "friendship" would stop at being friends.

Thirteen

DEAN RETURNED HOME from his run with Sarah to a sheriff's car parked in his driveway. The sheriff himself stood on the doorstep, his back leaning against a brick pillar as if he'd been there a while just waiting. Dean paused for a moment. Maybe his grab for freedom was over already, and still, the sheriff pushed away from the pillar and strolled closer, his wavy gray hair swept back and his weathered face unreadable.

"Dean Holloway?"

Adrenaline spiked, and Dean's pulse climbed to a galloping pace. He could stay and find out what the sheriff wanted, or he could run while he had the chance. Except the sheriff's car blocked his, so running would have to be a literal run. In a place like Harlow, his best chance would be hiding in the woods, but not before trekking across miles and miles of high grass plains.

He took a steadying breath and met the sheriff's direct stare, relaxing his body one tense muscle at a time. "That's me."

As far as he knew, this was just an innocuous visit to say hello. Best not to incriminate himself just yet.

The sheriff pointed to the front door. "Mind if we talk inside?"

Okay, so maybe not innocuous after all…

Shit!

Dean nodded, resisting the urge to say no.

Hope wasn't dead yet. Maybe the sheriff had no idea about his unintended involvement with Ms. Bonacci's home invasion.

"You're new to town." The sheriff spoke from behind Dean's shoulder, while he unlocked the front door.

"That's right."

The two men made their way into the sparsely furnished living room, and he took a seat in one of his new armchairs.

"I'm Sheriff Peter Marlin." The sheriff sat on the matching couch perpendicular to Dean, the lines either side of Sheriff Marlin's mouth anything but welcoming. The man had to be somewhere near his sixties. "I'm here to talk to you about the recent shooting. I assume you've heard about it?"

Dean put on a calm appearance and forced his breathing to slow in a bid to continue enjoying his new life of freedom. No way was he ever going back to prison. Certainly not again over a crime he'd wanted nothing to do with.

The sheriff's probing stare seemed to size Dean up, or the intention here was to psych him out. Either way, the silence chipped at his nerves since he had no idea what this man already knew.

"One death and a serious gunshot wound. Yeah, I heard." He curled and uncurled his fingers in his lap, stopping the second he noticed the fidgeting. He needed to give away as little as possible. To not fall into any traps. "I bet something like that doesn't happen around here very often."

"No. Never." The old sheriff gave a restless exhale and shook his head, the wrinkles over his forehead deepening, his brown eyes exuding a level of wariness. "As you can imagine, there's a lot of people worried and riding me for answers. It looks like a simple case of an ex-husband wanting revenge, but certain details don't add up. At a local level, I can't let up until I at least try to find some answers."

Dean lightened his pitch slightly, feigning surprise. "And your visit here today has something to do with that?"

"You're here from LA?" The sheriff angled his body toward Dean, as though he aimed for a better look at him, the goal being to weigh Dean's every reaction.

"That's right."

No point lying about information easily obtained.

"And are you aware the man killed in the incident, Anthony Stucco, was also from LA?"

Dean shrugged. "Of course. People here like to talk, and this whole thing is the current topic of choice. So yeah, I've heard. But LA is a big place. What are you trying to say?"

Sheriff Marlin cleared his throat, and he frowned down at the biscuit-colored carpet at his feet. A sign he wasn't so easily led astray. "You arrived roughly around the same time as the deceased. A strange coincidence, don't you think?"

Dean leaned forward and raised a brow, making it clear he wouldn't give in either. "Around that time, Harlow also had a town fair and a bunch of tourists from all over passing through. So, what do I think? I think it's highly likely two people from one giant city like LA could be at the same big gathering, yeah."

The sheriff leaned in, mirroring Dean's move; at the same time, mirroring his attempt to intimidate. "I'll come right out and ask you then, Mr. Holloway. Is there a connection between you and the deceased?"

Dean shifted back, an unnatural stillness taking him over, while sweat clammed up his palms. He pressed his hands to the sea-green armchair material and turned the question over and over in his head.

The last thing he needed were more felony charges added to his already dismal rap sheet. After ten damn years, he'd only now gotten his life to a point where he somewhat liked what he saw. Then again, a clever but evasive answer now would be the only way to avoid hanging questions over his honesty should someone ever manage to link him to Anthony.

"I understand you have a job to do, Sheriff, but—six degrees of separation and all—it'd be impossible for me to rule out having any overlapping acquaintances with Anthony."

Sheriff Marlin narrowed his eyes and held the expression of a man much more astute than his faded uniform and modest country surroundings implied. A man unwilling to tolerate ambiguous bullshit. "You know, son, I've done some research on you."

A bitter taste filled Dean's mouth, but he pressed his lips into a firm, flat line, still trying to give nothing away. "And what did you find?"

"You're ex-army. An infantry sergeant." The sheriff kept his brows low and his stare hard. His research had clearly paid off. "You did time in military prison for assaulting an officer. You were discharged for bad conduct. You then dropped off the radar for a solid ten years before resurfacing in Harlow in the aftermath of a shoot-out. See how all that doesn't sit well with me?"

Fuck. Holy fuck.

Still, this was stuff a background check *would* show up. So maybe all hope wasn't lost.

Dean had no control over his past, including what had happened after his incarceration and discharge. The many instances he'd tried to rebuild, failing over and over and over again…

"I did my time." He controlled his tone, his simmering anger nearly undetectable beneath his still delivery, despite the searing sensation expanding in his belly. "What's your point?"

"You have no employment records since your release." The sheriff lifted both brows, lightening the severity of his face but not the weight of his suspicion. "How have you survived all these years without any income?"

"What can I say? I did a bunch of cash-in-hand jobs, not too dissimilar to what I'm offering now that I'm in Harlow. Good thing you're not the IRS, huh?" He gave a casual smirk, the lighthearted gesture intended to distract from his thundering pulse and the sweat beading at his temples.

If he concentrated too hard on the effect of his nerves, the shallow pull of each breath alone would send him undone.

"I can arrange a call to the IRS if you'd like, Mr. Holloway?" Sheriff Marlin gave a dry reply, one that held the flat frankness of someone who'd been on the job for far too many decades. "I'm not sure you appreciate how bad this looks for you. Mr. Stucco left no evidence of having driven to Harlow on his own. No trace of a car. No keys on his body. He didn't have the resources or ability to find Ms. Bonacci on his own, either. But perhaps a man with a military past would. Now"—the sheriff leaned in farther, pointing a finger in Dean's direction as if to demand his total attention—"if Mr. Stucco *had* survived his attempts to extort money, he'd be up for a number of charges, including attempted murder. That's one hell of a charge, don't you think, Mr. Holloway?"

The sheriff didn't wait for a reply, and Dean didn't get the feeling he'd ever really wanted one. The older man scowled now, harsh wrinkles scoring his age-freckled cheekbones. "You should understand, if someone delivered Mr. Stucco to Ms. Bonacci's door here in Harlow, I need to know. I need to ensure they're caught, or at least that they've left. I won't have any murderous criminals loose in my town."

Murderous criminals? Dean's face and hands burned with an instant rush of blood. Emilia and Harlow had nothing to fear from him, not even back when he'd been in on helping Anthony get here.

Dean's work with Luciano had always been about finding people. Not *killing* them. He'd said as much to Anthony on the drive over. Hell, the entire syndicate knew that he never stooped that low. He'd had more than his fill of blood, guns, and gore in the service; his need for money was the only reason he'd justified working for Luciano. The syndicate had been mostly about rich criminals screwing over other rich criminals. Innocent civilians were rarely involved.

The Bonacci job was different. He'd nearly begged Luciano to keep Anthony distracted in LA while he worked that one alone. He would have been quick. He would have figured out if there was even any money to be had. And everyone would have survived the ordeal, shaken, but very much alive and unharmed.

But Stucco had always been a loose cannon, even as far back as when he'd hired Dean a decade earlier to help find and pry some girlfriend away from another man. Hell, he probably should have bowed out of that trivial job, too. He couldn't blame that woman for choosing literally any guy who *wasn't* Anthony.

Maybe all of this *was* Dean's fault. He should have bailed out of the syndicate earlier. Should have suspected that Anthony would sneak a gun on this latest trip.

"If someone helped Mr. Stucco, wouldn't it make sense for them to return to LA?" Dean drew a slow inhalation. He'd been half banking on the syndicate and law looking for him anywhere but here, though perhaps a little resigned now to whatever came next. "This whole mess has stirred up a lot of attention."

Sheriff Marlin's gaze darted about Dean's face. "Maybe, but it's still a little too convenient that you, Mr. Stucco, and Ms. Bonacci all originate from the same city."

"Like I said, a coincidence at best, but I appreciate you have a job to do. In fact, I'm grateful to live in a town where keeping the peace is a priority." Despite the sharp prickle raking over his skin, he shrugged, a small semblance of fight returning. He'd known nothing of Anthony's intentions that day and wouldn't take the heat for another man's crime. "So, tell me Sheriff, what can I do to put your suspicions to rest?"

The sheriff inched his posture back. "It'd help if I knew your movements in the hours leading up to the shooting."

Dean drummed his fingertips on his armrest and bit back a smile because, once again, meeting Sarah turned out to be a stroke of, for him, hugely unusual good luck. Perhaps he wasn't quite so done for after all. "I'm not sure the woman I was with would appreciate me saying."

The sheriff jolted his chin back in poorly hidden surprise. "You were with someone?"

Dean gave a slow nod, trying his best not to come across like a smug bastard. Not because of *what* he'd been doing that night, but because for once in his goddamn miserable life, he had a genuine alibi. "We met before ten p.m. at the soiree, and I left her house around three the next afternoon. As far as I know, that time would overlap Mr. Stucco's foiled crime spree, am I right?"

Sheriff Marlin didn't bother to answer. He instead dug a pen from his light brown shirt pocket as well as a small notebook, his movements a sudden flurry of activity. "I'll need this woman's name and address."

Dean opened his mouth, then pulled it shut again. Not an hour had passed since he'd promised Sarah he'd keep quiet about their night. As sketchy as his morals had been over the years, a sharp pang still knocked at his heart. He'd be betraying her trust, and so quickly too.

So much for turning over a new leaf.

Then again, the LAPD had suspicions about the syndicate, and the sheriff knew about Dean's past. What future did he have with Sarah if he *didn't* speak up?

He scrubbed a hand over his face and let out a low groan. "You know what sort of trouble you're getting me into here?"

Sheriff Marlin gave a stiff smile, one that didn't belie much sympathy. "You don't have any other choice."

A low and incredulous laugh broke from within Dean's chest, his last shreds of integrity sliding away.

Maybe my confession will buy me enough freedom to apologize, you know, right before she ditches my ass.

"Her name's Sarah." His ribs compressed and a churning sensation took over his stomach. "She lives on Lincoln Drive and works at Maynard's, and she likes to run, and"—he flicked his gaze up in time to register the sheriff's astonishment—"that's all I know about her."

Or at least, as much as he was willing to say, which was still far more than he'd wanted.

He peered down again, avoiding the sheriff's scrutinous stare, breaths changing to hollow puffs of regret. He never ratted others out. Much less others he liked.

"Sarah Overton?" The sheriff didn't even bother to scribble anything in his notepad, which now hung loose between his fingers. His wary stare inspected Dean as if to wonder what a woman like Sarah would be doing with a punk like him.

The sheriff was right.

He and Sarah Overton didn't belong together, but she liked him, and he damn well wanted her all the same.

He nodded to confirm the sheriff had the details correct, but also in silent agreement with the man's critical wonderings.

"Well." The sheriff rose from his armchair, his movements stiffer than when he first walked in, as though he carried the extra weight of this exchange. "I'll let you know if I have more questions."

Dean walked the sheriff to the door but paused before opening it. "Please, about Sarah, she didn't want anyone to know."

The sheriff turned, his expression taut before the muscles over his brow gradually softened. For the first time this meeting, the guy gave off a fatherly air. "It's my job to be discreet, Mr. Holloway. Enjoy your day, I'm sorry we couldn't meet under happier circumstances."

Fourteen

"I'll have the chicken and mushroom pie and a glass of your house red. And I'm sitting myself down right over there." Aggie McKey peered up at Sarah from the other side of the bar, her hand pointing to one of Maynard's empty dark wood dinner tables, the octogenarian's cheeks a tad rosier than usual.

"A red wine? Are you sure about that?" Sarah raised a brow and held a lighthearted smile. "You're usually a gin drinker, Aggie. Celebrating something special today, are you?"

Aggie's eyes glittered, and she looked about as excited as a teenager who'd inexplicably found herself seated next to her high school crush. Except no one else was beside her, and she and Sarah had done this dance a number of times over the years.

"Today's the day Walder and I had our first date, all sixty-four years ago, and I love the man more than ever." Aggie gestured down to her pink floral dress, a crocheted white shawl over her shoulders, and her long, white braid perched on top.

Truth was, Walder Aaron McKey had been dead for a solid twenty years, seven years shy of how long Sarah had been alive, and *still* Aggie celebrated every first date and wedding anniversary.

"Well, in that case…" Sarah gnawed on her lower lips as if to weigh up her next words, even though this was still part of *the dance.* "This meal's on me."

Aggie wasn't the only one to think her relationship with Walder deserved celebrating. That kind of love just didn't exist anymore. Sarah could always spare a meal and a glass of wine as her own little tribute.

"Oh, you're always such a dear." Aggie chuckled and reached across the bar, soon wrapping her age-affected fingers around Sarah's palm. "Walder didn't always make life easy for me, don't cha know, and I sure didn't for him either. Heck, I sure am happy I met him, though. You'll see just what I mean for yourself one day."

Aggie's stare turned still and all-seeing, as it tended to do from time to time, her blue-green eyes seeming to peer into the depths of Sarah's soul. The weird part was the old woman did tend to get things right with a freaky level of accuracy, but in this case, Sarah wanted her to be wrong.

She returned a half grin, certain she'd never come to understand the kind of love Aggie spoke of. Not with the way her luck went. Not that she intended on skipping down that brimstone-covered path of delusion, anyway.

"I'll look forward to it." Her lie now was about not letting her somber view of reality dampen Aggie's moment. "Until then, I'll go get you that wine and tell Gordon to serve you some pie."

She spun away to avoid any more of Aggie's sage advice and pep talking, making a beeline for the back of the bar where food orders piled up one after another. The dinner crowd was building, and as usual, she needed to stay on top of her staff. She was short on bar staff as it was, at least until more cover arrived in another hour. No time to think about absent family. Or injured exes. Or even Dean. Or his promises of "friendship"… *whatever that meant*… thank goodness.

"Sarah, I need to talk to you."

She jumped at Peter Marlin's voice, the old sheriff half-shouting across the bar at her, his face sporting an unusually serious expression. Her heart strained, and the ruckus around her seemed to die. Peter didn't usually come in wearing his uniform—and paired with his sober glare, *and* demanding she talk to him—something was wrong.

The order tickets in her hands slid from her fingers and onto the bar top. "Why are you here? What's happened? Is it Blaine?"

The sheriff frowned over his shoulder and then back at her. "Blaine's fine, but is there somewhere private we can talk? You won't want anyone hearing what I have to say."

She paused at the sheriff's softened tone, a tone that hinted at sympathy. What would he have to say to *her* that was urgent enough to disrupt the dinner service *and* required a private meeting?

She tilted her head, gesturing for him to follow her through the kitchen. A kitchen that ultimately had Gordon clinging about in his usual flurry of activity, the sounds short-lived by the time she and the sheriff made it outside to her usual quiet spot behind Maynard's.

"What's this about?" She spun around to Peter. Despite his assurances, she couldn't shake the fear that something terrible had happened. Something with Blaine.

The cool night air brushed her face, and the sheriff cleared his throat, his gaze pointed down in clear avoidance. Her heart jolted. What was there to avoid?

Blaine had been nothing but good to her. He'd been safe and reliable, nothing like Dean with his love of crushing her carefully constructed and controlled little world.

Blaine, with his unflappable morals—he would have stayed with her if she'd so demanded—even if his love belonged to Emilia and staying caused him total misery. His selflessness came back to haunt her now. Despite their clumsy ending, anything that hurt him still hurt her.

"I have some... um..." Peter peered past the beige brim of his sheriff's hat and over to her. "Sensitive information."

"Okay." She stuffed her hands into her dark denim pockets. "Shoot. What is it?"

His lip stiffened, as though he tried to hold on to whatever he had to say for as long as possible. "I need you to confirm where you were on Sunday, around midday to be exact."

Her muscles turned rigid and her thoughts stalled. "You mean when the shooting happened?"

The sheriff nodded. She'd known the man her entire life, regarded

Peter as her father more than her *actual* father. He was the last person she wanted to talk to about where she'd been.

Her face turned cold, and this time not because of the cool air. "Why do you need to know? It's not like you suspect me of anything, do you?"

She shot forth a smile, one designed to deflect, whilst giving the impression she had nothing to hide.

"No, no." Peter swiped his hat off his head, turning it over in his hands, his light-brown stare still avoiding hers at all costs. "Just a couple of details I need to clear up. You know, to corroborate another person's story…"

His attention continued to skitter about, the wrinkles over his cheekbones deepening, like he'd rather interrogate a serial killer than have this conversation with her.

Oh no. Surely Dean didn't say anything…

Maybe her neighbors saw him leave her house. *Mrs. Byrne.* She'd driven past earlier today, just as Sarah had been talking to Dean. Though, why would she call the sheriff over *that*?

"Oh shit." She ran her hand hard over her face. "Dean. He *did* rat me out!"

Her face went from cold to burning, but aside from her embarrassment, there was something else she wanted to know. "Why? Why would he do that?"

The sheriff shook his head. "You know I can't share any details on an ongoing investigation."

"No way, you think he had something to do with what happened to Blaine and Emilia?" *One thing at a time. Exonerate the man,* then *kill him.* "Well, if you're trying to ask if Dean and I were together, then yes, we were. We were at my house till midafternoon the next day."

Silent seconds ticked by, and it was her turn to peer away awkwardly, even as Peter's disapproval took the form of a drawn-out sigh. "Sarah, going home with a stranger, this isn't like you. Is everything okay?"

She kicked a pebble on the ground and watched the sheriff from under her lashes. "I'm fine, just bummed he couldn't keep his mouth shut."

"I didn't give him much choice." The sheriff offered a tight smile, one that said he wasn't judging her, just concerned. "Believe me, he didn't want to tell me."

She peered away again, making it clear she wasn't willing to discuss the reasons for her behavior that night. "Should I be worried you were interviewing him?"

"I didn't get the impression he's here to cause trouble, but..." The sheriff pushed his bushy brows together and glared at the ground. "What I did gather is that you could do a whole lot better, Sarah. Just promise me you'll be more careful. That man—"

"Dean and I aren't a permanent arrangement." Even as she finished speaking, Peter Marlin peered back up at her, his hands pushed into his hips, just above where he kept his firearm and portable radio.

"Two-forty on 325 Main." A female voice crackled over the radio. "May need medical assistance. Over."

Sarah recognized that address and her eyes widened. "What's a two-forty?"

Sheriff Marlin held her stare, but spoke into his radio's receiver. "Copy that two-forty, proceeding to 325 Main. Out."

He turned, already rushing around Maynard's perimeter toward the parking lot.

She raced after him, her heart clambering. "Peter, what's a two-forty?"

"Never you mind." He threw himself into the driver's seat of his brown patrol car. "And don't you even think of telling Aggie what you heard. You know she'll race over to the nursery with that big ol' rifle of hers. I'll speak to her in good time, you understand?"

She didn't get to answer before Peter sped away, sirens blaring.

That chilling wail followed her through the parking lot and back into Maynard's, where she buried her concerns in work and putting on a convincing display of external calm.

The bar's cheerful chatter made its way into her ears, and she skipped her gaze over to Aggie, a small horde of smiling locals now sitting at her table because they, too, were in on her annual Walder celebrations.

Sarah didn't like keeping quiet in an emergency or that she couldn't decipher what she'd heard on the sheriff's radio. More than anything, she didn't like that Aggie's special night was on track for a likely bad ending.

Fifteen

ANOTHER CLAY POT shattered with a dull clunk as Dean jammed his phone into his back jeans pocket. The last time he'd inserted himself into a bad situation, he'd paid far too costly a price. But here he was again, marching onward through the darkness and past the nursery's broken wire gate.

"Hey!" He yelled to three teenagers a few yards ahead. One kid's arm was wound back, ready to release another glass bottle at a plant pot balanced with others along a narrow beam.

The kid turned and flung the bottle at Dean's head instead.

Dean ducked, and the bottle exploded along the edge of a metal shelf behind him. Glass shards cut through the cotton of his dark gray t-shirt and into the back of his bicep. Just as he'd expected, no good deed went unpunished.

"Fuck." The curse hissed through his gritted teeth, and he stormed forward, the kid's angry green scowl shifting to wide-eyed fear, the two other boys behind him bolting away in opposite directions. "Got to work on your aim, don't you, you little shit?"

The kid tried to run after his friends, but Dean grabbed the kid's collar, the one attached to his hooded sweat shirt, and the kid dangled for a moment.

I've seen these boys before. Those weren't his friends. They were his siblings.

The kid directed a kick to Dean's shin. He jolted back in time to sweep a foot under the kid's one supporting leg, sending the little weasel well and truly onto his ass.

Outweighing the kid by about a hundred pounds, he pinned him down to the cold concrete, the wiry teenager wriggling and grunting, his dirty-blond hair flopping about his face. "Shove off, asshole. You're hurting me."

"Stop struggling, and it won't hurt so much, Weasel."

Dean peered down to his right arm pressed into the Weasel's chest, blood pooling around the crook of his inner elbow, his blood-slicked bicep not agreeing with this struggle.

"Get off me." The boy's voice twisted in pitch.

"You think I'll let you just run free?" Dean leaned in, though he did ease his weight off the Weasel's chest in favor of pressing an elbow into the kid's spindly throat, their faces now barely an inch apart. "You're lucky the worst I've done is call the sheriff."

"You snitched on me?" Despite the harsh language, the kid's voice screeched even higher and broke under the pressure of his panic, the redness in his cheeks fading to a shade of sheet-white. "You can't. My mother, she'll—"

"Hopefully kick your ass all the way into acting right. You don't look like you've hit fifteen, and you're already screwing up your life." Dean shook his head and made a light *tsk* sound. "Shit, boy, count this as your wake-up call."

A look of wide despair spread across the kid's face. A look that reminded Dean of himself at that age. He'd had no one to guide him, no one but a couple of other hooligans. Then again, he'd tried to change his life. To rise above his zero prospects—the army his ticket to that freedom. At least, that's what he'd been told. A spectacular failure that turned out to be…

Still, he had a chance right now to do one good thing in all his years.

"Please, I was just following—" The boy snapped his mouth shut, about to rat out his brothers.

Dean shoved the kid a little harder into the ground, garnering a helpless yelp. He hated being needlessly rough, but this wasn't all that needless if it worked to scare the boy into making better life choices. "You were following when you should have been thinking. Trust me kid, no matter how big and bad you get, there will always be someone or something stronger to stop you."

Like prison. Or the syndicate…

A stinging guilt wound through his conscience, but he pushed that useless emotion to the background.

The boy looked up at him, jaw tight as if attempting to silence a cry. An internal war raged beneath Weasel's terrified exterior. The kid shook his head, as though he wanted to speak but couldn't.

Dean shoved the boy again. "You don't need to tell me who the others were. They're your brothers. You're the Chadleys, and I saw you throwing rocks at Miss Overton at the soiree. But look around you, kid. Where are your brothers now?"

"Gone." The boy gave a raspy whisper and blinked once, twice, his movements slowing after the third, as if he processed the deeper meaning to Dean's question. "They left."

"That's right, they left you here on your own. Some brothers, huh?" Dean eased off the kid and gave him room to sit up, though he continued to grasp the front of the kid's shirt to ensure he stayed put. "You're the youngest, right?"

The kid nodded, his gaze dropping to the ground, his fingertips connecting with a cluster of loose pebbles atop the path's worn concrete.

The wail of a siren prompted Dean to stand and wrench the kid up with him. "Listen, while you're chilling your heels in the back of the sheriff's car, I want you to think about something I wish someone had told me when I was your age. You don't have to do what everyone else is doing, you got it? Especially if, like your brothers, everyone else is setting the bar way down low. Heck, if I could do things over again, I'd pick the most impossible thing I could become, and I'd go do that. Scaling back is always easier than dragging yourself out of a pit."

The kid kicked the earth with his scuffed and dirty sneaker and gnawed on his lip as if to think. "I've always wanted to be a sculptor. You know, make cool shit outta metal and stuff?"

"Good start, kid." Dean clapped the kid on the back while the sheriff's vehicle squeaked to a stop just yards away.

Sheriff Marlin jumped out. His gaze flicked between the kid and Dean before his stare hardened back on Dean, and he rested his hand over the gun in his hip holster. "Let the kid go."

Dean let out a sigh but did what he was told, slowly uncurling his fingers from the kid's shirt while mumbling, "See what I mean about life choices?"

The kid stumbled forward, both hands outstretched. "Sheriff Marlin, no."

But the sheriff's focus didn't budge an inch from Dean. "Put your hands behind your head where I can see them."

Again, Dean did as told. Clearly, the sheriff hadn't formed a glowing opinion of him earlier in the day.

The sheriff stayed stock still, his hand remaining over his gun. "Step away from the boy."

The boy stirred in Dean's peripheral vision. "You're making a mista—"

"Stop talking, Thom, get behind me." The sheriff shuffled closer to Dean. "You might know from experience how this goes."

"Sure I do." Dean narrowed his eyes at Thom, challenging the little weasel to own up anytime now—all while pain radiated from Dean's wounded bicep, the weight of holding his hands up not helping to stem the flow of blood.

"Good, then." The sheriff toyed with a clip on his belt, a clip that held handcuffs. "Lay face down, hands behind your head."

Dean knelt, extra slow.

"Sheriff." The kid's voice trembled now.

Dean turned to catch the kid's shaky movements, his shoulders rounded in a cowering sort of stance. He looked about ready to faint or pee himself. Dean couldn't decide.

"I said, get down." The sheriff barked the order at Dean and took a quick step closer.

The kid screeched and stumbled forward. "Don't shoot."

Thom wrapped a hand around the sheriff's forearm. Dean slammed his eyes shut, preparing to die, Thom's sudden move a gateway to the sheriff taking an accidental shot.

When a bullet to the brain didn't eventuate, Dean opened his eyes to the kid curled in a tight ball on the ground, his knees tucked to his chest, his hands pressed to his face while he screeched and sobbed. "Don't shoot him. I did it. It was me. I broke into the nursery."

The sheriff stepped away from Dean and removed his hand from his gun, his silent glare on Thom.

"My brothers and I, we thought it'd be a bit of stupid fun to break into the nursery. Then this guy came along." Thom thrust a hand in Dean's direction. "I was being a smart-ass and threw a bottle at him. That's why he's bleeding. It was me, not him. Don't shoot. Please."

Thom lifted his tear-streaked face to the sheriff, only for the sheriff to turn to Dean.

Dean shrugged his confirmation of the kid's story. The sheriff stepped back even more, his entire expression relaxing before he hunched down next to Thom and mumbled a few things too low for Dean to hear.

The boy nodded along to what the sheriff said, seeming to find calm while Dean rose to his feet.

Soon, the sheriff hooked a hand under the kid's arm, helping him stand and turning him toward Dean. "Thomas Chadley here would like to say something to you."

The sheriff held on to Thom and waited.

"I'm sorry." Thom blinked, sending his attention down before lifting it to Dean again. "I'm sorry for your injury there, and I shouldn't have thrown anything. I'm sorry I got you in trouble with the sheriff just now too. My mom will cover the costs of a new shirt and whatever medical bills you get, and I'm sure she'll see that my brothers and I pick up extra chores until we're like ninety years old and can pay her back."

Dean pressed his fingers to the back of his arm, the blood having slowed, but not altogether. "I hope you *do* get chores till you're ninety, if that's what it'll take to keep you out of trouble. But I can take care of this wound myself, so don't worry about any bills. I accept your apology, though."

The sheriff gave Dean an unreadable prolonged stare. Maybe the man hadn't expected him to be reasonable, much less the good guy in this whole mess. He turned Thom toward the patrol car and pressed him against the dusty exterior, the click of handcuffs coming next.

Dean frowned as a sniveling Thomas Chadley hunched into the patrol car's caged-off backseat. "Is that necessary?"

The sheriff slammed the door shut with an overly dramatic thud. "Nope, but if we're going to scare him and his brothers, we might as well do it right."

The sheriff strolled around and opened the trunk of his car where he dug around for a while before producing a folded bandage, presumably from a first aid kit Dean couldn't quite see.

"I owe you an apology too." The sheriff extended the bandage to Dean. "I made a snap decision, and it was the wrong one."

"And our chat earlier today had nothing to do with that?" Dean went about winding the bandage around his arm, occasionally flicking his gaze back to the sheriff.

"Could be." The brown of the sheriff's eyes brightened—an odd reaction given Dean's criticism. "Or could be I saw a giant man dragging a petrified teenager around by the shirt. Poor Thomas looked like he was about to pee himself."

Dean choked down a laugh, eyeing Thomas through the cruiser's window, his ashen face still pointed down to his lap. "I guess I can see how that might have looked."

The sheriff strode closer to his car. "I take it you called this in?"

"Yeah, though the brothers scattered, which is why I've only got Thom for all my trouble."

"Ehh, never mind about that. I'll catch up to them soon enough and get your statement tomorrow, after you've had a chance to see to your wound. Now"—the sheriff pounded an open hand to the cruiser's roof, before sliding in behind the steering wheel—"get in. I'll drive you home."

Sixteen

"Hello? Hello?"

Luciano squinted at the computer on his black marble desk, a bunch of icons on the laptop screen staring back at him, none of which made any sense. So much for technology making life easier. When had using a phone become a hassle? And what was with all this video-calling bullshit? All he wanted to do was talk to his cousin over in New York, but right now, he could hear Mark, but Mark couldn't hear him.

Not sure what to press, he stabbed at the trackpad hoping that might fix the issue. "Can you hear me?"

Still no reply.

"Luc, you haven't got your camera or microphone on." Mark's voice cut through the laptop speaker. A laptop Luciano rarely used since he had a personal assistant to handle pretty much everything to do with computers.

He'd grown up pre-internet era, and even though he'd missed the 1950s by decades, he figured America had only lost its shine since the days of Dean Martin and Frank Sinatra—video calls and technology included.

He shook his head at the computer and ran his fingers down the laptop's sides, then over the keyboard, looking for where the camera or microphone buttons might be. "Where the fuck are they?"

He stabbed a finger at the keyboard some more, but that just made a bunch of gibberish letters fill a typing field on the screens right. Maybe it was time to get his PA back in here so she could set up this stupid call.

"Luc, see a red microphone picture on your screen's bottom left?" Mark paused a beat, then added, "Click on it with your mouse."

Luciano searched the screen again, an agitated fire filling the space beneath his ribcage before he saw what his younger cousin talked about. "Can you hear me now?"

"Yes, now do the same with the camera icon just next to it."

Luciano did just that, only to be met with the moving image of Mark shaking his head—with his thick, light brown waves swept back, his open-collar powder blue business shirt matching his eyes.

Luciano peered at the top right corner, a smaller square beaming his own moving image back at him. He was about a decade older than Mark and about a hundred pounds heavier, his hair dark and gelled back, and unlike his pretty-boy cousin, he put in the effort to wear a suit and tie for work.

"So, what the fuck is all this about?" Mark held up his phone and flicked through article after article on his screen, each time pausing to push the phone closer to the camera so Luciano could read the titles.

Mark turned the phone back to him and read out loud, "There are signs Anthony Stucco didn't work alone. Authorities say they are on the hunt for anyone who might have aided his failed attempt to extort money from his ex-wife, Emilia Bonacci."

Mark lowered the phone and stared back at Luciano. "First failure, and now you fuckers left evidence that Anthony had help?"

"Look"—Luciano held up both hands, the muscles at his jaw bunching with a desire to unleash his temper—"even we don't know what happened, which is why I wanted to talk with you."

"Oh, so let me guess, you want *me* to figure out what happened?" Mark raised a brow, glaring ahead like he thought Luciano had lost his fucking mind. "Seems Anthony's was the only body found, so what happened to the guy you had assisting him?"

Luciano scoffed and shook his head. "Like you don't know, you arrogant piece of shit."

Mark gazed up at the heavens, gaping in a hammed-up oblivious act. For years, he'd pushed to modernize the syndicate, wanted each branch to become more tech savvy. But none of that bullshit made much sense to Luciano and the other top honchos. Why fix something that worked well enough?

"Let me guess." Mark's expression hardened, his moment of sarcastic humor over. "Your guy bailed."

Luciano clenched his jaw together, working his teeth against each other in another attempt to hold on to his cool. Despite what Mark liked to think, Luciano wasn't stupid or a loose cannon. He was just some poor immigrant kid from one of LA's scummier outer suburbs, a kid who the whole world had looked down on until he did what he could to get ahead.

If dealing drugs had given him his start, so what? He'd opened a door, met people like Anthony Stucco, who'd then opened doors with Rudolph Manzinni—the enigmatic man behind the entire syndicate.

Fact was, despite Mark's attitude right now, he owed Luciano for the college education neither of them could have afforded if Luciano had kept his hands clean. He'd gotten Mark into this gig too. Gotten him the New York branch. They both had power and money now, enough to keep their families rich over multiple lifetimes. There'd be no worrying about where the next meal or medical treatment might come from. Whoever said crime didn't pay, was a fucking moron. So, he wasn't about to let Mark or some pissant cog like Dean Holloway put a dent in what he'd built.

"I'm in over my head here, okay?" He paused, not for the first time in his life, doing what fucking needed to be done to get ahead. "I need your help."

For this one time, he agreed with his cousin. A little tech savvy had helped Dean Holloway find Anthony Stucco, so maybe it had helped him escape the syndicate altogether too. Now it was time to fight technology with technology and have Mark, with his army of eggheads, find Holloway.

"To find your interloper?" Mark gave a mocking sort of laugh. "Don't you have your own man for that?"

"Yeah, and he's the one we need to track."

Mark's short, mocking laugh turned into a boisterous roar, and he slapped his hand repeatedly over a desk Luciano couldn't see on screen, the hard thud and rocking of Mark's computer making that desk "visible" either way.

"You're an ungrateful little punk, aren't you?" Luciano glared into the tiny camera on his laptop, finally releasing his frustration, his words loose but his tone controlled. "You think it's fucking funny that one dissatisfied employee might blow a big, fucking hole into the syndicate's side? If you don't help me, you'll be guilty by association, and we'll both be knee-deep in shit with Rudolph, you got it? Man, for all your education, you're a fucking dead brain, you know that?"

He shook his head in a slow and condescending motion, while pressing his lips together in a tight line. Meanwhile, Mark held a long silence, his stare unreadable but hinting at thought.

"Okay, fine. I'll see what I can do." Mark leaned back in his chair, no apology given but the decision made. "But if I find him, Luciano, no more fuckups. You deal with Mr. Holloway and anyone else helping him. You make them all disappear."

Seventeen

SARAH POUNDED her fists against Dean's thick, red, wooden front door, her patience wearing thin since his car sat parked at the top of the driveway. He'd either gone on a late-night stroll, or was intentionally ignoring her.

She took two steps back and scanned the double-story brick house's exterior. No lights through the windows. No sounds either. No sign of life at all. And still, her hot temper refused to die. She wanted to stay. More importantly, she wanted to fight.

Maybe he's still inside laughing his ass off at my pathetic demands for him to come out.

What happened to Miss Self-Control?

Standing on this man's doorstep like a lost puppy, clearly.

The loss of control was Dean's fault. He'd promised to keep her secret. The one about their night together. Then again, he'd also lied about leaving town. Stupid her for believing him *twice*.

Oh, she'd make him pay. Lost puppy or not, both she and puppies could have sharp teeth, and she'd rip holes through Mr. Holloway for betraying her trust.

Though… maybe not tonight…

She kicked at the door and growled again at his absence, releasing some tension, before turning for her car. She should have stuck to her instincts about not trusting anyone.

"Miss me already?"

She halted at Dean unfolding his large frame from the open door of Sheriff Marlin's patrol car parked at the end of the driveway.

What the hell?

He plodded toward her in the dark, her tummy churning that, of course, Peter Marlin had to be here to witness her standing on Dean's doorstep at an ungodly hour.

The sheriff gave her a tight smile and a slight nod through the windshield, a reminder of his earlier warning for her to be careful with her heart.

Dean trudged closer, his stare fixed to the ground like perhaps he avoided her.

Maybe he just has other things on his mind. I can't tell, and I'm not sure I care.

Unlike many in Harlow who would have sat back to enjoy the show, the sheriff steered his car away, giving her the good fortune to speak with Dean alone. "I need to talk to you."

Dean stabbed at his front door's lock with a key, missing the first few times, before dropping the set completely.

Was he drunk? He'd come home in the back of the sheriff's car, after all. But he didn't strike her as a big drinker. Besides, Maynard's was the only bar in town, and she'd just come from there. Where had he been drinking?

She crossed her arms and waited for him to pick up the keys and try again. "Did you hear me? I need to talk to you."

"Yeah." He groaned as he pushed his door open, the crescent moon and lack of street light meant she couldn't see much beyond his severe glower. "I heard you."

He disappeared deeper into his house, leaving the heavy wood door wide open. She followed and pushed the door behind her. "I got an interesting visit from the sheriff today. You told him about our encounter. I want to know why."

"Sarah." He strolled across the large living room, and his lowered tone hinted at fatigue. "Now's not a good time."

"You promised you'd keep our night a secret." She continued after him, up a set of stairs with a painted white banister. "Of all people, did you have to tell Sheriff Marlin? It would have been less awkward if you called my dad and told him the gory details."

"Leave your dad's number on your way out and I will."

She stopped in her tracks while his broad back disappeared around a corner. *What a jerk.* Not once did he bother to turn and look at her, and now this snarky reply? Heck, he didn't so much as turn on any lights so she could see where she was going.

His dispassionate dismissal had her releasing a soft growl. She marched onward, now indifferent about her intrusion in his house. He'd intruded on her entire life. Exploited her trust. She *would* get an answer.

A bright white light came on at the end of the upstairs corridor, and she called after him, "I'm talking to you."

"I know."

She strolled through a door and rested her hand on the frame, pausing. Dean stood within a fully tiled bathroom, a heavy stream of water filling the sink and disturbing the quiet.

He scrubbed his hands in quick motions under the taps, again, not looking at her, though he did speak. "Given how fired up you are, I'm sure there's not much I can say right now that will make you hate me less. The sheriff asked where I was that night. I couldn't lie. Can we drop this now?"

His left bicep rippled from beneath his dark gray t-shirt, though she could only see one side of him since he stood in profile. Her breath quickened at the size of him, his clear physical strength and unrefined air. Even when in a prickly mood, he still got to her.

He should be the last man I want right now.

"You could have at least warned me." She dipped her attention to the occasional flash of a white hand towel in the sink, unable to figure out what the hell he was doing or why. "The surprise official visit came while I was at work."

"I don't have your number, remember?" He turned to her, his face pale and sporting a somewhat clammy sheen. "Though, you're comfortable enough to follow me around my house, so maybe I should?"

Her gaze dropped and snagged on the state of his right arm—a bandage at the top with a crimson bloom soaking through, his forearm streaked in red despite his covert scrubbing.

"Holy shit!" She charged forward, her anger collapsing as she reached for the towel in the sink—a towel that, on closer inspection, was tinged pink. "What happened to you?"

She wrung out the towel and began wiping at the remaining blood down his arm, working her way up to the ineffectual bandage.

Dean's iceberg gaze didn't waver from hers, though it took on a harder edge. "I happened to be strolling by the nursery just as the Chadleys were trying to demolish it. One of them threw a bottle, and I got this."

He lifted his arm, gesturing to his concealed injury.

"And the sheriff didn't call the doctor for you?" She yanked off the bandage and winced at the open wound there. No wonder the sheriff had asked her not to tip off Aggie about the nursery. "This wound needs stitches."

He shrugged and pulled off his bloodied shirt. "The sheriff tried to call the doctor and got no answer. Anyway, I can handle this. I've had worse."

She shook her head at his overconfidence and the sheriff's lack of action. Dean lowered his injured arm and grimaced through the effort.

"The way I see it you have two choices." She tossed the stained bandage into a small trash can near the sink. "I can get you to the nearest hospital, but that's a good hour away, or you can take a seat on the edge of that bath over there, and I can stitch you up myself."

She nodded at the bath but kept her attention on him. Even covered in dirt and blood, Dean drew her in, enough to make her forget her earlier anger. Enough to make her launch into action just so she could stop staring at him, and because she also didn't like to stand idle when someone clearly needed help. "Do you have a first aid kit?"

He pointed to the sink. "Drawer to the left."

She turned away and found a navy-blue case about the size of a toolbox and somewhat larger than the usual home first aid kit. The damage to his bicep appeared small, but the area would get lots of movement, and the constant seeping meant the cut ran too deep to heal unattended.

"We'll sterilize your wound and the needle first." She balanced the case on a wide ledge on one end of the bath before throwing the case open and assessing what supplies he had, stopping to frown at a plastic pack containing a suture needle and thread. "You especially accident prone or something? These don't come in your standard kit."

She waved the pack in his direction, snatching up a small bottle of rubbing alcohol while she was at it.

His hooded eyelids narrowed before they relaxed. "Something like that. Seems you have some experience with wounds too."

She coated the needle with alcohol and dropped some onto a cotton pad for his wound. He groaned at her touch, and not in a good way, his muscles taut with a clear desire to escape the pain. "Glass injuries come with the territory of running a bar. Besides, I grew up in the country with a clumsy younger brother."

"And where were Mommy and Daddy while little Sarah was saving the day?" Dean's voice echoed against the small bathroom's walls, somehow highlighting just how alone they were together, despite his all-too-clever lift of a brow.

She took the threaded needle and gleefully dug the first stitch into his arm.

He hissed, muscles again clenching. She did her best to hide a satisfied smirk. "If you must know, Daddy was a doctor, a surgeon actually. He worked at the hospital I mentioned and taught me how to do this. A skill I've used on occasion over the years."

Especially after Daddy Dearest disappeared to a new city, with a new woman, leaving Sarah alone with her brother and shell-shocked mother.

She tied the first stitch and moved to the next, figuring she'd need about six to finish the job. "And we weren't talking about my family.

We were talking about you and your propensity to cause more trouble than I bargained for."

"Right. That." His attention rested on her hand pressed to his naked shoulder from behind, the careful stroke of that attention sparking a dance of nerves inside her tummy. "Look, the sheriff came to me. It's not like I went searching for someone to share our story with. And if I had wanted to talk, it sure as shit wouldn't be with Sheriff Marlin."

She cleared her throat, seeking distraction. "Really? So now you're getting visits from the sheriff and lifts from him too. What am I supposed to think?"

His lips lifted into a slight smile, and his stare trekked up until he held her gaze. "You're right, I'm sorry. I'd promise not to get you in trouble again, but I seem to have a knack for it."

A frustrated sigh broke from her lips, and she sat behind him on the tub's edge. The scent of his skin, including the earthy musk of outside, teased her. The man seemed set on making light of her secrecy, and still, something about him, about the way he looked at her when his mouth wasn't moving, tugged at her sympathy.

Maybe she made the connection up in her head, but she got the sense Dean here hadn't had a whole lot of second chances in life either —missed opportunities being something she identified with.

She moved to bury the needle for her third stitch, but he grabbed her wrist, dragging out a long silence before he spoke again. "Sarah. I really am sorry."

A small hollow grew deep within her. She bit the insides of her cheeks, attempting to come up with a smart reply, only for nothing but a rough croak to escape her mouth.

His low, soft tone. The sincerity in his apology. She wanted to believe him, but she shook her head and tried again. "It doesn't matter."

Of course it does. Otherwise, I wouldn't have raced over here.

"It does matter." His words echoed her thoughts, and his grip on her wrist tightened by the slightest margin. "It does to me, and I made you a promise that I didn't keep."

She slid her wrist free of his hold and sank the third stitch in, that sinking in perfect harmony with whatever happened within her heart, the all-too-familiar plunge of disappointment. "I'm a grown woman. I'll survive."

His little stumble today really wasn't the worst thing ever to happen to her, and she genuinely did forgive him, so maybe she needed to bail from his house as soon as she could.

His gaze burned into her face, creating a heat there while she fastened a new knot.

She did her best not to return the attention, even wincing as he spoke again. "The sheriff has a soft spot for you. Why?"

She dabbed blood from his wound through her ensuing lie. "Harlow's a small town. Everyone's invested in everyone else's business here."

"Sheriff Marlin showed more concern than your average. Is he family or something?"

"Something."

She dropped the cotton pad she'd dabbed him with onto her lap. What was with his sudden questions, anyway? Though, even as she got what she wanted—uninterrupted silence—that silence provided far too much space for her to think… of her father, the sheriff, her erratic mother, Sarah's failed engagement, and her recent forced solitude.

Heck, even her solitude wasn't all *that* recent or forced. She kept to herself more than any normal person, even when she *was* in a relationship. Blaine hadn't minded. Perhaps that should have rung alarm bells since he'd held his own secrets, ones that hurt her in the end.

So, maybe keeping quiet wasn't the best thing for her. Maybe opening up to this mysterious stranger would help somehow.

Or maybe the breakup has affected me worse than I thought, and I'm starting to lose my marbles…

Maybe.

Still, she had a choice here. Say exactly what bothered her, or clam up as she always did, which hadn't gotten her all that far, now had it?

She swallowed hard and readied to speak, her thoughts snagging on the man beside her and how the heat from his skin seared into hers. In that moment, she wished for their usual scuffles or for him to kiss her again—to pull her from the everyday humdrum of being sad, unfortunate, and bitter Sarah Overton.

The silence here was too dangerous. So, she drew back the intrusive self-pity long enough to decide that talking beat overthinking.

"For a time there, I was both Mommy and Daddy."

Eighteen

SARAH'S FINGERS paused around the needle, just before she placed the fourth stitch into Dean's wound. She pressed her lips together and second-guessed what she'd just admitted—that her childhood had been weighed down by far more stress and responsibility than she should have borne.

Dean turned and took hold of her hand. She winced, his touch the very thing she needed to avoid.

"You're shaking. Take a break."

Her heart strained at his open stare and hushed tone, a tone that matched his gentle hold and echoed within the tight confines of his bathroom.

"You're right." She struggled to look him in the eye, so she dropped her attention to his large hand over hers, a strong hand that belonged to someone who'd lived a hard life, perhaps not too dissimilar to hers, though maybe in different ways.

What is his story, anyway?

"I can probably manage the rest, if you like." He moved to take the needle from her, but she snatched it away. No chance she would make him stitch himself up simply because she was having a moment. She'd be okay. She always found a way to be okay.

And seriously, who was Dean? What with visits from the sheriff and the next-level first aid kit, then Dean's seeming comfort with patching himself up…

"The sheriff's invested in me because he's looked out for me since I was seventeen." She met his gaze, not one to shy away now that she'd made the decision to open up. "My family were model citizens here in Harlow. Dad had a respectable job, and the bar belonged to my mom's family, who'd been in Harlow for as long as anyone can remember. So, when my dad skipped out on Mom, it was a shock to everyone, especially her. She had a breakdown, and Sheriff Marlin was there the day she threw all our furniture out onto the front lawn, including smashing every antique in the house. It was a huge scene that no one's forgotten, though I wouldn't say she was angry, so much as manic and completely broken."

"And that's why you said I should have called your dad?" Dean's brows squeezed together, his expression contorted in a look of concern. "That's how you see Sheriff Marlin, like a father?"

She nodded, the strain in her body easing a little since at least *she* was the one telling this story and not one of the townsfolk. "Peter got Aggie McKey to swing by and look out for my brother and me, while he drove my mom to the nearest hospital. To this day, Mom still struggles to look after her own basic needs. She was never the same after that. Our entire family has never been the same."

"That's why your brother lives in Boston?"

She nodded again. "Our family is scattered across the country. With Mom no longer an option, Chip was too young to stay in the house with me, so he had to live with my dad and his mistress."

The intensity in Dean's stare grew. "And you stayed in Harlow, alone?"

"My dad destroyed our family, and no one dared force me to stay with him. I was less than a year from being legally independent, not that I wasn't independent already. So, what I couldn't do for myself, Sheriff Marlin and Aggie took care of, including running Maynard's."

Dean settled back, as if her explanation somewhat satisfied his curiosity. He handed her the needle. "And while you already had too much on your plate, you also promised to keep an eye out for Ally?"

Sarah rolled her eyes. The lead-up to Chip leaving town had been a frenzied affair. "Ally and Chip were always close. He was devastated to leave her, more than anyone else in this town besides me. And while I lost a brother, she lost her best friend. She's been somewhat socially aimless ever since, though we've gotten closer over the years."

Dean frowned at the ground before his attention landed on her, his expression quick to lighten. "I like this."

"What?" She let loose with a big smile and made her fourth stitch. "Me repeatedly stabbing you with a needle?"

He hissed, a rich chuckle soon rumbling through his chest. "Well, you are exceptionally good at that, and I like your confidence, but what I really mean is, I like when we're not fighting. When we're just talking and I get even the tiniest glimpse into who you are."

"Yeah, well, I'll just be another moment. So don't get comfortable with any of that."

Despite her cynical reply, she too liked the ease of this exchange, even if she did focus on the needle in order to avoid his intent stare. Besides, maybe part of why she found it so easy to talk with him was that he didn't already know her entire life, unlike ninety percent of people in this town, so he didn't have a stack of town gossip weighing down his opinions of her.

She tugged the needle out of him and tied the thread's end. He outstretched a hand and cupped her cheek. She nuzzled into his touch for the briefest second before her heartbeat seemed to pause, and she pulled back, scared he might kiss her again.

"Don't."

He flexed his brow, seeming more concerned than annoyed. "I wasn't going to."

"Don't touch me."

He took his hand back. "Now you're touching me."

"I'm patching you up. There's a difference." She swallowed against the thickness gathering in her throat and peered at her fingers around the needle, bloodied and shaking.

"Listen." He turned to her more fully, his widened pupils pleading for her attention. "You were honest with me, and I want to be honest with you. We've established that when I first got to town, I had no intention of staying. What I haven't told you is that you're the number one reason I'm still here. Sarah, my past isn't so rosy either. I want a new start."

She scoffed, her heart rate exploding at his certainty when she was everything but. "And you figured I'd be your fresh start?"

"Why *shouldn't* you be my fresh start?" His direct stare held hers, awaiting a reply, which only came in the form of her taking her final stitch and him squeezing his eyes shut against the pain.

"That's a lot of pressure to put on a relative stranger." Again, she focused on her stitching, her movements quick but tight.

"We're more similar than you'd like to see."

She lifted her attention to his weak smile. She schooled her face in what she hoped would be a flat stare. "That sounds truly ridiculous. You know that, right?"

"Not ridiculous. *Simple.*" He gave a small shrug, eyeing her work. "In that, I like you, you like me."

"Not so simple." She snipped the final stitch and wiped down his wound with a final dab of alcohol. "You'll only break your own heart."

An aching silence stretched between them while she washed her hands and everything from the kit that she'd used, her face hot the entire time. She wanted to steer clear of him and his plans—overly idyllic plans she'd heard a thousand times from various other people. She'd learned to guard her heart, and she was right about him also needing to.

"Sarah."

She kept herself busy returning to the bath's edge to jam tools back into the first aid kit.

"Sarah."

She swiped up the kit and ferried it back to its drawer, eager to hightail out of there as quickly as possible.

"Sarah." He grabbed her wrist before she could get too far, spinning her back around to face him, that cobalt stare not leaving her face. "Like you, I haven't been all that in control of what happened to me. All I meant is I want that to change."

His tone had turned softer, and he gave his head a slow but certain shake. The quiet expanded between them in an unexplainable and never-before-felt pull—one that seemed to halt time and draw her in—despite her resistance. "What were you thinking that night at the soiree, the moment just before you bumped into me?"

What had she been thinking about? About how alone she was and how she always seemed to get the rough end of any relationship she dared to engage in. And why would any of that change now? Especially with a man as enigmatic as Dean?

I have zero reason to trust him.

She blinked, the moment bursting like an overfull balloon. "I've said enough about me and still know nothing about you."

He stood and she backed away, the action increasing the unspoken distance between them. "What do you want to know?"

"I'm not sure. Why did the sheriff call you a person of interest in the shooting?"

"He went digging around in my past and figured he found something." He stared at her a moment, his expression unreadable, before he turned to the door.

Despite getting what she wanted—a reason to leave—she slammed the first aid kit to the sink's counter and picked up her pace, following him down the hall and stopping just shy of the room he'd entered. *His bedroom.*

"And what did the sheriff find?" She peered inside. Though his house didn't have much furniture, her attention caught on two small shelves either side of his bed. Not just shelves, but *bookshelves.* Filled to busting with books.

He reads? This man reads?

Her thoughts slipped to the soiree and his suggestion that "ninth-grade English" was about as far as his exposure to literature went—that memory alighting an inkling that he maybe tended to downplay his more refined points by a whole lot.

He let out an exasperated sigh, which made her attention shift back to him as he turned to her with a clean shirt in his hand and shadows taking up space under his eyes. "He found out about my old job, and that it didn't end well."

He tugged his shirt over his head and down his body. His sharp movements were a strong hint she should let the subject go for now, even while the information provided new details about this man, only to awaken more questions.

He has a story. One he isn't so eager to tell.

Seems he's not all that wrong about our similarities…

He drew near, and his gaze connected with hers in what could only be described as a molten stare. Her pulse quickened, his grin suddenly easy and bracketed with deep dimples. "You and I both know I wasn't there when Blaine Callaghan got shot."

There was Blaine's name coming from Dean's lips. An unwanted dose of reality. This sultry man's reminder of what they'd been doing when all hell broke loose.

A weak ache gripped her chest, but his close proximity held her in place. "In our own ways, we could be good for each other."

"Except in this small town, people will see us together and get to gossiping. With all that's happened, I don't need whispers following me everywhere I go."

And still, a light fluttery feeling worked through her tummy and out into her limbs, as though she actually considered his proposition, if for no other reason than she wanted to know his story.

Oh no, don't lie. It's so much more than that.

Right. Like remembering just how alive, and wanted, and seen she felt in his presence, especially when he made love to her—fanciful emotions ill-fitted to her or her reputation. But she was a living, breathing woman, wasn't she? And maybe. Just maybe. There were things she *did* want.

He saw her waning resolve—like he knew that all he had to do was push just a little harder and all her protests would fold to his feet—and he lifted his hand to her cheek again and said, "Sarah, no one else needs to know."

Nineteen

"WHAT ABOUT THE SHERIFF? He knows about us."

Sarah ran her attention over the details of Dean's face, who stared back at her. Maybe he could read the clash of desire and doubt churning her tummy. Maybe his offer that "no one else needed to know" about this relationship meant she could have what she wanted, *him,* and keep that *want* a secret. Or maybe his proposal was all too simplistic.

"The sheriff won't tell anyone, and you know it." He shrugged, his hand still resting on her cheek.

"You're right, he won't." She clawed her fingers into the bedroom door frame, her focus unwittingly shifting to his bed with its masculine plain white sheets and dark blue throw. "But nothing stays a secret in Harlow."

"Sarah?" His attention followed to where hers had been, to the bed and back to her, her heartbeat skipping since it didn't take a genius to know where her mind had gone.

He held her, even as the tight tugging in her chest told her to step away from him and his bedroom.

She blinked up at him, slow and heavy, regretting every second she failed to run. "What?"

The breathiness in her voice alone opened a hollow within her. She didn't want to leave. Begged for a reason to stay. Even if staying should have been the *last* thing she wanted.

And of course because of that conflict, she *didn't* run when he leaned in close—so close that the smallest nudge would bring their lips together. "We could pretend we hate each other."

She slammed her eyes shut, feeling stupid and numb and exhilarated all at once. "Sorry?"

He'd reduced her to a bumbling mess, and all it took was his simple touch—a simple touch that permeated through her body in gentle waves, seizing her ability to do the smart thing and leave.

"What if we let people believe we hate each other?" His thumb rubbed a firm line over her cheek, that caress seeming to plead with her to hear him out, to tip her chin upward and just kiss him. "We'll trash talk each other to anyone who'll listen, throw in a few public squabbles. No one will suspect a thing."

"Dean…" She shook her head.

"It could work."

"It could, but—"

"If outright hate is too strong, then we can fake indifference." His voice was a soft whisper, words meant for her alone, words that melted her so much that she didn't hesitate to close her eyes the moment he leaned in and pressed a soft but quick kiss to her lips.

How had she gotten here? She'd stormed into his house in search of confrontation, fully prepared never to speak to him again, and here she stood now, caving to the low thrum of need spreading roots throughout her body.

"Just give my idea a try. Can you at least do that?" His attention swept over her face, his soft focus pleading with her. "Tomorrow night, I'll come to Maynard's. You'll get to pretend to be the biggest bitch you can muster—"

"Would it even be pretending?"

His lips stretched into a grin. "No comment. Either way, whatever you dish out, I'll take and I'll give right back. We can have fun with this. If my plan doesn't work, we'll call this whole thing quits. I promise."

A slow smile tugged at her lips. She could unashamedly slam Dean's pride in public, while having her fill of him in private. *The best of two worlds.*

She gave a small nod, only for his lips to crash down over hers like that small nod was something he'd been waiting for his entire life. And maybe it was. Maybe she'd been waiting her whole life too. Not for Dean exactly, but to give herself permission to be free, even if it was with just this one thing. With *him.*

He scooped her up and carried her to his bed.

So much for him putting on a new shirt. Even as his mouth ravaged hers, her fingers clawed and pulled at the loose cotton over his shoulders. She wanted him and his naked body over hers, and within moments, that's exactly what she had.

He made love to her hard and fast—taking his fill, while she took hers—two people who'd waited far too long. Two people who could only ever be themselves around each other.

She arched into him. Clung to him. Her cries were wild and unabashed and a release in more ways than one. All while he took her, his stare pitching a challenge for her to break first. Or maybe there was more to her need and his demanding than two people seeking a thrill —a universe of buried pain and unspoken dreams.

He wanted. She wanted to run. That much was clear. But there was no escaping this—this moment where she relinquished control and relished all he had to give—his breaths exploding against her skin, his length swelling within her and pushing her to her limits.

Her heartbeat climbed at the intensity of it all. Of Dean and everything he drew from her.

She couldn't hold on any longer, and her eyes slammed shut, her hands coming away from him to claw at the bedsheets. Every muscle in her body bunched as a deep cry tore from low in her chest. For once in her life, she was happy to lose. Happy to break.

He picked up the pace and broke along with her, his face buried at her neck, his kisses tracing the tendon there.

This wasn't love. Not by a long shot.

But she loved how he felt, how he let her be someone else, or perhaps more herself than ever before. Either way, if tonight was all about making love, tomorrow would be nothing but all-out *war*.

Twenty

"I DON'T CALL BEING in the wrong place at the wrong time heroic."

One day after making her pact with Dean, Sarah put on her flattest, most bored expression and leaned a hip against the bar, even as Ally's cheeks took on a sudden red glow, her eyes flaring in disbelief.

"Gee, Sarah, ease up." Ally flicked an apologetic cringe to Dean sandwiched between her and Aggie, while an out-of-uniform Sheriff Marlin sat farther to the left. "If Dean hadn't interrupted the Chadley boys, Aggie might not have a nursery left at all. And what about my painted pots? Those things take me ages to make, and they're kinda spendy to put together too. Those little vandals could have smashed the lot."

Sarah drummed her fingertips over the bar, her face hot because Dean's stare refused to leave her whenever the others weren't looking. "From what I hear, he didn't do all that much. Besides, who decided to hold this sappy lovefest at my bar, anyway?"

Aggie reached out and gave Dean a firm pat on the back, his smug grin spreading wider the moment Sarah caught his gaze. "I did. The least I owe him is a free drink. Heck, he's been looking for work, and with Emilia busy taking care of Blaine, I sure could use some extra help at the nursery, don't cha know?"

Sarah rolled her eyes and shuffled over to the bar's glossy brass taps to pull that "free drink" for Dean, a row of confused faces narrowed her way.

"You owe him nothing. And will you all stop scowling at me like I'm crazy?" She focused down at the amber liquid rising in the glass she held at a forty-five-degree angle. "Unlike you all, I'm not about to worship some man who would have kept walking if not for one of the Chadleys swinging a bottle at his head."

She shot Dean a sarcastic look, his eyes lighting at her short-sell on his efforts. "That's not what hap—"

"Dean, not all of us are gullible." She shook her head at him. "I know it sucks not being able to convince everyone in this town that you're a stand-up guy."

The muscles around his eyes stiffened, hinting that maybe she'd hit a nerve, though his lips still held that jovial upward curve. "I hear those Chadley boys were throwing rocks at people at the soiree too. That they've been harassing people for months. Any normal person would show some appreciation, Sarah."

He held her gaze for a beat too long, his gaze flicking down her body and back up again, like he sought to remind her of how they'd met and just what sort of appreciation he'd received and still wanted.

She mumbled something about never being more glad to be considered *abnormal*, only for Sheriff Marlin to clear his throat and draw her attention back to the group. "I know you two have your differences, but Dean's actions might have saved this town a great deal of trouble. After I dropped Mr. Holloway at home, I tracked down the remaining Chadleys. Their mother was in on the idea of them spending the night in the station's holding cell, and she was mighty glad for the intervention. Maybe this time, they'll get to acting right."

The sheriff held his usual warm and even tone, his world-weary brown eyes sending a tight pang to Sarah's chest. He of all people didn't deserve her deception, but perhaps the truth of her friends-with-benefits relationship with Dean would hurt Peter more.

No doubt he'd think she was rebounding from Blaine, perhaps even consider her actions dangerous and self-destructive. Maybe he'd be right on both counts, but being with Dean felt good. She just wanted to feel good.

"You see, Sarah?" Ally's semi-famous wide smile lit up, and she threw her arms around Dean's broad shoulders, the sudden movement knocking him briefly off-center. "He's a hero."

Ally maintained her stronghold, and Sarah clapped her hand over her mouth to keep from spitting forth a hard laugh. Meanwhile, Dean's eyes widened, and he mouthed what she thought looked like, "Help me!"

Sarah shook her head at Ally, which was really just her attempt at aiding Dean's escape. "Gross. I think I'm going to vomit."

She pushed a beer toward a patron farther down the counter, catching the sheriff's puzzled stare bouncing between her and Dean. His lip pitched at one corner, and the two lines between his brows deepened.

He suspects something.

She swiped up a dish cloth and spun around, making busy with polishing glasses. Long minutes passed while she averted her gaze from the sheriff and Dean, all the while feeling both stares burning into her and for polarizing reasons.

Her heartbeat thundered loud and fast, and nothing she did slowed it down. One awkward and way-too-candid conversation with the sheriff had been bad enough. Maybe her "sworn enemies" charade with Dean wasn't working after all.

But I wanted it to. For a short while, at least.

"Hey, Sheriff!" Ally's overly bright voice shattered the strange silence, but Sarah continued her fake interest in the glass in her hand. "Didn't you say you were looking to retire but couldn't find someone to take over? I bet Dean would be a perfect candidate."

Sarah snapped her focus back up, her mouth slipping open. How could Ally be so rude to bring up the sheriff's retirement?

"Based on what?" The question shot from Sarah's lips far more abrupt and abrasive than she intended. Especially since she'd intended to say nothing at all. "One act of half-hearted and coincidental bravery?"

The sheriff sent Sarah another quizzical stare before turning his gaze to Dean, then Ally. "I'm sure that would make my wife very happy, Ally, but there's more to being sheriff than you think. Besides, we don't know how long Mr. Holloway here will stay in town."

The sheriff's subtle change in demeanor had his jaw muscles twitching and his cheeks hardening. She'd seen that look a million times. Every time the sheriff wasn't all that sold on a person's character. Though she couldn't condemn his skepticism, she too didn't yet know all that much about Dean Holloway. Only that she enjoyed spending time with him, and he seemed to notice things about her that so many didn't.

Dean sat forward, arms crossed over the bar, his attention fixed on her, and his wicked smile daring her to… to what? Her heart hitched, and she refused to finish that thought.

The dragging seconds had her forgetting to breathe, which then hung doubt over her recent deal with Dean the Devil. Her mind already worked over time to second-guess what every person around her thought—whether they knew of her relationship to this man.

Aggie reached out and pinched Dean's black stubbled cheek. "He'd make one handsome sheriff. Don't cha think, Sarah?"

The old woman stared at her now, increasing the erratic rhythm of Sarah's heart. Meanwhile, her attention slipped to Sheriff Marlin, and her breath shallowed for a reason beyond the need to escape his scrutiny over Dean. "I like the sheriff we have. Peter's been flawless at his job for decades. Besides, no one knows Harlow like Sheriff Marlin, and the role of sheriff isn't a beauty competition. We all know he would have stopped the Chadleys himself, eventually."

The sheriff's cheeks turned slack, and he tilted his head to one side in seeming shock, like he hadn't expected her compliment.

Dean cleared his throat, disrupting the exchange. "Sarah's right, and I wouldn't say I came to Harlow with sheriffing in mind."

For the first time during that conversation, his tone relaxed and he spoke with all seriousness. Though even as he backed up her argument, he at least had the smarts not to look at her while he did so.

A sly smile pulled at her lips, and she turned to Ally, partly to distract from the warm-fuzzy sensation taking up space in her torso. *Hormones. It's just hormones.*

"You see, even Dean agrees. Besides, you've been so focused on Mr. Holloway right in front of you, you've completely forgotten about Sheriff Williams over in Moresley." She gave Dean an overly sweet smile. "Now, those are some smoldering brown eyes. Not to mention his diamond cut abs and those plump lips that look like they could kiss the life back into a three-thousand-year-old mummy." She shrugged, turning back to Ally. "Sheriff Williams makes Dean here look like a week-old dropped pie."

Dean's shoulders shook in her peripheral vision while Ally let out a quick gasp and pressed a palm to her mouth, her other hand swinging out to land on Dean's chuckle-affected shoulders. Like that would save him from the sting of Sarah's barb.

At least she could say she'd upped the ante on dousing anyone's suspicion. And there was the added bonus of having a mighty internal laugh at Dean's expense...

"Bit harsh, girl. *Uff-dah!*" Aggie shook her head, her weathered forehead crinkled further in a *What the heck is wrong with you?* sort of glower. Understandable, since Sarah was putting in her absolute worst show of manners.

Meanwhile, the sheriff diverted his focus to his drink, face pale, while a heavy quiet cut the bar's bustling background noise.

She lifted a brow at Dean and gave him a weak smile, begging him to hit back with an equally bruising reply, or at least save her from the hole of total awkwardness she'd just dug.

"I don't know, Sarah." A wicked grin lifted his cheeks, his eyes glinting in a way that said he was more than happy to oblige. "What with your general uptight and soulless personality, I get the feeling even Sheriff Williams' lips would fail to resuscitate you."

The sheriff, Ally, and Aggie all spluttered against flawed attempts to conceal laughter. Blood rushed to Sarah's cheeks, and she glared at Dean, not all that sure how much of that glare was still for show. The insults hurt more as the receiver than the one doling them out, that was for sure.

She took a deep breath and slumped her shoulders, handing Dean her defeat. This was all part of their game. At least, she hoped so.

Otherwise, she'd have to consider the amount of truth in his comment about her being uptight and soulless.

"So, how's the arm, Dean?" The sheriff's question cut through her thoughts, and he eyed her in a sidelong way that said he timed the intrusion to keep her from saying anything more.

"It's fine." Dean kept his stare trained on Sarah.

"You hurt your arm?" Ally frowned at him, her voice a little too sullen.

"Ricocheting glass." The sheriff nodded to Dean. "Though this one insisted on going home to stitch himself up."

"Jesus, Mary, and Joseph!" Ally pressed her hand to Dean's meaty forearm. "You did your own stitches?"

His wicked smile returned, and he pitched his pale blue stare back to Sarah. "It's amazing what a skillful pair of hands can do."

She felt her eyes go wide, and choked back a splutter of her own, not one of stifled laughter but of buried astonishment.

The man's provocations reached a whole other level, one that would get them both in trouble one day. Even Ally's moon-white face took on a sudden deep blush. Hell, Dean laid on his charm so thick, Ally probably figured he'd directed his flirting at her.

A light ache, maybe of jealousy, wound through Sarah's tummy, extending upward into her chest, that ache deepening to a distant pain. The jealousy and the pain were two things she refused to entertain. "I think I hear Gordon calling me."

She turned toward the kitchen, bailing before Dean said anymore. But even as she made her exit, Dean's overly confident and booming voice followed her. "I'll see you later then, Sarah."

By the time Dean got to Sarah's house, the ink-black sky hosted little more than a thin, crescent moon. Her shift had ended an hour ago, and her front door swung open. She waited for him beneath the eaves and under the porch light—the glow of her amber-green eyes competing with her bright smile. Maybe, just like him, she rejoiced at their competent skills in fooling her friends.

From now on, night would spell the time for her to be his. A time where mystery and seduction came out to play. She sure as hell was all of that to him. Mystery. Seduction. Maybe more… though she wouldn't want to hear about being "more".

She wanted schemes and aversion. But he had just the scheme for her.

Play slow. Play dirty.

If he were lucky, win her heart. With all her bravado and hidden kindness, he didn't deserve her, but he'd come too far to step back now.

Her smile broadened at him, and his heart took on a deep thud. He picked up pace over her porch and swept her up in his arms, taking her inside and away from anyone's view.

No matter how many times he had her, he wanted more. *Always more*. No matter how many times he insisted he had control here, a quieter voice told him that was a lie. Because Sarah, in her beauty and strength, held all the power.

Twenty-One

Sarah paused under the hospital corridor's stark white fluorescent lights, the air a touch too cold and her mind a muddle as she stared at Blaine's door just ahead.

"I wouldn't go down there."

She spun around to Emilia's pretty brown gaze, the scent of vending-machine coffee wafting from the paper cup in her hand. "Not unless you want to see the nurse cleaning out his wound. Trust me, it's not pretty."

Emilia nodded at a row of gray-blue plastic chairs along the wall. "Would you like to sit and wait with me? The nurse won't take long."

Sarah dropped her chin and gawped at Emilia, a dull pang of guilt expanding high in her tummy. "Oh. I. Yeah, sure."

Eight days after the home invasion, word had gotten to her that Blaine was taking visitors, but for some reason, Sarah hadn't banked on meeting his new girl again. Though she had no major issues with Emilia, the woman's presence added weight to what was already a confronting task.

But Sarah *had* to be here to show Blaine her support. That there were no hard feelings. To dispel any guilt he might have over what had happened with her, in case that guilt impeded his recovery. Though even with all those reasons, a deeper part of her questioned whether, more than anything else, her own guilt prompted this visit.

Dean. His mere presence in her life, plus the fact that he made her happy, call it survivor's guilt, even though her ex had no idea she was moving on too…

Emilia sat and took a slow sip of her coffee. Her weak movements and distant stare belonged to a woman who carried more than she could handle. She flicked her attention up to Sarah and gave a small smile.

"I keep telling myself I'm going to cut back"—she lifted the cup in a resigned sort of gesture—"but then something new happens, and well, I fall back to this trusty old crutch."

Sarah wandered over and sat too, her chest muscles squeezing because Emilia had always shown more vulnerability than she ever could.

Maybe that's why Blaine didn't pick me.

She slammed her eyes shut at that thought, before opening them again and pasting on a smile for Emilia's benefit. "I know more than a few people who would drink my bar dry over less than what you've been through."

Emilia's doe eyes relaxed into warm chocolate pools, and a slight smile lifted her lips. "I thought… Blaine… I thought he would die for sure."

Her lower lip trembled, and she turned away, her thick lashes beating together as if she fought off tears.

"But he didn't." Sarah curled her fingers in her lap, wanting to reach out and comfort Emilia, to clasp the woman's hand and say something meaningful, but she couldn't.

Not because this was Emilia—her replacement with Blaine—but because Sarah didn't do tears.

Besides, she wasn't the best support person, anyway.

She'd been so busy with work and Dean that she hadn't had time to fully come to terms with what had happened. *Heartbreaks. Gun fights. Near-death experiences.* Yeah, that was a lot for any person to work through.

Emilia pressed her lips together, the edges lifting in pained acknowledgment, like she saw that Sarah tried but failed to offer help.

"You're right. I'm very lucky." Her whispered tone matched the paleness of her usually warm skin tone, that same skin red and splotchy around her eyes. "Blaine was a part of your life for so long. You must have been beside yourself too."

Emilia reached out and did the thing Sarah had struggled with, the woman's hand landing over Sarah's on her lap and giving a gentle squeeze.

You must have been beside yourself too.

Had she been, though?

She frowned, unable to remember a time when she'd *ever* been beside herself… about *anything*.

Even in the wake of the worst of the worst. When her dad had abandoned her along with the other members of her family. When her mother had fallen apart. When Sarah had been forced to give up her dreams… she just kept going.

What other option was there?

Emilia withdrew her hand, and Sarah tore her frown away, directing it to the floor. "Blaine's yours now. Maybe he's always been yours, anyway. Don't worry about how I'm doing, okay?"

What a charitable offer. Letting Emilia know she had nothing to feel bad about, so she could focus solely on her immediate problems. But really, Sarah didn't like fuss. Much less over her. Much less since asking for help usually invited a barrage of unwanted intrusions.

"You know, I don't expect you to cut him out of your life because of me."

"No. I know that." Sarah rubbed her fingertips over her temples and squeezed her eyes closed again, as if that might work to shut out this conversation. "I didn't think you would, but you've got enough going on without me encroaching."

She opened her eyes. Emilia still cupped her hands around her coffee. "You must think I don't deserve him. Maybe you'd be right. You stepped aside so Blaine and I could be together because you thought that was the best thing for everyone, but I'm the one who brought trouble into his life. I'm sorry."

Sarah flicked her attention over her left shoulder, to Blaine's door, hoping the nurse might be done. *No such luck.*

She pressed her hands hard against her dark blue jeans, losing herself a little in the tiny threads and woven pattern. "Don't apologize. You weren't the one holding the gun. I'll be fine, and I don't hate you. Soon enough you and Blaine will go back to living happily ever after, okay?"

As foolish as those words felt to say, she honestly hoped Emilia would believe her. After three years of sharing her life with Blaine, he'd become her best friend. Three years of planning a future together, and now, would they continue to even be friends?

In an uncharacteristic move she couldn't quite explain, she reached out and grabbed Emilia's hand from her coffee cup, the woman's skin clammy and her fingers stiff. Despite the voices in Sarah's head screaming for her to let go, she held on, needing to feel at least a little better about herself.

She didn't do emotion. She didn't offer comfort either. Doubly so with a relative stranger such as Emilia. But Sarah hadn't been there to help Blaine. His life had imploded, and she'd been busy hooking up with Dean.

And yes, her logic here was all screwed up. Blaine was the one to move on first. But guilt had a strange way of making little sense, and being kind to Emilia felt like atonement. Sarah's gift to Blaine. Even if he never knew.

Emilia eyed Sarah through an eerie stillness, her expression wilting like a crushed flower still trying to bloom. Before long, she lowered her head under an avalanche of fat and wrenching tears.

Sarah snapped a hand out and caught the coffee cup before Emilia could drop it, the woman listing to one side to bury her face against Sarah's shoulder.

"I'm sorry." Emilia sniffled and then hiccupped. As ill-timed and unintentionally vain as it seemed, Sarah was heartened that Emilia was capable of an "ugly" cry. "I didn't expect you'd... I've held myself together all day, and then you... You're here, and you're being nice to me. Any other woman—"

"I already said you don't need to apologize." Sarah patted Emilia's back awkwardly while eyeing Blaine's door again. Genuinely, she was the least capable person to help with anyone's grief. *What was taking that nurse so long?*

Emilia slumped back and swiped at her tears, her breaths slowing. "Blaine says the same thing, you know? I apologize too much. Even now, I'm biting back a need to say sorry for that too. I just don't know how I'll ever repay you for being here now, and for—"

"Honestly, don't mention it."

Sarah launched from her seat and feigned a desire to pace in front of Blaine's closed door. She didn't want to hear Emilia finish that sentence. To hear her say, "for stepping aside and letting me have your man."

This was all too much honesty. She couldn't wait for everyone to forget. To just move on already. No broken engagements. No pitying looks. No screwball gunmen. No hospitals. No secret lovers…

Blaine's door clicked and a nurse stepped out, stopping Sarah's thoughts on just how complicated life had gotten.

"You can go in now." The nurse gave an easy smile, but Sarah's stomach churned all the same.

The kidney-shaped dish in the nurse's hand had a pile of bloodstained bandages. *Blaine's blood.*

"You go in."

Sarah jolted at Emilia's voice and pulled her attention away from the dish and onto the woman beside her, with her upturned stare and washed-out complexion. "I don't want him to see me like this. He'll know I've been crying."

Lacking in words, Sarah nodded and stepped forward. No matter how many "moments" she took to gather her thoughts, no moment could erase what had happened—much less forever delay her encounter with the man on the other side of that door.

Twenty-Two

"Oh, don't give me that look." Blaine's emerald gaze twinkled back at Sarah in undeserved excitement. "I get enough sympathy from Emilia."

Sarah stood in the doorway, her lips parted, while she took in the scene. Despite the bloody gauze the nurse had carried out earlier and that his smile wobbled a little at the corners, he didn't look anywhere near as bad as she'd expected.

Her silence lingered a beat longer. The scratches over his face, and especially his nose, brought doubt to even that positive train of thought.

She shook her head and forced a level of control over her reactions, strolling deeper into the hospital room. "Sorry, I'm just not used to seeing you so, so…"

He quirked a brow and a cheeky grin took over. "Irresistibly handsome?"

Her chest jolted with laughter, one that betrayed the conflict churning a mild sick feeling within her belly. "Yeah, that's it."

She'd meant to say "fragile," but Blaine's joke offered her a merciful escape.

She pointed to his pale blue hospital gown. "Does that thing come with a back or are your ass cheeks just hangin' in the breeze most of the time?"

He choked out a laugh, only to wince and clutch at his side. "Damn it. I keep forgetting that laughter hurts."

She stepped around the bed and lowered herself into a chair at his side. "Sorry about that too."

He swatted a hand, dismissing her apology, then dropped that hand to the bed's edge nearest to her.

A brief and instinctive moment took over. One that made her want reach out and clasp his palm in hers. Call it a habit, maybe. But she opted to interlace her fingers together in her lap.

"How are you feeling?" She focused on his disarray of auburn hair and the long stubble peppering his jaw, more signs that his good humor merely hid the damage he'd suffered. Somewhere beneath his white cotton blanket lay a deep bullet wound, its existence a tragic ode to how close he'd come to being erased from the world.

"I feel..." His eyes glittered again, that friendly and uncomplicated glimmer that had drawn her to him years ago. "I feel like a guy who just got shot."

She huffed a short and staggered laugh. "Right, stupid question."

"Don't think about it. I'm hearing that stupid question a lot lately." He jutted his chin at her. "Anyway, how are *you*?"

She frowned down at his hands, her tummy hollow at how much had happened in so short a time. The genuine care in his tone made her heart twist where it sat. He'd been one of the few people she could turn to, and yet in the wake of the breakup, an entire gulf stretched between them.

Losing Blaine meant losing more than a fiancé. She'd lost her number one fan. A firm supporter. The direction in which her entire life would go...

Even at the best of times, she didn't *do* uncertainty, and this, right here, was far from the best of times.

"I'm fine." She lifted her chin and gave him a wide smile.

He kept a long pause, his stare holding hers, and when he did speak, it was with an analyzing sort of stillness. "Anything fresh from the Harlow rumor mill? This hospital saved me from my injuries, but it's killing me with boredom."

She shrugged. "You *are* the Harlow rumor mill, right now. The hottest topic we've had in a long while. Though many people send their regards. Aggie, Ally, Maureen, Frank, Gordon, just to name a few."

"That's nice and all, but"—he gave a twisted sort of smirk—"I'm going to need more than kind regards."

She let out a sigh, shoulders sinking. She would give him the gossip he'd wanted but hide the finer details. "Some teens were caught vandalizing the nursery the other day—"

"Oh, let me guess, the Chadleys?" He sat a little taller in his bed, grimacing as he did so, the action a hint on his high levels of boredom.

"Yep." A light sensation worked through her body. At least she could give him this small reprieve, even though they both tended to dislike gossip.

"So, the sheriff finally caught them doing something he could pin them with?" He shook his head, still smiling. "I bet that just about made his year."

"Well..." Her chest sank, her face turned to ice, and she fought hard to keep eye-contact. "Actually, Sheriff Marlin wasn't the one to stop them. There's a new guy in town. He caught the Chadleys mid-reign of terror. To the sheriff's credit though, he did track them down for a much-earned night in the station's holding cell."

Blaine pressed his brows together, a hint that he needed a second to process. "A new guy in town?"

She gave a sharp nod, though her heartbeat thundered at the dreaded prospect of having to discuss Dean with her ex.

And of course, Blaine's silent side-glare prodded for more, so she resigned herself to giving him something. "Thomas took a swing at him with a glass bottle, and things didn't play out well for the kid after that."

He laughed, groaning and clutching at his side again. "I never thought I'd see the day someone finally beat those bratty Chadleys at their own game."

She nodded again. "The guy even gave Thomas a motivational talk on changing his ways."

Blaine let out a high and impressed whistle. "All the interesting stuff happens when I'm not in town. I'll have to buy the new guy a drink when I finally bust free of this hospital bed."

"At this rate, you'll have to get in line." Muscles she didn't know she'd been holding, relaxed. For the first time in this exchange, she felt she could truly breathe. "You're old news and he's taken over as Harlow's new hero. Everyone's fallen in love with him."

Blaine shot out another laugh and then slapped his hand over his ribcage. "Ahh, Jesus. You're no good for my health, woman!" He jutted his chin at her. "And what about you, anyway? Are you *in love* with the new hero too?"

She reeled back a little, shaking her head. "Hardly. You know I'm not that easy to impress."

He pressed a knuckle to his lips, as if to stem off more laughter— her flippant comment heavy and uncomfortable in the air, like wearing a thick blanket on a hot day. She *was* hard to impress. The last person within miles ever to fall "in love." Which meant when she did, starting over was even more difficult.

Sure, she liked Dean. But love? Not if she could help it.

She frowned down at her hands in her lap, her fingers locked together in a rigid knot, her throat tight around an insidious emotion she refused to name or analyze.

"Sarah, with everything that's happened, we haven't had much chance to talk." Blaine's soft tone churned at her insides.

"There's nothing to talk about." She unlocked her hands and struck her attention back to him in a false show that everything was just peachy.

"And we're still friends?" The quick dart of his gaze said her answer did still mean something to him. "Right?"

And the fact that he did still seem to care, meant that despite the weight taking up space in her tummy, the light smile she offered was a genuine one. "You know we are."

"And you're okay? You got someone to talk to?" The sympathy in his tone, his question, though well-meaning enough, stirred the bile in her stomach, lending a heavy sick feeling.

He'd seen her in her weaker moments, and still, she resented his pity.

Anyone's pity.

Pity abraded against everything she'd fought all these years to keep.

Not build, *keep.*

Nothing in her life had grown over the years. She'd spent the better part of a decade just trying to hold things together. Not to lose more than she already had.

Her throat muscles pulled tighter, her thoughts switching to Blaine's question about whether she had anyone to talk to—now that he wasn't really an option for her anymore—or at least, not while their breakup was still so fresh. Not while he still lay in a hospital bed.

So, she couldn't decide which was worse, the truth or a lie. She *did* have someone. *Dean.* He'd helped her to talk more than anyone had in so long. She even *liked* talking to him. That fact alone made her want to clam up once more. To revert to safer and more desolate waters.

Who was Dean to her, anyway? *A casual fling.* Someone she would step away from should she find herself investing more than she wanted…

But maybe I already have…

The weight in her tummy sank even deeper, the churning building in aggression. She turned her mind to Blaine and their longstanding past, none of which made her want to invite him into her present. Not because she held a grudge but because she wouldn't even know where to begin.

The unpredicted one-night stand. No way could she tell him about *that.* Her knee-jerk decision that night would come across as a desperate post-breakup rebound move. Maybe it was. Yet another reason to keep recent events private.

"Like I said, I'll manage. You don't need to worry about me." She stood and patted his knee, the good-humored gesture designed to erase his worries.

His pinched and unwavering stare said he wasn't convinced.

"Promise you'll tell me if whatever's happening in that head of yours gets too much."

She stilled for a beat or two longer than appropriate before she shook off her surprise at his astute observation. "I'm a big girl. Just concentrate on getting better, okay?"

She was a jerk for withholding the truth but leaned in to land a gentle kiss to his brow, before turning to leave, anyway. Still, he grabbed her wrist, halting her exit. "Emilia and I are thankful for all you've done for us. You know that, right? Don't you be a stranger."

She angled back to him and ruffled his already messy hair. "I understand perfectly, Mr. Callahan. You can count on seeing me again sometime soon."

Twenty~Three

"WELCOME TO HARLOW." Ally stood on Dean's doorstep, her usual exuberant smile and chipper tone crossing the landing.

"I've been here over a week." He frowned and squinted against the bright spring sun, the harsh rays hitting his bare torso above his gray pajama pants. "Aren't we past the introduction phase?"

He held a hand over his brow and tried not to smile too hard. Not because of Ally, exactly, but because he'd never had so many chances to sleep in as he did in Harlow. Speaking of Ally, the woman's face was a few shades rosier now, her wide-eyed stare frozen on his chest and her lips slightly parted.

"I... ahh..." She shook her head and blinked up at him, raising the woven basket in her hand. "I... I brought breakfast... You know, since I extended the same courtesy to Emilia when she first moved in. It's only fair I do the same for you."

He glared into her bright blue eyes, her rapid blinks changing to a more intentional and less innocent flutter.

Ally, as smooth as she thought she was, seemed to attempt to make herself at home in his life; but then, maybe that wasn't it. Sarah had mentioned that Harlow people didn't believe in privacy or personal space, so this little intrusion could be just the way things were done around here.

Ally's sunny yellow dress seemed to conspire toward that logic. The young woman was like Mary Poppins and a ball of sunshine rolled into one. Not exactly his kind of woman, but pretty nonetheless.

His empty stomach growled for him to step aside and handle whatever Miss Sunshine here threw at him, so she and her basket could make good on the promise of breakfast.

"Thank you." Ally skipped past the second he moved aside.

He closed the door and trailed after her into the living room. "Has anyone told you it's not a good idea to invite yourself into strange men's homes?"

"You saved Aggie's nursery and my plant pots. Those aren't the actions of a bad guy." She plonked the basket down on his coffee table and swanned into his kitchen. "Besides, as you said, we're hardly strangers now, are we?"

He frowned and sat in his armchair, tugging on a sweater he'd tossed there last night. Meanwhile, she set his kettle to boil and then rummaged through one cupboard after another in a probable search for cups.

Yep, definitely making herself at home...

"I have a few things to get through today." He kept his voice flat and non-emotive, not wanting to lead her into thinking this interaction meant any more than it did.

"Oh, no worries." She dug around in his fridge now, two cups waiting on his counter, while she pulled out a carton of milk. "We'll make this quick."

So, for the sake of "quickness," he added, "There's a jar of instant coffee in the cupboard above the stove."

Ally scrunched her nose, as if he'd told her his cupboard contained a human head. "It's okay, I brought my own grinds."

She strolled over to the coffee table, deposited the carton of milk, and then pulled out a tall, glass coffee plunger and a metal tin from her basket.

He shook his head but kept his mouth shut while she popped the metal tin open at his counter and scooped the contents out with one of his spoons, the grinds going into the plunger. "So, what are your plans for today, anyhoo?"

"The sheriff hired me to do some odd jobs over at the station, though it's hard to tell if he trusts me or just wants to suss me out some more."

"*Pfft.*" She swatted her hand in a dismissive gesture, still focusing down at her coffee making. "Old Marlin is like that with everyone he doesn't know yet. Besides, I saw your advert up at the general store, and it's great that you already have some interest. Aggie sounded eager to have you help at the nursery too, yah?"

He waited for the kettle's burble to die down before he answered, the mention of Aggie's work offer adding a sharp prickle to his skin since he had something to do with Emilia not being around.

His cellphone gave a loud buzzing sound over the glass of his coffee table, the glowing screen showing a concealed number. The only people he knew who used those were telemarketers and anyone from the syndicate. Even though he'd changed phones since leaving, only giving his new number to Ramos, he sure wasn't about to pick up any concealed call.

Rudolph Manzinni, Luciano's boss, the one who oversaw all syndicate branches from East Coast to West, would be riding Luciano for answers. Luciano would be sweating buckets looking for news on Dean.

With any luck, the syndicate would realize he wasn't causing them any trouble. They would get distracted with some bigger drama and leave him alone.

"Not going to answer that?" Ally navigated her way around the couch, placing two mugs of coffee down while nodding to his phone.

"Probably nothing important." He snatched up the phone and shut it off completely, distracting Ally by jutting his chin out toward the contents of her basket, open and also on the coffee table. Strawberries, a plate of homemade biscuits, even a small vase of wild flowers... "You've gone to a lot of effort there."

She went about pulling everything out, wild flowers included. "It's no trouble."

But a deep blush ran up her neck and into her cheeks, telling him otherwise.

"Did you bring Emilia wild flowers?" He took a sip of coffee, minus the milk or sugar on offer, and waited for her reply.

"Yes." Her gaze skittered away from him, indicating she lied, but he let that observation slide. No point embarrassing her.

Still, at some point I'll have to set her straight…

But Ally had her own special charm. An innocence he didn't want to shatter. Innocence being a luxury he'd been denied at far too young an age.

Harsh reality could wait.

He'd let this woman, with her positive outlook and her heart on her sleeve, have her moment.

"Well, thank you for this." He gestured to the collection of food, and she grinned at him, her attention dropping to his lips and holding seconds too long.

His heart did a dampened thud and a distinct coldness washed over him. He dropped his attention to the coffee table. Sarah's warning wailed in his ears. How did the saying go? *The road to hell is paved with good intentions.*

As much as he wanted to put this visit down to country kindness, his hope shifted to something else. To their encounter not ending with him shoving her out his door. To her not clinging to him or storming away in a fit of tears.

He lifted his focus to her sitting in the armchair perpendicular to him, her gaze bouncing around his face like she'd been staring at him the entire time he'd been thinking.

"I'm embarrassing myself here, aren't I?" Her eyes took on a soft sheen while a wide chasm imploded just beneath his sternum.

"No." He sat taller, clearing his throat and scrubbing his hand over his mouth to buy an extra few seconds. "But I get the impression my feelings don't match yours."

Her stare held a long and silent moment longer before she nodded, the strain over her cheekbones dropping as though she acknowledged what he'd said. Perhaps even accepted his sentiments a little.

"I don't really know what I'm doing here, either." She huffed out a tight laugh, her gaze falling to her lap. "It's just… I had hope, you know?"

He took a moment to absorb her words—or more so, the meaning in them—then gave a slow nod. He *did* know. About hope. About pursuing what he wanted despite the odds. At least, he'd come to know, after years of just accepting his lot. For that. For Ally's ability to put action to her ambition, even though she was a good ten years his junior.

"Listen, I'm sorry." She shot to her feet, quick to swipe things off his coffee table and shove them back into her basket while more words rushed out. "I won't take up anymore of your time."

"No. No." He lashed out a hand and grabbed hers, halting her packing, while her wide and overwrought stare hit his. "It's okay, you don't need to—"

"It's just hard, you know?" She ripped her hand from his and turned away, continuing her hurried exit. "Being my age in *this* town. There's no one around, and you have no choice but to hope… to hope that the next guy to stick around is *your* guy."

She paused, turned her attention to him, eyes still wide, though this time the pointedness in her stare said she hadn't planned on being so candid.

He shrugged, trying to let her see that her honesty didn't faze him. "Maybe the answer to your problem isn't in this town?"

She gave a taut chuckle and gestured to the world at large. "But what would I do anywhere else? Everything I know is here. How do I leave without hurting everyone who loves me?"

He didn't know.

Not because he lacked a list of alternative things Ally could do anywhere but here, but because he didn't know what it was like to have anyone want him to stay.

Ally drew back her shoulders and tilted her head to one side, her eased posture suggesting she'd figured he had no answer either.

"It's about time for me to head out too." He launched himself out of his seat and helped her place a few final items into her basket, last being the wild flowers.

Ally held a hand in front of him. "No, keep those."

The pinched edges of her stare told him to just accept the peace offering and say nothing more. So, he nodded and replied, "Thanks. That's kind of you."

She let out a sigh, her expression cheerier, and she snapped the basket closed before leading him to the front door. He stood with her on the landing, his green lawn sending a mild glare into his eyes, the familiar thud of fast foot falls drawing closer from his right.

He squeezed his eyes shut and waited for the inevitable. Sarah usually ran past his house right about this time most days. He shot his gaze to Ally, just as she spoke again.

"Thanks for the talk." She rose to her tippy toes and grabbed his face, landing a lip gloss–heavy, wet kiss to his cheek.

The nearing footfalls came to an abrupt stop. He jolted back and turned to Sarah, her hands on her hips, brows raised, and a bemused look on her face. He could only imagine what this looked like—him on his landing, disheveled and half in his pajamas, with Ally's lips attached to his face.

And as usual, Sarah didn't give away her feelings. She merely shook her head and kept running.

Twenty-Four

Night came and Sarah leaned against her open front door. She made a show of eyeing Dean slowly up and down as he took the few steps up to her porch. Her TV blared in the background, announcing the football game he'd come here to see, though football would likely be the last thing on her mind.

"I'm surprised you made it." She turned for the living room, leaving space for him to enter, trusting he would close the door. She battled an internal debate over why she'd agreed to watch a game, rather than just sticking to the easy limits of this being a purely physical relationship.

"Why's that?"

"Oh, I don't know." She peered at him from over her shoulder, not even bothering to hide her smirk. "I figured Ally would have you tied to a bed by now, all while she had her wicked way with you."

He gave a slow shake of his head, even though he smiled. "Your mind is even more sordid than I thought. Ally hasn't got it for me as bad as you think."

He kicked off his shoes.

"She's paying you personal visits, kissing you on your landing…" She stood over him while he sank back into her couch, both arms outstretched across the back and near spanning the entire length. She tried to sit too, only finding enough space to perch on the edge farthest from him, a dull pull in her gut indicating she didn't quite know how to feel about his clear comfort in her home. "Sounds like a done deal to me. You might just have to marry her now."

The deflection seemed right, given her thoughts on "comfort," not just his, but hers too.

He reached for the remote and cranked the volume, yet another sign of his ease around her. "It's a crush. Ally will get over it."

She grabbed a cushion and swatted at him lightly, her silent way of telling him to make room for her on her own damn couch.

He moved to the right a little, and she huddled in beside him. "You're right. She just needs to see you hoard all the curly crisps and couch space once, and she'll know any future between you two is sunk."

"Is that why we're having popcorn tonight?" He tipped his chin toward the white ceramic bowl on her small wooden coffee table.

She shrugged. "I figured you needed some variation in your diet."

A slow smile grew on his face, those scintillating dimples making a welcome appearance. "So considerate of you."

That hot look in his eyes, that analyzing stare paired with his deliciously wicked smirk, spun a warmth within her belly that turned her everyday thoughts about kissing him into a burning need to actually do so.

Because of that need. Because of the cold fear setting roots within her, she turned away from him and feigned a sudden urge to open the two beers also on her coffee table. "Seriously though, be careful with Ally, okay?"

An overly long silence dragged out before he tossed the remote to the table and spoke again. "Like I said, I'll do my best."

I killed the spark bringing Ally up again. He knows I'm holding back.

She nodded to herself and handed him the bowl of popcorn as a peace offering.

"Thanks."

More silence, so she peered up at him looking her over a little too closely. "You didn't have to dress up for my sake."

She focused down at her loose, pink-and-black striped pajama pants with the tattered hem because they were just a *bit* too long for her. She'd paired those pants with a pale orange, baggy t-shirt.

A laugh shot past her lips. "Hey, I've been pouring beers all day, and this is comfortable. Shoot me."

The smoldering look returned to his stare, and his gaze paused at her chest. "Oh, I'm not complaining."

She should have taken the hint and had *her* wicked way with him, should have launched herself into his lap. But she groaned and played up her fatigue, flopping back against an armrest and propping her bare feet onto his lap.

Way to kill the mood again…

With every encounter, something changed between them, and even her evasion spoke of that change. The natural ease, despite all her prickly edges, those prickly edges mostly about *everything* but him.

He let her wriggle out of anything too deep. Never pestered her into being more than she was. The fact that he did only deepened the needling guilt taking up space in her body.

Her gloomy thoughts disintegrated at the heat of his large hands engulfing her feet, feet that hadn't stopped all day. His strong thumbs pressed and ran over her tired arches, his strength channeled to nurturing.

She closed her eyes and groaned, the sensation soothing, the man providing the soothing somehow aware of what she needed without being asked.

What have I gotten myself into?

"Thank you." His voice was a soft murmur, and his palm warmed the top of her foot.

She took a deep breath, reveling in the massage. "Shouldn't I be thanking you? This feels amazing."

"Oh no. I'm definitely thanking you." He paused, the silence purposeful. "For not wearing a bra."

She kicked out a foot and sat bolt upright, that foot connecting with the solid wall of his stomach. He laughed, heartier than before, and grabbed her foot again, his fingertips brushing her sensitive sole.

Laughter and panic twisted her voice. "Please. Don't."

"Don't what?" He ran a finger down her foot's center. A sharp tingling shot through her body, and she kicked but to no avail. "Is this Sarah Overton's weakness? She's ticklish?"

More strokes, which made her wriggle and laugh harder, both of which forced her into a slow slide off the couch. Well, except for the foot Dean held hostage and the arm she outstretched to keep her propped above the floor.

She fought, despite her chuckles. "If you don't stop, I swear, I'll pee myself."

The tickling stopped. She caught his eye.

"Revenge peeing, huh?" His grin held strong and even grew a little, wrinkling the tops of his cheek bones.

She shook her head, and he moved to tickle her again. "No!"

She thrashed even harder than before, uncontrolled, as her free foot slammed into the bowl of popcorn on the coffee table.

The white, salty snack exploded everywhere like a miniature snowstorm. She flailed and swatted at rogue pieces falling about her face, unrestrained laughter billowing out of her.

Another wriggle and she freed her foot from Dean's hold, an ill-thought-out move as a high-pitched squeal escaped her lungs and her supporting arm buckled, sending her to the floor with an ungraceful thud.

"Well"—Dean chuckled and reached out, helping her back onto the couch—"at least you didn't pee yourself."

She gave him a side glare, albeit a half-hearted one, through her laughter.

"Yeah, and I didn't crack my skull on the floor, either. So today is all about winning for me." Dean leaned in to pick out popcorn bits from her hair while she spoke. "I'm surprised you're not the one peeing yourself. I'm sure watching me fall on my ass was hilarious."

"Only a little hilarious." He finished removing popcorn and gave her a light kiss on the lips. "I didn't want to see you fall, though."

She blinked at him, stunned and silent. The man was so close his breath lapped at her skin while his spicy, warm scent wound its way through her nostrils and spread a sensual heat throughout her body.

His lower lip sat fuller than his top, and the outer corners held their natural upward curve, calling for her kiss.

His piercing blue eyes held her too—held her from looking away and prodded an internal battle that had her wanting to run to him and run away, all at once.

"I should probably vacuum this mess." The weak excuse rasped past the tension in her throat. She tried to move again, but his iron-strong hand wrapped around her waist and rested over her hip, refusing to budge.

"The mess isn't important."

She opened her mouth to protest, but even she could see the futility and weakness in that. Dean wasn't the sort to let anyone weasel out of an honest conversation, so she offered her version of honesty instead. "Whatever's happening here, it's going to end in disaster."

"That's what you said the first time we met, remember?" He drew in and she didn't move, allowing him to brush his lips over hers. "And look at us. Still getting along."

His hand stayed at her hip, his thumb drawing tantalizing circles against her t-shirt's super thin material. Something within her melted, and heat pooled between her legs. What she wouldn't give to give in. Not to the sex. Sex with Dean was the easy bit. The other stuff though… the unspoken demand for promises. *That* required something else entirely.

"I know you're not sure about any of this." His gentle, rumbling tone made her heart jolt and squeeze. "But don't run, okay?"

Her mind blanked, and he lifted his free hand, his fingertips making contact with her collarbone and sweeping a delicate line over her skin. A sharp breath pulled at her lungs. His rapt focus stayed on her, as if each minor reaction fed his need—those reactions betraying her feelings about him. Feelings she wasn't all that clear on.

"I just… I don't know what this is." She pressed her lips together, holding onto her next words just a moment longer. "Are you my rebound guy?"

What if she was beginning to like him, as in, *really* like him? Was that even possible, so close to being engaged to another man and having her heart stomped all over?

"What do you think?" His attention shifted over her face, suggesting the vulnerability in his question, like her answer truly meant something to him.

"I don't know." She frowned, pausing to gnaw on her lower lip. "I don't trust anything I feel anymore."

His gaze landed on her chin, and he gave a small nod. He read the subtext in her statement, that she'd trusted her feelings before only to find she'd been wrong.

Equal parts of her were happy and sad. Despite his tough exterior, Dean wasn't the knuckle-dragging Neanderthal that she'd first assumed. He understood her, at least to some extent, but that understanding further exposed her limitations.

But she was human after all, and like any human, solitude came with drawbacks. And because of her humanity, she also didn't want Dean to believe he was *just* her rebound guy, which was why she undertook her next move—a move with the extra benefit of pulling her away from having to overthink her connection to this man.

"But if it makes any difference—" She launched herself at him, and he released a surprised *hmph* sound.

She unleashed a fevered kiss on him, and before long, his hands swept her body, and she tugged at his clothes. Through all that followed next, the same disingenuous chant tumbled over and over in her mind. "We're just friends. We're just friends."

Twenty~Five

"What makes you think we hire just any clown off the street?"

Luciano bit into the end of his cigar and scowled at the schmuck sitting in the black leather chair across from his desk, this guy somewhere in his early thirties with dark hair and dark eyes. Not Italian, though. Latino, maybe. And he'd literally walked into the building demanding a meeting with Luciano.

"Word on the street is you're down a man, and I need work."

A harsh laugh burst past Luciano's lips. Was there anyone in LA who *didn't* know about his missing guy?

"*You* need a job?" Luciano dropped his cigar to the crystal ashtray on his right and ran his gaze over the fucker ahead. Granted, the guy *looked* tough. Tall, broad shoulders, and solid build. He was either appropriately confident about his worth to the syndicate, or a total ignorant asshole, given his insistence and relaxed stance despite *where* he sat and *who* he sat before. "Why the fuck would I care what you need?"

"Because you're going to need me more than I need you."

Luciano threw his head back and barked out another laugh. "Arrogant fucker, aren't you?"

The guy shrugged, his black leather jacket shifting above his fitted black t-shirt and jeans. "Maybe. Or maybe I know *who* you lost, Mr. Conti, and I know for a fact I'd be an upgrade."

"Oh, yeah?" Luciano pitched forth a tight smile, allowing a moment to warm to the guy's arrogance.

Four days had passed since his talk with Mark, and he still lacked a location for his missing man. Either this schmuck would make good on his "upgrade" claim, or Luciano would have a new candidate to inflict his frustrations on. "Wanna tell me how you're an upgrade? Besides, what makes you think I'd trust you?"

"We both know you have people everywhere, even in the force. Run a background check on me. And as to my worth to you, just like your missing man, I have military experience—two extra years of it. Plus, five years in private investigations." The guy leaned back in his seat, somehow appearing even more easy about this meeting than before. "Hell, if you're having trouble finding Dean Holloway, I might be able to help there, too."

Luciano took a slow puff at his cigar, the tobacco smoke hot in his lungs and soon swirling around his face, in contrast to his office's dark furnishings. He narrowed a stare at the man before him. A man who had not only found his way to this building but knew the name Dean Holloway.

Maybe he did have his ear close enough to the ground to make good on his claims. With Mr. Holloway gone, Luciano was down a tracker.

"Like I said." He tapped the spent ash off his cigar and into a small pile in the ashtray. "I don't hire fresh off the street. Usually my guys come recommended."

"Sounds like a piss-poor reason to pass up a good hire." The guy shrugged but stood all the same, leaving doubt over his claim about being desperate for work. "Unlike Mr. Holloway, for the right price, I don't care about getting my hands dirty."

So, it was less about work and more about the money to be made? Maybe private investigations didn't pay so well after all. Either way, the guy turned and marched toward the black glossy door behind him, setting off Luciano's own desperation. Desperate to find Holloway. Desperate to ensure word of the syndicate's involvement in the Stucco fuckup didn't get out. Desperate not to taste the metal at the end of Rudolph Manzinni's gun.

"Wait."

Luciano scowled, and the guy spun around.

That this guy was willing to do things Mr. Holloway hadn't, well, maybe hiring him *would* be an upgrade. "Fine. You got a job. At least once we know your story checks out." He jutted his chin toward the door. "On your way out, get my PA to point you to our head of security, Mr....?"

"Ramos." The guy pulled at the door handle, ready to leave. "Adrian Ramos."

Twenty-Six

"So, the usual for you today?"

Dean buried a deep sigh over Sarah's unaffected gaze directed at him from across the bar, an unaffected gaze she kept just for his visits to her here. Two weeks. Two weeks of watching TV sports and sharing passionate nights together, and he didn't know how much longer he could keep pretending.

Her motivations for holding back made sense. She liked her privacy. Wanted to avoid judgment. Heck, she was fresh out of a major relationship and wasn't ready for another. Problem was, everything she couldn't commit to, he'd been waiting for his entire life.

He was more than her rebound. He knew enough about Sarah Overton to see she wasn't a "rebounding" sort of woman, and that the way she was around him, all those open exchanges and moments of laughter and raw need, went beyond what she'd give just any man.

She liked him. Genuinely liked him. And he sure as hell liked her. Still, he couldn't ignore the missing pieces. Couldn't continue the public farce that he felt nothing. That he didn't want anything more. And then there were all his unspoken words...

A distinct pulling drew inside his belly, maybe less a sensation than a physical warning.

"Yeah, the usual's fine." He stared into her beautiful eyes but got nothing back, so he shook his head and frowned down at the bar top, allowing her to get on with her job.

Maybe her reservations were less about anything missing in this relationship, so much as *him*. He wasn't a prize catch. He had one friend in the entire world, a mountain of secrets, and a not-so-rosy future. What exactly *did* he have working for him?

She's not the only one holding things back, now is she?

I'm a hypocrite.

"Fancy seeing you here." Ally squeezed up against the bar and onto the stool next to him, her beaming grin lightening his mood some.

"You mean at Harlow's one and only bar?" He returned the smile and tried not to hate himself when her moonstruck eyes lit up further. "Fancy that, indeed."

His old self would have been just fine with the pact he had with Sarah. His old self wouldn't have given a damn about the limitations. But then, his old self wouldn't have gone missing in action the night he'd met her, either…

Even then, I liked her too much.

Ally patted his hand, her sweet perfume something akin to a freshly opened bag of candy, and in his opinion, no competition for Sarah's scent of orange blossoms and something more floral, like lilies.

"I appreciated our chat the other week. I've been so busy at the store, what with Blaine still in the hospital and all…" Ally pushed her hair from her face, as if to bring attention to her glowing, pale neckline, a simple, thin gold chain sinking into the dip at her throat. "It's nice seeing you again, Dean."

Sarah set a bottle of beer before him, not even the gentle curve of her athletic body and her skin-tight jeans enough to distract from her straight stare on Ally. "Why not get Wayne and Jacob to take up the slack?"

"They're doing their best, but really, I'm not much of a morning person and the longer days are killing me." Ally's gaze fluttered over to Dean, her blue eyes glinting in an adoring sort of way.

He focused on Sarah, her hip leaned against the bar and brow raised at him, the slightly jealous expression sparking the smallest sliver of hope.

She eyed Ally again. "I hear Emilia's dad is in town, and he's pulled strings to get a fill-in carpenter at Oak Tree for you."

"As if one Blaine, with his endless list of demands, wasn't enough?" Ally laughed. "But seriously, the new guy won't get here for a couple of days yet, and in the meantime, we're running out of stock and racking up more orders. Who'd have thought Blaine making national news as a crime victim could be good for business?"

"The world works in mysterious ways." Sarah shrugged.

"Way too true, which brings me to another reason I came in tonight." Ally patted his hand again, the soft smile she extended denoting appreciation more than affection, as though her feelings for him had mellowed some, though Sarah's subtle pout said she didn't see the difference. "I know you've been looking for some handy work. I wanted to offer you some part-time money if you're interested. The work would just involve loading deliveries with Wayne and Jacob, and if you're up to it, helping the fill-in carpenter with basic tasks until we're all caught up again."

Sarah's gaze flicked once more down to Ally's hand over his before her stare hit him again, her silent seething something he was willing to draw out since it might make her reevaluate her feelings for him. "Sounds like a great opportunity. You should take it."

Her flat delivery turned her suggestion into a dare, but she peered back at Ally now, a fraction more at ease. "Are you here to see Dean, or can I get you a drink?"

"Oh, no. I'm here to stay for a bit." Ally's tone held an obliviously chipper edge. "Budweiser, please."

Sarah gave a habitual-type smile and turned away, but not before raising both brows at Dean in a, *you'd better watch yourself* stare.

"What do yah say?" Ally leaned her shoulder into him, her voice lowered like they shared some kind of intimate secret. "Sheriff Marlin raved about your work at the station, and we'd love the extra help at the shop."

"I can't imagine Sheriff Marlin raving about anything." Dean took a long swig of his beer, not sure how he felt about once again stepping into the shadows of Sarah's ex, much less accepting his money in the wake of an injury incurred, in part, due to Dean's negligence. Then again, Ally had used the word *help*, and no one knew of Dean's connection to the home invasion. So maybe he could *help* keep the man's business afloat while he recovered. "Okay, sure. I could do with some steady work for a while."

A light squeal squeezed past Ally's lips, and he twisted the long neck of his beer bottle between his fingers, already anticipating the talk Sarah would have with him. He tread a fine line here, no doubt about that. Somewhere between awakening her true feelings for him, prodding her issues with Ally, and now working for her ex… all this while trying to make a living in a town that wasn't exactly awash with opportunity.

I'll find a way to pay the man back someday. Shit. This whole mess just keeps getting bigger.

He couldn't keep living off odd jobs, that much was clear. At some point, he'd need to come up with a permanent plan. One where he got to stick around and build a life with Sarah. If she would have him.

"This is for you." Sarah dropped a folded piece of paper in front of him and slid a beer over to Ally.

"What is it?" He turned the paper over and stared across at Sarah, her posture decidedly more relaxed than before.

"The sheriff called and asked me to take a note for you."

The lifted corners of her mouth said she was lying, but he stared at her anyway, for no other reason than he loved looking at her. The sheriff had no reason to call him, and still, the amber glimmer in her eyes invited him to play along.

He unfolded the note and read it.

"Say you have to make a phone call and come meet me out back."

He peered up again, slow this time, using his frown to cover his amusement. "I need to use your phone. I left mine at home. This sounds important."

An instant grin tore across her face, and she flicked a thumb over her shoulder. "Sure, just through the double doors and in the kitchen. Don't mind Gordon, no matter what he has to say."

Dean did as instructed and strolled through the kitchen doors. A wave of steamy air hit him, an active stove in one corner of the room, a guy with a tall and solid build standing before that stove, his shaved head twisting toward Dean with an open expression. "Hey, you can't be back here."

"Hi, Gordon." Dean didn't break stride and headed for the metal door at the back with the EXIT sign above it. "Save your complaints for Sarah. This is her doing."

The man shook his head and went back to work. Dean stepped outside, the fresh night breeze cooling his skin while he waited for Sarah. The metal door behind him crashed open, and he spun around to Sarah slipping through toward him. "I thought you said you'd do something about Ally?"

Hard tension drew at his chest, and that tension spread to his jaw. What with Sarah's cheeky smile at the bar and the ruse to meet outside, he'd hoped for an intimate moment together, not for her to chew him out. "I did, and I have."

She jerked back a little, as though his short reply hurt her, but she simply jutted her chin at the metal door and continued her indifference. "What was that in there, then?"

He glared at her. "Why do you care?"

She frowned, further depicting pain over anger. "You know why I care."

"Because Ally's your friend and you made a promise to your brother?" he scoffed, shaking his head. "Right. Got it."

A long silence brought out the sounds of cicadas and rustling grass. She stared at him, her gaze darting about like she tried to fit a multitude of pieces together. "Want to tell me why you're the one who's pissed?"

He kept his jaw pressed shut for a moment longer. "I'm not pissed. You're jealous."

Again, she didn't say anything, just blinked at him with her wounded expression turning stony, her foot tapping against the dry gravel.

He scrubbed a hand through his hair, trying not to growl his frustration. "Look. I don't understand you."

Her brows dipped and her tapping picked up pace, her stoniness changing to agitation coupled with a terse laugh. "I'm not sure I understand me either."

Not the clear answer he'd hoped for, but closer to an admission of her true feelings. He stepped in and placed his hands either side of her upper arms. "Fine then, let's concede that as the newbie in town, I can't afford to go around making enemies, so you'll have to trust me when it comes to Ally. If that's too much of a stretch, then trust your instincts. You know there's nothing there."

She gave a heavy sigh, and her shoulders dropped, her gaze dipping to his chin and her sharper edges smoothing out. "Trusting my instincts hasn't gotten me far."

"Why?" He offered a weak smile, hoping to ease her doubt somewhat. "Because you didn't bank on your ex's long-lost love stumbling into town?"

"Well, when you put it like that—"

"When I put it like that, you're not to blame for any of this. No one is. Sometimes shit just happens."

She dropped her attention to the ground and nodded, though not all that convincingly since her lower lip did a tiny wobble. Yet another sign that he got to her, even though she'd never admit as much; her reservations and personal wounds were something he could identify with, and in part, why he'd been drawn to her in the first place.

"Now, don't get me wrong." He allowed the fragility in his smile to give way to a full-bodied beam. "Ally's not bad to look at—"

Sarah snapped her gaze back to him, a breathy laugh soon falling from her as though she grasped his intended humor.

"But..." He moved in closer and pressed a soft kiss to her lips. "We've talked, and she knows nothing's going to happen between us."

"She's a good kid."

"She's a grown woman, and we both know it, but yes, deep down you know you've worked yourself up over nothing."

"It's not nothing to me." Her husky tone betrayed that poorly hidden vulnerability again. One that reminded him of her recent heartbreak, and that he'd been too quick to get defensive.

"I know." He kissed her again, brushing his thumbs over her temples. "I know that."

"Either way." She stuffed both hands into her jean pockets, shifting under his hold. "I'm acting irrationally, and that's unfair to everyone who crosses my path, especially you. I'm sorry."

"Sarah." He touched his nose to hers, sinking under the sensation that he could drown in her eyes and never escape. "I simply take your irrationality as a sign of how much you must really like me."

She laughed and slapped a hand against his chest in a playful gesture. "You better get out of here before we tip anybody off."

But he liked that he'd been able to change her mood, so he didn't let her go right away. Would it be so bad if someone did see them together? No. So, he reveled in the closeness for a while, despite the air of sadness wafting from her.

Maybe it would be bad if someone saw... if they know who I really am...

He stepped back, even as he acknowledged that in her presence, he was someone else.

Someone worth her affection.

Someone without a dubious past.

Someone worth being seen with in public...

For all my fakery alone, I deserve her mistrust.

The worst part? No doubt she held her own guilt over all the hiding. She blamed herself for holding back, for being the height of his current frustrations, while unknowingly being his salvation too.

But he could pretend with her. Pretend he was normal. Pretend everything was well and good, and that it was safe to have dreams and allow someone to fall for him. Pretend that it was only her issues keeping them apart...

What an asshole!

He made room for her to get to the door, signaling that he would leave too, though to the parking lot so Gordon wouldn't see them enter Maynard's together. Maybe this relationship *should* remain a secret. Maybe it didn't deserve to continue at all. He had no place wanting more. Still, he wanted—and just once—he wished that what he wanted and what he got could be one and the same thing.

Twenty-Seven

"Well, don't you look like a glowing ball of sunshine?" Blaine stood beside his hospital bed, his pride in his ability to stand evident in his smile, even if his posture wasn't completely straight.

"If you like, I can always turn right around and leave." She threw him a pinched glare, but held a smile and strode deeper into his overly white room, anyway.

"And I could threaten to chase after you." His sea green-eyes sparkled. "But we both know you'd kick my ass. That said, I *was* about to go for a walk in the courtyard. Wanna come with?"

"It's good to see you're making progress." She doubled back but waited at his door for him to lead the way down the quiet hall, chuckling at his blue hospital gown, which thankfully had a closed back. "Even if I've seen tortoises move faster."

He laughed, not grimacing from any pain unlike last time, yet another sign he was improving. "Hey, three weeks ago I thought I'd be dead, I'll take my tortoise pace in a heartbeat."

She crossed the short corridor with him, then held a glass door open at the end that led to a red-brick path and the tiny courtyard, a heaviness settling in her chest. "Everyone in town will be glad to hear you're doing better."

Blaine shuffled past and across the linoleum floor, his gaze turned downward and his smile dropped by the smallest margin. His knuckles atop the walking frame were white, the veins on his hands bulging. "They should be more concerned about Emilia. She obsessively uses up every second of her hospital visiting hours. It's a miracle I convinced her I'd survive while you visited today. She blames herself for Anthony returning. For me getting hurt. There's no convincing her none of this is her fault."

Sarah skimmed her gaze around the simple garden ahead, the manicured yellow roses, the lush green grass patches, and wooden benches that offered a hopeful view despite the subject matter. As usual, she came up dry of any supportive words, so she offered him a gentle pat on the back. Silent reassurance would have to be enough.

Blaine paused and drew a long breath, the task of walking taking its toll, even as his focus landed on her, pinched and a little gray. "Something's bothering you. What is it?"

Her heart did a slow, dread-heavy beat. Blaine was still on the mend, and she wouldn't bother him with her inane problems. But even on an off day, he read her like a book. "Nothing's wrong with me."

He strolled toward a bench, and then groaned as he sat. "How long have we known each other? The last time you came here you were off your game too, but I said nothing because I figured you were in shock like everyone else over what happened to me. But you're even more rigid and cagey today."

She shrugged and nudged a stray leaf on the ground with her foot, choosing to remain standing. "A lot's changed, that's all. I'm just trying to adjust."

He lifted his gaze to the bright afternoon sun and squinted against its glare. "And these changes aren't all because of me, are they?"

"If you ever want to give up being a carpenter, you could try for a career as a professional psychic, you know that?" She kept her tone flat and her expression on him light, hoping humor would distract him.

He did laugh, shaking his head like he appreciated her levity, but then a prolonged silence took over, giving her dreaded moments to think.

Even though she stared at the ground, the sting of his gaze burned her skin, bringing a harsh heat to her cheeks. He'd always had a way of seeing right through her attempts to hold on to her true thoughts, though Dean seemed to have the same talent.

Or maybe I'm not half as cunning with keeping my thoughts to myself as I figured.

The funny thing about this silence, it made her want to say something, to free herself of all she held on to.

There'd been a time when everyone in Harlow knew everything about her. Knew *too much* about her. She'd gone from being a golden child living it up in Florida and on her way to a spot on the pro-tennis circuit, to a sad outlier everyone pitied. One minute she'd lived a teen dream, and the next, a futureless nightmare.

The truth had hung around her neck like a concrete target, an impossible-to-hide drag that had turned her emotions and privacy into a precious commodity—a rare gem never to be shared.

Maybe that's why she held her interactions with Dean so close to her chest.

Yes, she didn't want the judgment. No more pitying looks…

Poor Sarah, ditched by her fiancé and now rebounding with the new guy in town.

But also, she had no idea what her feelings for him were, and if she did, she sure as hell wasn't about to admit to anything.

And then there was something else entirely. A more innocent truth. That she reveled in having something all to herself. The joy in her secret intensified because her "something" was actually a "someone".

But secrets had a way of growing bigger and bigger and needing somewhere to go. If she wasn't careful, control of this particular secret would slip from her fingers. She'd lose the ability to determine what others knew.

Then again, even if she wanted to talk, now was not the time. Blaine had his own problems, and he was also her ex-fiancé, as well as Ally's, and now Dean's, employer. Her truth telling could wait for another time.

She peered down and gave him a tight smile, wanting to offer at least some kind of explanation. "I need to mull a few things over before I can put what's going through my head into words. Does that make sense?"

He gave a slow nod and patted the empty spot on the bench next to him. "It does. Though I hope you won't let whatever it is get you too down."

She sat and bumped her shoulder playfully into his. "I think I can handle this."

Even though her throat constricted from the crush of her overwhelming emotions and a desire to get her thoughts out. But as always, she picked stubborn bravery over anything else.

"There's something I wanted to talk to you about." Blaine's hushed tone broke through her inconvenient doubts, his expression open, yet somehow unreadable. "You're the first person I'm telling this to, and I hope it won't cause any extra pain."

A tight band constricted around her ribcage, and she shifted her position toward him, her movements jerky. She tried to predict what he might say, her thoughts darting to something negative, but what exactly, she couldn't decide.

"The moment I get out of this hospital..." He studied her face, as though measuring her reaction before adding, "I'm going to ask Emilia to marry me."

Sarah's face turned suddenly cold and was doubtless pale, her lips parting of their own volition. She wanted to believe he wouldn't notice her unchecked shock, but she wasn't so naive to pretend Blaine, of all people, wouldn't see.

"Wow." Her voice came out breathy and weak, and she struggled for more words.

She should have expected this, but Emilia had been in town only a couple of months, and Sarah had been with him a solid two and a half years before he'd asked her to marry him. "Are you sure about this?"

"After all that's happened..." Blaine nodded. "Yeah, I'm sure."

She swallowed hard, and her mind flicked through all the years she'd been his girlfriend.

A hard and heavy ball of *something* made a home in her belly. She refused to call that *something* anger or spite, though it may well have been.

She wanted to be the bigger person here. To take Dean's advice and believe none of this was about her personally. Just a series of unfortunate events that led to her stepping aside before she'd been *tossed* aside. Yet another move taken to preserve her pride.

And so, being the bigger person, she plastered on a smile and took Blaine's hand, as if this news didn't bother her.

"Why did you want to tell me first?" Even she could hear the thinness in her tone. "You don't need my permission to marry Emilia. I'll be happy for you either way."

That much was true. She *was* happy for him. *Did* wish him the best. Even as she once again shoved herself through yet another closing door.

"I know you'll be happy. You're a survivor, Sarah Overton." He squeezed his hand around hers. "But you still deserved to hear the news straight from me, and also, as ill-timed as this is, I need your advice."

Tension drew at her forehead, and her brow flexed at the pressure. "Advice about what?"

Blaine's eyes held an expectant glow as he spoke again. "I'm thinking maybe I could hold the engagement party at Oak Tree, since the showroom is big enough to hold everyone. Maybe Ally could do all the invites and preparations while I'm stuck in here. What do you think?"

"Oh no. No, no, no. You can't do that." She shook her head. Maybe she'd misheard him, though his nervous cringe didn't support that theory. "Firstly, as nice as Oak Tree is, you can't hold an engagement party at a furniture store—especially not if you're planning to marry Emilia Bonacci, the heiress to a jewelry empire. Second, you and I both know Ally can't keep a secret. The details of your proposal are bound to reach Emilia before you even get the chance to ask."

His gaze slipped from her, and his lips formed a tight line. "Yeah, I guess you're right. Shit."

A long silence took over, and she watched the disappointment play out across his face, disappointment being something he'd had a lot of lately. And because she hated to see that look on his face, because she had a megaton of guilt to escape, and maybe simply because she wanted things to be all right for a change, she opened her mouth and offered the unexpected.

"Let me take care of the party. We'll host it at Maynard's. I'll even post the invitations for you."

"Sarah." His eyes pleaded with her, exhaustion dulling his complexion. "You know I can't ask you to do that."

"You're not asking. I'm *telling* you I'm doing it." She gave him a tight grin and patted his hand. "Though it might seem a bit weird that your ex-fiancée is organizing your engagement party."

He gave an easy chuckle, his grin giving him an air of renewed lightness. "Some might say weird, I'd say unique. You sure about this?"

She gave a quiet nod, even though she wasn't all that sure, but willing to help either way. "Just tell me when you plan to propose. I'll do the rest."

He took a deep breath, as though he needed a moment to accept her offer. "With any luck, I'll get discharged on Sunday this week. The plan is to propose at Mirabelle Falls but tell everyone the party is just to celebrate my recovery. Hopefully she'll say yes, and then I guess we'd head straight to Maynard's, where maybe she'll have a chance to take her mind off how tough these last weeks have been."

He gave his head a slow shake and held her gaze for another while. "I don't think you know just how much Emilia and I appreciate you. Anthony kept her isolated in LA, and it's been so long since she's had friends of her own. She keeps telling me how lucky she feels that you, Ally, and Aggie took her under your wings. For this, for everything else, thank you, Sarah."

A soft tingling spread through her chest, filling the bitter moment with a layer of sweetness, reminding her she'd done the right thing in instigating the breakup, since her personal sacrifice meant two people were together and happier now.

In a round-about way, she was happier too. As in, she wasn't with someone who would have come to seeing her as his second, and therefore, lesser choice.

"You owe me some boxes of tissues and numerous tubs of ice-cream." She nudged Blaine, producing a genuine smile for once. "I'm supposed to go into mourning now, aren't I? Now that my ex is marrying someone else…"

"Ice cream, I can do, but the tissues? No. You and I both know that almost nothing makes you cry." He reached for his metal frame and gave a groan as he stood. "Though I guess given the month I've had, I should be mighty glad you're not the type of woman to seek revenge over this. God knows, I've fielded enough revenge."

He took a few lumbering steps and gave her a grin from over his shoulder. "Are you coming? It's almost time for Oprah reruns."

She spat out a crackling laugh and shook her head before standing. "Is this what hospital life has reduced you to?"

"Jealous?"

"Hell, no." She laid her hand between his shoulder blades and helped him walk, mostly just delighting that for the first time in this whole ordeal, they had a chance to find a new place with each other. A place where they could move on. Be genuine friends again. That she really could organize his engagement party and *not* feel weird about it.

"Oh and, Sarah—" He led her into the corridor before pausing, his grin still in place, though significantly wider. "Say hi to the new man for me."

Twenty-Eight

"Hey." Dean trailed behind Sarah, the blue sky dotted with a few jagged gray clouds overhead, her usual quick steps taking her across a small road on the way to Main Street.

She stalked onward, not stopping to look at him. "Sorry, can't talk now."

He frowned at her back and pushed for a longer stride to catch up. She tended to keep to herself most times, but she also wasn't usually outright dismissive either. "What's happening?"

"Nothing, just busy." Her staggered phrasing made her seem pissed more than busy, though over what, he had no idea.

He tried not to growl because Sarah wouldn't play into growling, so a more nonplussed reply would have to work. "Okay. Well. Want to tell me what you're busy with and maybe I can help?"

"I'm not sure you'd want to." She swatted hair from her face, the light spring breeze working against her seeming need to get away from him. "I'm handing out invites."

"Invites?"

"Yeah, invites."

"Invites to what?

He wanted to roll his eyes at himself. He'd never been all that talkative, and this game of twenty questions only highlighted how far he'd fallen.

Fallen? As in, for Sarah? Have I really gone that far?

He couldn't seem to shut up when it came to this woman, that much was clear. Then again, if she alone didn't send him off-kilter, her evasive act right now did.

"Invitations to Blaine and Emilia's engagement party." She held a casual tone but by now he had a good view of her profile, as well as the tension pulling at her jaw. "Though we're not supposed to call it an engagement party, so try to keep that bit a secret."

Her tight tone had his brow sinking heavy and his muscles turning slack. At least her cageyness wasn't about him, and still... "You're handing out invites to your ex's engagement?"

"Yes." Her steely stare pinned on the street ahead, and her stride didn't slow.

She clearly didn't want to talk about it, and somehow, he couldn't let it go. "I guess that explains a lot."

She sent him an unreadable stare before ripping her attention away again.

The Main Street storefronts flicked by to her right, and he marched alongside her, his hands clenched into fists in an attempt to keep from reaching out and grabbing her arm. She wouldn't appreciate him forcing her to stop, much less forcing any kind of direct conversation. Was it even his place to talk exes with her?

But he had an endless list of things to say and wanted to cut the love-sick-puppy act, so he planted his feet and waited to see if she'd make room for him too. "Will you stop already and talk?"

She halted and swung around, her wide gaze darting about as though checking no one else heard his loud demand.

"We had a deal, remember?" She held a tight whisper, gaze still moving about her. "No public displays."

"You want everyone to think we don't get along, don't you?" He crossed his arms, hinting that this current terse display would suit her goal perfectly. "Though I'm not so sure either of us is pretending right now."

She swore under her breath and grabbed his arm, tugging him

toward a narrow alleyway at the side of a coffee shop. She stared at him for a while, her jaw tight, before some of that tension slipped away and she gave a heavy sigh. "Blaine knows about us."

The strain throughout his body dropped too, and he stared at her in stunned silence. "You told him about me?"

She sank back and shook her head. "No. He figured it out, which is worse."

Well, yeah, that was worse, though probably not for the same reasons she figured. He'd wanted her to claim a stake over this relationship, over him. Telling someone, especially her ex, would have gone a long way toward that.

"He didn't figure I was seeing you exactly, just that something had changed, and I was probably seeing *someone*." She shrugged, not looking at him as she spoke. "I can't help but wonder, if he put the pieces together, how long until everyone else does?"

He held silent for a moment, trying to decide what her true motivations were. "Would people knowing about us be so bad? We've been seeing each other for weeks now."

"Maybe not, but it wouldn't be fair." She peered up at him, even as she began pacing in a short line back and forth. "Not for you."

A heavy weight pressed on his lungs and breathing took extra effort. "Why me?"

"Because…" She bit her lower lip and stared at the ground. "I don't know how I feel here, and…"

"And what?" He took a quick step forward, then stopped himself from going any farther. "You're afraid you'll have to end things, and that would be mighty embarrassing for me, is that it?"

She pressed her lips into a hard line and drew a slow breath. "I don't know."

"Despite your 'tough-woman' act, you sure care too much about what other people think."

Lines sank between her eyebrows, hinting at her simmering temper. "We were meant to be a secret, now we're not. So, sue me if I'm a little shaken about this."

He shook his head, a slow warning for her not to insult his intelligence. He wouldn't be so peeved about the privacy thing if she were willing to let him in at other times. Her vague approach extended to their moments alone together, and he wanted that to change. He wanted to know what she was thinking, didn't always want to be on the outside, searching for a way in. "One person knows. *One person.* So, what's really upsetting you here?"

"One person is a bad sign." She shrugged, like his argument was no big deal, but it was and he refused to be dismissed.

He scoffed, wanting to call her a coward, but caring too much about her to say it out loud. "So, you're spooked now? You never struck me as someone to wilt at the first sight of an obstacle."

Her lips made that flat line again, her indifference on display, only for a soft sheen to wash over her eyes.

For the longest time, she said nothing, only gave a small and repeated nod, her throat bobbing as she swallowed and eventually found her voice. "Not because of what they might say…"

A sudden stillness washed over him. For the first time in his life, a mild ache formed within, taking up space inside his chest and expanding outward. Her reaction, the watery look she gave was less about impending tears, more an expression of being uncharacteristically overwhelmed. But by what?

"Why does everyone just assume that because I don't appear to be falling apart, I'm handling things just fine?" Her words answered his unspoken question, and she pressed her palm to her forehead, turning from him. "I wish I could be an open book like Ally or Emilia, but I'm not, Dean, I'm just not."

"What *things* are you not handling?" He remained still, unwilling to curse this rare candid moment. To be fair, he'd never assumed she was just fine—more of an incoming storm hidden beyond the horizon… bound to roll in sooner or later. "Maybe I can hel—"

"I'm not over the hurt of being ditched for another woman, okay?" She dropped her hand and gave him a direct stare before her expression crumbled, and she turned again like the shame of snapping at him hurt her too. "Telling everyone the engagement was off, it was humiliating and my confidence is a mess. And here you are"—she shot a hand out to him, still not making eye contact—"just sweeping into town and asking me to be ready, because, why? Because you're ready.

Well, I'm not. I'm telling you I'm *not.* But believe me, there's nothing wrong with you. It's all me. Me being broken and hurt, and just wanting my life to stay the same."

This time her gaze did meet his, but there was a harder, more defensive edge in her eyes. "Is it too much to ask to be left alone? For everyone in this town to just back up and give me some space?"

Twenty-Nine

"Is that what you really want?" The question fell from Dean without much thought, but the deep, gnawing ache in his gut said he hung on her answer. "You want to be alone?"

She shook her head, her silence drawing out.

Someone he didn't recognize crossed the alley's entrance, past the coffee shop's large windows, their quick pace taking them farther down Main Street and out of earshot. "The scary part is, as much as I tell myself I'm unsure, I *know* how I feel about you, Dean."

"And?"

"I like you." Her gaze fell from him again, like she'd just spoken the most devastating words of her life. "I like you a lot."

Her overwrought look had the corners of his lips twitching, but he held down any genuine smile, still too uncertain where this conversation was heading. "I can see why that would be a problem."

She scowled at him, though the lopsided clench of her cheeks suggested humor. "The thing is, I like you way too much for this to be healthy. I've come to realize hiding you is becoming less about what people will say, and more that, just once, I want something that's all mine."

He took a hurried step forward, reaching to give in to his longstanding urge to touch her, but she stepped back, her hand held out in a gesture for him to stop. "Not yet. I'm not done. In realizing how I feel about you—that this is more than just friends with benefits and a fun trick to play on the local gossips—there's something else that's holding me back."

Her attention worked over him, as if she appraised him and whether she should say more, the narrowing of her eyes confirming his theory. "As much as I consider you more than a friend, I know significantly less about you than any friend. You also know less about me than anyone else in this town. See how that could be a problem?"

"Sure." He schooled his face, keeping his response minimal, despite his quickening pulse. She was about to ask him for the one thing he couldn't give. "So, you want a heart-to-heart?"

She tucked her hands into her jeans pockets, the action an easing from her earlier defensive tact. "I guess. I can't rightfully say I trust you if, when I get down to it, I don't know much about you."

"Right." He nodded, more to himself than to her, his joy somehow fizzled to a dry and deathly reality.

Reality. Something he failed to escape, time and time again.

This was the bit where she asked questions he couldn't answer. Not truthfully, anyway.

He didn't want to lie. Didn't want to lose her either.

Once more, a good thing teetered on the edge of disappearing from his life completely, all because his past didn't make such a pretty picture. In fact, his past was downright hideous.

He turned toward the alley's entrance and slowly but surely trudged out.

Gravel crunched behind him, Sarah's hurried footsteps. "Dean? What's wrong?"

"I can't give you what you want." He tossed his voice so she could hear but kept on walking all the same.

"So, you're leaving?" She grabbed his bicep and turned him around. "Just like that?"

Her glare held him, out on the pavement and just outside the alley. Now he was the one peering about the street, concerned about what others might see or hear. "Not 'just like that'. I… I need a minute to think."

She stepped back a little, her narrowed stare taking him in anew. "Well, that's a bad sign if ever there was one. You know about Blaine. I've told you a bit about my family. It's not too much that I want to know a little about your history and problems."

The angry heat blooming in his chest dimmed a little, and he found it in him to reply. "You've never asked."

Her expression remained unmoved. "I'm asking now."

He spun away and ran his fingertips through his hair, his greatest wish being that he'd never have to tell anyone, much less *her*, the truth. So now he stood with his mouth clamped shut, his reasons for secrecy as strong as ever.

If she knew the truth, she would leave. If he said nothing, she would leave.

"Exactly." She stepped around him and shook her head, confirming the impossibility of his predicament, the drop of her shoulders a show of familiar disappointment.

Even then, even as he'd been the one to walk away—walking away from Sarah wasn't straightforward—and just like the night they met, he searched for a way to prolong his time with her.

"Let me start with this, then." He held a hushed tone and took her by the shoulders, turning her to face him. "When I look at you, I remember what it's like to be human. You give me things I haven't had in years—dreams, desires—the things that made me stay in this town to begin with."

Her lips parted, like she meant to say something, but abandoned that idea, her cheeks hollow and pupils wide.

He drew her in more, allowing himself the privilege of running his thumb over her cheek, despite the public setting, despite the selfishness of his move. "My past, it's not a pretty story to tell."

Her gaze held his, like she didn't want to let go as much as he didn't. "It's still something I want to hear."

"Why? Tell me, why?" His tone turned unintentionally rough, but as much as he didn't deserve her, he wasn't beneath trying to keep her. "So you can decide if I'm someone worth being with?"

She shook her head. "So I can trust you'll be open with me about the *not so pretty* stuff. I deserve a chance to understand the man I'm dating."

"Isn't the man, himself, enough?"

"Do you know how unreasonable you sound right now?" She blinked at him, her expression still and not at all denoting humor.

He let go of her. Backed away. All the while, nodding to himself. He was being unreasonable, and just as she asked too much in wanting the truth, he asked too much expecting she could live without it.

"There's not much between us that isn't beyond reason. Starting with the way we met." He held her gaze again, his small offering of honesty. "The stupid charade we've been playing around everyone..."

Her brow ticked upward, a small challenge of sorts. "You want to stop the charade?"

She tested his resolve. A test he deserved in light of his secrecy, a test he might just fail.

"The charade was fun at first"—he gave a fake, easy shrug—"but it's not anymore. I know as the man here, I'm supposed to be the one chasing you. Just to break with tradition, what if I told you that I'm not ready yet? That I need a little more time?"

Hell. What a lie. If it were up to him, he and Sarah would be a done deal. As in, she'd be his forever. No ifs, no buts. But little was up to him here, even if she, and the future this town promised, did happen to be everything he'd ever wanted.

She lifted her chin and peered up at him with a dry and analytical stare. "I think that whole 'chasing' tradition extends to getting it on, which we've already done more than a few times. But yes, I can understand some things aren't easy to talk about, and I'll give you more time."

"Thank you." A sudden and fulfilling breath filled his lungs, her offer of more time an unexpected gift.

She squeezed her eyes shut, hinting she wasn't done yet. "But someday soon, Dean, you'll have to give me something to work with."

Thirty

Sarah was only two hours into her shift and already this night dragged like no other. She handled each order with mechanical efficiency, gave a few mumbled words to appear somewhat social, her confidence meanwhile twisting in the wind.

To her mind, she'd reached a crossroads with Dean. Not so much that she wanted to step away, but that she had a decision to make on how close she could and should get to him.

He'd started out as someone meant to mend her battered ego, her breakup with Blaine still so raw and fresh, all while she decided whether to trust her judgment. She'd been wrong before, chased the wrong dream, and in this case, man.

For years, her life had been an immovable wall, except now she wanted to move. She wanted change. Small change. Not more than she could chew. She was open to being wrong. Not so much about Dean—she trusted him—but where her initial feelings for him lay, as well as the trajectory of this relationship.

Sure, that first meeting had been everything impulsive. She wasn't a dreamer, had never been one to take a risk. But what if she tried? What if she gave in? Just once. And let there be more to that initial spark at the soiree.

She squeezed her eyes shut and shook her head, the whole dreamer thing so ill-fitting. If she wasn't at work, if it wasn't so late, she'd go for a run and let the confusion settle around her.

A thud sounded behind her and she opened her eyes, turning to three plates now waiting on the pass. Down a server, she welcomed the chance to move, grabbed the plates, and took a short trip through the dim bar, where two unfamiliar college boys sat at a table with Ally nestled beside them.

Sarah paused, something about this scene instantly off. Something about the way Ally shifted her gaze to the tall, blond, football-player type next to her, or that he used Ally's shoulder as an armrest. *Arrogant prick.*

Sarah forced back a frown and lowered the plates to the group's table, the sudden silence churning a sick feeling just below her ribcage. The shorter guy peered up at her, his frosty gray eyes shadowed by his flop of muddy brown hair.

His emotionless gape changed to a lopsided smile, and he dragged his stare over her in unguarded appreciation. "I'm Marcus Martin."

She narrowed her eyes at him, at his expensive-looking knitted blue sweater, but turned away before she could unleash her desire to tell him she didn't care what his name was and that he should keep his leering to himself.

A high whistle cut through the bar's noise, that irritating whistle of course coming from Marcus Martin's direction. "Now that's a firm piece of ass."

She stopped in her tracks and spun around, the muddy-haired little jerk leaning his elbow into his table, his gaze still at her hips, like he had no intention of hiding his staring.

She scowled at his woolen sweater again, the upturned collar with a white shirt underneath somehow annoying her more while he drummed his stubby fingers over the tabletop. "What did you say?"

His gaze finally lifted and met hers, and he pitched forth a greasy smile. "My buddy and I hear Mirabelle Falls is the place for an intimate night swim. We're heading down there later. You should come, honey."

He looked her over again, his arrogance still ringing in her ears since he'd used an obnoxiously loud tone. Meanwhile, Ally's overt laugh pinged across the space, her head now resting on blond boy's shoulder.

What was she doing?

Sarah grimaced at the stumpy guy before her and muttered nothing more than an abrupt, "No."

She turned away again. Having dealt with countless sleazy types over the years, she wanted nothing more than to return to the bar and for Ally's strange choice in companions to leave already. What was with the strange choice, anyway? She'd need to talk to Ally. Find out why she'd suddenly decided to drop her standards.

Then again, hadn't Sarah done similar the first time she'd met Dean? Taken a risk on an out-of-towner? Not that Ally knew anything about that. Still, at least one of these guys was acting like trash and that didn't bode well for Ally's safety.

"Is she always such a sour prude?"

Once again, Marcus's dull-brained words stalled her exit, the volume and vileness of those words enough to send a blanket of silence over the other nearby patrons. Some stared back at her, mouths agape and hands frozen mid-air as though they dared not complete their next bit of food or sip of drink.

"I don't know about that." She turned slowly and tucked the frostier edge of her mood behind a tight smile before swanning closer and adding a little extra sway to her hips, along with a brightness to her tone. "I guess it depends what's on offer, Mr. Martin."

She rested a hand on Marcus's table and leaned in, giving him a healthy view down her t-shirt's V-shaped collar. The tension across his cheeks subdued, and he sank back in his chair, a smirk taking over his expression. "Like I said. Mirabelle and a swim. You and me. Naked. I'll take things from there, honey."

His smirk inched higher. A man used to treating people like shit and being rewarded for it, but she refused to slink away and hide, so she bit her lower lip and played coy instead. Let the fucker underestimate her. Let him believe that was the smuttiest thing a small-town woman like her had ever heard.

The room's eerie silence grew, and she couldn't escape the stinging awareness that most people in the bar watched her now. At least that meant someone might back her up if this turned sour. Maybe Ally would also rethink who she spent the rest of her night with.

Sarah leaned in farther, not stopping until her face was mere inches from Marcus's. "How old are you, sweetie?"

His gaze bore into her, predictably over-confident. "Twenty-two."

"Hmm… I just don't know. The river sounds mighty crowded…" She lifted her hand off the table and ran a fingertip over his non-existent bicep, biting her lip again, this time to keep from laughing. "I mean, what with your friend there and all…"

Marcus leaned in closer, his lip brushing her ear before he whispered. "He'll be too busy fucking his new bimbo to notice anything we're doing."

She winced before she stopped herself, wanting to reel back, wanting to smack this smug bastard across the face, and not stop smacking him until he left Maynard's and Harlow altogether.

Her stomach roiled, and she clenched her fingers on the tabletop, forcing herself to stay and pretend what he said didn't bother her.

Even then, her gaze unintentionally slipped to Ally. Sarah had made her brother a promise. As archaic and ridiculous as his request had been, he'd warned her about looking out for this very thing. Maybe there was something about Ally that he knew and she didn't, or maybe he was more of a knuckle-dragging caveman than she'd ever figured, and his warning was based purely on possessiveness. Either way, nothing about this situation seemed right, and warning or not, she would never stand aside without trying to stop a looming wreckage such as the one staring back at her now.

"You see, the problem is"—she slid her hand forward and grabbed Marcus's wrist, digging her fingers hard into his overly soft flesh—"I have a few extra years on you, and I don't think this would be an even exchange."

His pupils spread to wide pools, and his face lost color. Her terse tone was not lost on his privilege-addled brain since he twisted his wrist and tried unsuccessfully to break free of her grip.

So, she pulled him closer, adding to his misery and whispering in his ear. "Not so fast. I'm not finished."

She'd spent her teen years training to return two-hundred-mile-per-hour serves, then her years working the bar, and her efforts maintaining strength through exercise. All these things buoyed her decision to grip tighter, to level a threat this dirtbag might comprehend. "That 'bimbo' your friend is with, is *my* friend. If I hear even the slightest complaint about how she's treated tonight, I'll make sure the meanest people in these parts find you and your buddy and break all your legs and other appendages. Understand?"

No one in Harlow actually ran around breaking pieces off other people, but Marcus wouldn't know that. And still, her thoughts switched to Dean since, for some reason, she could imagine him being really good at hunting people down and breaking legs.

Marcus pulled at his wrist again, his nose wrinkled in a disgusted sneer. "What the fuck is wrong with you, woman?"

She let him go now but patted him on the cheek just to return his condescension from earlier. "I mean it. Be a good boy now, okay?"

Marcus's friend rose from his chair, the legs releasing a high-pitched scraping against Maynard's old boards. "Is mega bitch here laying down the law?"

"Yeah." Marcus jutted his chin out at her. "Seems she doesn't like you hooking up with her *friend*."

Ally rose and wrapped her arm around the blond guy, her glare burning into Sarah, like she was an embarrassing parent scaring away the cool kids. Somehow, Ally looked angrier than Marcus. Then again, she'd hadn't heard what Marcus had said about her earlier.

"Your friend here has issues." Blondie scowled down at Ally before shaking his arm and pushing her away.

Her taut look of panic dropped to slack disbelief. "But I thought—"

Blondie rolled his blue eyes and marched over to Sarah, poking his forefinger into the hard plate just below her collarbone. "If you knew who we are, you wouldn't be threatening us. One word to my dad, and I'll have this whole shitty backwater flattened." He scoffed and peered down at her in disgust. "This sad excuse of a bar will be the first to go."

Despite the pain from where his finger stabbed at her, she drew herself taller and rolled her shoulders back.

"You're really leading with the, 'I'm gonna tell my daddy' approach?" She slapped his hand away, the action designed to highlight the weakness in the toffee-nosed brat's threat. "And over what, some small-town girl insulting your feelings? I'm sure your poor dad, whoever the hell he is, lost hope in you years ago."

"Sarah!" Ally's cry broke the moment, and she squeezed in between the action. "What are you doing?"

Blondie's face paled from its angry shade of red, the muscle twitching along his jaw easing too. His mouth lifted to a toothy grin while he pulled his gaze from Sarah and onto Ally. "You're right, honey. What *are* we doing? You and this crazy bitch aren't worth our time. Enjoy your days milking cows in shitty paddocks, or whatever the fuck you hicks do. We're outta here."

Before he left, he took a second to shake his head at Ally in a pitying sort of gesture, Marcus laughing and trailing behind him on their way out of Maynard's.

A slow minute ticked over and Sarah watched Ally, her eyes sparkling and her thick eyelashes batting back tears. She took two quick steps as if to follow the boys, but Sarah lunged forward and grabbed Ally's elbow. "No. Stay."

Ally swung around, the tears winning out and streaking down her face. "You don't get it, do you? You had no right to interfere."

"If you'd heard what that boy said..." Sarah clapped her spare hand onto Ally's shoulder, pleading for her to listen. "Besides, they insulted me too."

Ally shook Sarah off in a flurry of weak slaps. "Unlike you, not everyone wants the hermit life."

Sarah drew back, an ache hitting her square in the chest. Sure, she had a reputation for keeping to herself, but she'd spared Ally a likely horrible night, hadn't she? She peered around her, at the dozen or so patrons still staring at her, this whole public scene defying her comfort zone.

Maybe Ally's frustration didn't make all that much sense, but there wasn't any point talking this out in the heat of the moment. So, she eased back farther, nodding and conceding defeat as Ally turned her tear-streaked face and stormed away.

Thirty-One

Dean held his front door open, his words momentarily lost as Sarah stared up at him, a thick layer of sweat beading her forehead, and the late evening overly quiet behind her. "What's happened?"

"Honestly?" She pushed past him, leaving him to once again wrestle with the idea of just how many people in these parts were comfortable moseying into his home. "I don't know what happened. Only that I thought I was helping Ally, and she just flipped out at me for all my trouble."

He pushed the door closed and followed her in, where she kicked off her shoes and sprawled across his couch. For a woman so hesitant to call herself his girlfriend, she sure acted like one. At least when it came to making herself comfortable in his space. "I think I'm going to need more to work with than you tried to help, and Ally flipped."

"Just some out-of-town college boys, probably on some drunken road trip." She flopped her elbow over her brow, as though blocking the room's mellow light from her eyes, or maybe even just escaping having to look at him as she spoke. "They were being disgusting, and I told them as much. Except, Ally had her eye on one of them and seemed inordinately crushed when he did the predictable thing and bailed from Maynard's without her."

"Right." Dean lifted her legs off the couch and squeezed in beside her, depositing her feet back on his lap. That she'd come here for his support and the casualness of this exchange provided something he'd craved his entire life, but been deprived of for just as long.

A short silence drew out, and she dropped her arm from her face and half-sat, staring at him. "You know something about this that I don't, don't you?"

"I *do* know something about this." A slow grin tugged at his lips, just as her eyes narrowed into a scowl.

"And are you going to tell me?"

"Nope."

She growled and flopped back onto the couch. "Fine. But why does it seem like I'm always in the dark on everything lately?"

He let out a sigh, more annoyed at himself than her. No doubt the "darkness" she referred to was in part about the mountain of secrets he consistently backed away from telling her. So now he was left with guilt piled on top of his annoyance. "Look, it's not my place to tell you about Ally's business, okay? What I *will* tell you, though, is to cut her some slack."

"What about her cutting *me* some slack?" She turned to him again, her stare direct in a needling sort of scrutiny. "Why do people around here assume their tantrums and harsh words never bother me?"

"Because you generally don't act like things bother you." He shrugged.

Her stare held him, though the slight upward curl of her lips suggested she understood his point. "And what about when they do? What if, on the rare occasion, things do bother me?"

"You're never shy about telling people what you think, Sarah." He tucked his palm under the hem of her pant leg, rubbing her smooth skin, skin that had a gentle warmth snaking through his body, reminding him just how much he never got enough of this woman. "Maybe it's time to establish some new rules. Start with asserting how you'd like people to behave around you."

Her attention dropped to his hands now on her shins, and she took in an audible breath, her eyes fluttering shut, like she appreciated the attention on what would be tired muscles from hours of standing. "You know, there's a certain responsibility that comes with being this town's unfeeling robot."

He gave an unintended scoff, one he restrained from becoming a full-bellied laugh. "I'm sure there is. Though, I guess you could always quit."

"I know." She let out a sigh, still seemingly enjoying the miniature massage, her eyes closed. "I know."

"I get the feeling I'm not supposed to ask why you haven't yet."

She gave a tight laugh and flopped back, resting fully into his couch. "Because I'm an unfeeling robot, remember? See how this all works? It's a vicious cycle."

"But one you could stop." He held his hand still, vying for more attention, or maybe another clue as to her motivations. "So, why haven't you?"

She flung her eyes open and pinned him with a critical stare. "You speak from experience, do you?"

That stare of hers, daring him to come out with some truth too—about himself—a dare they both knew he wouldn't take up.

He looked away, the strain across his chest growing, a thickness taking up space in his throat. Of all the people he'd ever known, she was the one he lied to most, even though she was someone he didn't want to lie to at all. "Not experience. More like, it's something I'm also hoping is possible."

"Sounds like a story I'd like to hear." Her gaze softened somewhat, hinting at empathy, though she'd probably deny having any at all.

He raised a brow, his silent way of telling her to dream on. "You're not the only one who gets to be stubborn here. All I'm saying is, if you don't like how people perceive you, maybe it's time to shift their focus. Maybe shift a few of the things you're doing too."

"Please, tell me more, oh wise one." She gave a genuine laugh, her gaze lighting upon him while she prodded his hand, signaling for the massage to continue.

He reached over and tapped a finger to her forehead, his way of acknowledging her silliness, something she seemed to unleash more and more around him these days. That levity something he, too, needed more of. Yet another laugh escaped her, and he fought to stay on topic and not lift her into his lap and distract her in other ways.

"You don't flinch to accept the hard stuff. For one, your willingness to step aside with Blaine and Emilia. But when it comes to something that's just for you, you hesitate, Sarah." He rubbed her shin again, emphasizing his point and giving her what she'd asked for all at once. "Let Ally deal with Ally, and you deal with you, and I…" He leaned over and pulled her to his lips. "I'm more than happy to deal with you too."

"I'm sure you are." She pressed her lips to his, her tone lowered, warm and husky, despite her sarcasm. "But maybe I am a coward." Her voice wobbled almost imperceptibly, and she leaned back. "Maybe it's not so easy to switch off the parts of me that want constant and total control."

The pain in her words had him caving to his desire to pick her up, to lend her an ounce of his strength, so she could take a break from using her own. He shifted her into his lap and cupped her face, making sure her focus held him and only him, glad that someone in this world seemed to need him. "Do you remember that day by the side of the road? How I kissed you and you told me never to do that again?"

She gave a small nod, her breath stalling and her wide stare not leaving his.

"We've kissed and done just about everything else since then. We talk and see each other almost every day. All of that takes trust. Maybe not as much as either of us want, but you know how to give, Sarah, and—" an uncontrollable smile broke from him "—I bet I can get you to do it again." He pulled her closer and kissed her now, soft and slow, but still all too fast for his liking. "And again. And again. And again…"

She laughed and slapped a hand at his shoulder, laughing some more. "I see how you turned my misery to your advantage there."

"Very clever, right?"

Through her smile, she bit down on her lower lip and nodded.

He leaned in. "I'd prefer to call this taking mutual advantage."

She groaned, his excitement growing as she captured his lips and initiated the next kiss, confirming his theory that she was nowhere near as unfeeling as she pretended, her long fingers raking through his hair as she made those *feelings* blatantly known.

No matter how much he wanted to, he couldn't be honest about his past—or *not-so-past*—if Luciano and the syndicate still looked for him. Perhaps her courage did scamper away at times when it came to intimacy, but maybe he could help her there, give her the chance to find some freedom before she learned the truth and rightfully dumped his ass…

And one day, yet another man will benefit from my missing out…

He swallowed back the pain in that thought, of her moving on, and this thing between them ending.

"There's something I want from you. Something you've never let me do." He stroked a thumb over the curve of her hip, drawing light circles over the exposed skin there, aware he teased her with his words and his touch. A tease designed to softened her toward what he wanted to say next, making him the one to ask too much now.

"Let me love you, Sarah Overton."

Thirty-Two

EVERY MUSCLE in Sarah's body tightened at the strum of Dean's touch. His hand over her hip. That soft caress coaxing her to soften—as did her straddled position in his lap—even though a deeply embedded sense of restraint pleaded with her not to give in. But she wanted to. She *so* wanted to…

"Let me love you." His repeated and imposing words made adrenaline course through every one of her fragile nerves, his gentle kiss on her lips weakening the sting just a little.

She'd let a man love her before, but look how that turned out…

Blaine left me for Emilia, didn't he? But heck, had I really loved him too?

She squeezed her eyes shut, that whole situation too complex for her to work through right now.

"When I kiss you, I want it to be more than physical." Dean's easy tone smoothed her jagged edges once more, bringing her back to him, her chest sagging into his, his breath a hot summer's breeze over her neck. "I want all of you."

Her breaths stilled to short sharp intakes and heat pooled in her lower regions, defying her logic and overriding ten years of reason.

"Every last snarky word of yours, Sarah." His lips caught hers again, only to escape all too fast. "Every frightened thought. I want to hear it. As much as I try, I can't resist you and I want you to feel the same about me."

Her heart clenched so hard she feared it might implode altogether. The sneaky devil had her already and he knew it, but he didn't know what he asked for… Or maybe he did. And *if* he did, then he knew that he asked for the impossible. Not because she didn't feel those same things for him, but because she would have to give up far too much of herself to allow those feelings to run free.

"I want to." The words rushed from her mouth, and she moved to say more, only the slow shake of Dean's head halted her ability to speak.

"Don't let the next word be, 'but'. Can we just leave it at *you want to*?" The deep dip of his brow and his unrelenting stare spoke of his need to avoid disappointment.

Except, the tentative shift of his gaze over her face, that subtle but desperate search for another clue. Well, that gaze made her think maybe her initial impressions about him being an unbreakable tough guy were all wrong. That Dean Holloway's heart was capable of breaking. Much worse, that *she* could be the one to break it.

She pressed her lips together for a quick moment and jolted in an attempt to restrain a manic laugh. He'd come to the wrong woman if undying love and fluffy feelings was what he wanted.

But the tight clenching around her heart changed her protest to something lighter, more accepting. She wasn't one for "fluffy" feelings, but she wasn't a monster either. So, she blinked a few times to ease the sudden hot prickle behind her eyes—an unusual sensation—and gave him a quick nod.

We'll leave it at "wanting".

And just to soften things further, she lifted her hands and allowed her fingers to glide over his broad shoulders, her fingertips catching the short hair at the base of his neck. She'd fought her impulses long enough. The fire of his skin demanded she melt on every level, as did his words, and she yielded to that demand as she crushed her lips over his.

He met her desire blow for blow, his hands pressing into her back as he stood, and her arms latched around him for purchase.

Maybe he was right. She'd shelved so much of what she wanted, so much she left unexpressed, all to maintain a semblance of non-existent peace. Boring peace that required too much sacrifice.

Her version of peace had stolen her dreams. It had kept others from dealing with their issues. *Ally included.* Maybe this once she could try something different. Lay claim to her desires and see where that *different* took her.

Dean pulled his lips away. He stood in his bedroom with her wrapped around him, her legs locked around his waist. His gaze held her too, the steadiness of that stare seeming to read her change, allowing her time to have no doubt about what she wanted. No-holds-barred passion. No hidden agendas. Even though they still hid so much from each other.

Her blood raced at the imperfection of it all, when for so long all she'd wanted were things that were tangible and easy to answer. *Maybe Sarah Overton can be someone more.* Less a woman who people tiptoed around, more strength *and* fragility. Completely herself. Someone who wanted and needed others. Okay, less *others*, more *one man in particular*... Imagine that...

He carried her the few steps to the bed and lowered her to the mattress, the soft crush of sheets rustling in her ears. The hot press of his lips hit hers again, his stubble adding a prickle to her skin, one that sent need sweeping through her body.

The taste of his kiss matched the spicy, warm scent of him, and she groaned and surrendered to the sumptuous fever taking over, his kisses now tracing a path down her jawline.

"You smell like a bar." His teasing words skimmed her ears, his strong fingers making a mockery of the buttons at the front of her work shirt.

She gave a lazy chuckle. "And I can't even say I enjoyed a drink."

His deep chuckle joined hers. "I'm willing to drink for two."

His wide palm swept her shirt open and claimed her left breast from under her flimsy cream lace bra, his thumb brushing her nipple, drawing from her a hiss.

He'd touched her like this so many times before, but something changed here. The ache around her heart. The gnawing within her tummy. She lay beneath him, deliciously caught, her entire being connected to his every move. She constantly waited for what would come next.

Next was him leaning in, pushing her bra straps down, her arms caught at her sides, his lips meeting with her opposite nipple.

As caught as she was, she couldn't escape her assertive nature, and she bent her elbows and dragged her palms up and under his shirt, raking her nails over the hard surface of his waist.

His mouth countered her tease, his tongue enlivening her skin, his teeth nipping and scraping, and tightening her breaths so that she arched against him in a silent plea for more. And he gave more, that same hand rasping over her tummy and tugging at her jeans, his excitement protruding into her thigh.

She wriggled, helping him out, kicking the heavy denim fabric off her ankles and into a light thud on the floor. She figured he would touch her. Take away her frustration. But he merely sat back and took his sweet time staring at her.

He had a *look* on his face. A different air to anything she'd seen before. Like he didn't know where to start with her. Or maybe he was a man used to losing the things he cared about, and he wanted to freeze this moment in time. Or maybe she merely projected her own feelings onto him.

Once again, the hot, prickly feeling gathered behind her eyes. What an odd reaction and what an odd hunch. Why did these thoughts assault her brain? And why did the notion of having a man genuinely love or care for her feel the same as standing above a sea of hungry sharks, one small mistake from being devoured?

She gave a small gasp. A gasp that skirted far too close to a sob, as though just the *potential* of falling for someone, truly falling, could break her heart.

She didn't want to think about that.

Didn't *do* falling, much less love.

At least, not the untamed kind that Dean wanted.

Best to move on to the one thing they always agreed on.

She rose to her knees before him and removed the last of her underwear, then reached up and helped him lose his clothes too. His lips found hers, but still things were different, quieter, less hurried, like every detail and second mattered. Like the moment might grow wings and flutter away…

He shuffled back, taking her with him and seating her on the edge of the bed where he knelt on the floor before her like a man at worship. She closed her eyes against the swell of emotion taking her over, his attention all too much—especially as the silence continued—and he kissed her again, wrapping her legs around him, as though he might soon enter her.

"Sarah." His voice poured thick and low, husky with need. "Open your eyes."

She did as he asked, vulnerability hitting her so hard her heart jolted at the sight of him. His expression was taut and serious, as if her every movement required deep and unbroken study, as if he needed to chronicle every passing second. As if he *saw* her. Only her. And perhaps that had been the case from the very first night they'd met.

He entered her now, slowly, one tentative and evermore penetrating thrust at a time, each move sucking the air from her lungs and forcing her to fold forward into his arms.

Despite her best efforts, her eyes slammed shut again, and he held her and entered her again. Reassuring. Commanding. Her breathless state something new and all-consuming. He was only just getting started, so unrelenting and unrestrained with his desire, her body bursting and awakening like never before, no man ever having left her so defenseless and somehow flourishing.

She ground into him. Surrendering more, testing the new sensation of letting him have this. *Have her.* While she took, too.

Her need grew and she grew as a woman. She could feel it, the change. The strength she'd worn as a suit of armor, always believing it protected a fragile woman inside.

But none of that was true. Her façade of strength. Her hatred of fragility…

A surge of bone-melting desire overwhelmed her and her lips parted, allowing room for a low moan to escape. The guttural sound surprised her, but even this unintended release held strength. Maybe love didn't have to weaken her. No. Everything about being with this man felt like a bold victory.

She softened some more, one muscle at a time, losing her urge to resist altogether. He wanted to love her, and just once, she'd throw herself all in.

The pleasure shimmying through her rewarded her risk, and his lips pressed to her forehead, yet another reward, as ecstasy brought her undone—light flooding her eyes and her muscles bracing against the swell expanding and exploding within.

Even as that intensity settled, she didn't have time to gather her bearings. Dean pushed her back and pressed her into the bed, claiming her with his thrusts. Her fingers dug into his bulky triceps, and he repaid her with increased speed and intensity. More need took over, and she screamed out his name.

The pace he kept was just below punishing. He pounded into her again and again, as if making her pay for what she did to him. Well, the feeling was mutual. She needed him, when she'd never needed anyone, and for that she cried out again.

"Sarah." His lips poised at her earlobe, and his movements slowed. *Why?*

Was he trying to prolong this? Or maybe like her, he wanted to avoid facing the aftermath.

Something had changed here. But *what?*

She stared up at him, at the sweat glistening over his brow, tendrils of jet-black hair plastered to his skin, his lips poised so close to her, and his breath lapping at her skin. He was in her and all over her, and, that ache in her heart again…

He'd broken her open, but what about him?

What had changed for him?

Her pulse climbed, more panicked than anything.

"My beautiful, Sarah." His hushed tone acknowledged her inner battle, and there was the vise-like grip of his cobalt stare. "You promised me no holding back."

He buried himself in her again, a slow and rolling sort of movement that once again broke her apart, one stroke at a time, while he moved his hands to cradle the back of her head.

His kiss met the gentle curve of her ear, his thrusts maintaining intensity but more intentional and made to savor.

"Dean, I…" She had no escape, the intimacy of his embrace a heavy brick weighing down on her heart. That intimacy stole her breath and stole her ability to revert to her old ways of hiding.

He pushed within her, cutting off her words. Her legs closed around him, and she cried out again. He groaned, lighting an awareness that as much as she thought herself vulnerable, he was close to breaking, too.

"Come for me again." His words were a vulnerable plea more than a demand, soft and reassuring. He needed her. Needed to see she needed him too. In so many ways right now, they could heal or hurt each other.

"Sarah."

Her eyes slammed shut, and she tried to shut him out, but a tear rolled from her eye's outer corner and down her temple.

She wrapped her arms around him, unable to find words, but reassuring him either way. Her fingers pressed to his rippled back as he picked up pace, where every thrust drew from her new feeling.

As much as she tried to hold out, blinding light hit her eyes again, and her world shattered into a show of fractured sight and sound. She screamed for traction but tumbled further. Every cell, every piece of her, shaking and relinquishing control.

Dean's forehead met hers, his face crumpled with broken refrain. A wild groan tore from him, and his heat filled her—the gravity of his release frightening and thrilling—a rush of sensation and meaning she simply couldn't tame.

In time, her breaths slowed, though her lungs burned from the exertion, from the reality of what had just taken place. Dean sank against her, his head buried in the sheets at her neck, his back rising and falling from his sharp and heavy inhalations.

Each breath spoke of more than mere fatigue. He'd felt it too. The crumbling of barriers. That this relationship had irrevocably changed.

Thirty~Three

"I'VE NEVER DONE THAT BEFORE..."

Sarah smiled and turned her head to Dean, who now lay on his back, his broad chest undulating and warm under her cheek. "What? Had sex?"

His low chuckle reverberated in her ear, filling her with a renewed wave of need. "You know what I mean. What we just did. *That* was different."

She closed her eyes for only a moment and drew a slow breath, reticence holding her, even though she knew this man well enough that she should have guessed he'd cut straight to the point. To all that had changed between them.

That slow breath spilled from her lips now, and she opened her eyes again, rolling onto her tummy and pitching her chin on his pecs. "You know, around here, when someone says something is 'different', that's really just their polite way of saying they didn't like it."

His easy grin grew, and he ran a finger over her hairline. "Oh, I liked that plenty."

He shifted suddenly, pulling her up and catching her lips with his, driving in a deeper and more-passionate-than-expected kiss. Surprise ebbed and her body melted into him, an unintended moan breaking loose.

He pulled away and a full-scale beam took over his face, a beam she had the distinct feeling so few people ever saw. "See. You liked it plenty too."

A quick and shuddering laugh escaped her, forcing her to press her lips together, and a heaviness shifted in her chest. Something about his clear happiness now—it lit an awareness that maybe he wasn't happy all that often.

Then again, I'm no different. Though… lately…

She dropped her attention to the light sprinkling of jet-black hair across his chest. "Dean…"

"Sarah?"

She flicked her gaze back to his sparkling blue eyes, a tightness catching in her throat. "Tell me about your past… at least *something*."

She tried not to wince at her huskiness and that damn returning prickliness in her eyes. For some reason, learning about him had become so important. She wanted to know all about the people and events that had shaped the man she was quickly falling in—*No*.

No. Not yet.

Right, well, learning about him seemed important, anyway.

The cobalt in his eyes deepened, and he squeezed his brows together. She couldn't tell if he merely reacted to her strange behavior or genuinely resented her question about his past. "What do you want to know?"

She hadn't thought that far ahead, mostly just assumed he would shut down her question, so now she gnawed on her lower lip while she decided. "Let's start with what you were doing, say, at twenty-one? What sort of person were you then?"

The muscles over his forehead sagged, and he pushed out a rough breath, his focus snapping away from her and onto the dove-gray ceiling. A prolonged silence lingered, and she thought back to his previous insistence that he needed more time before he could talk about himself.

Granted, not much time had passed since that conversation, but he'd been the one to insist she *let him love her*, and she had, even though what he'd asked was huge. So now it was her turn to ask of him, and if he couldn't be honest with her now, then when?

"Let me see." He took a long pause, his gaze still searching the ceiling. "By twenty-one I was into my third year in the Marines. As for the sort of person I was—"

"Hang on now." She grabbed his chin and made him look at her. "You were in the Marines?"

He raised a brow but said nothing. In fairness, so much about him did scream, "former military", from his imposing physique to his shuttered demeanor, even his handling of the Chadleys the other week…

"Right." She nodded to herself and allowed him to continue.

"I wasn't too different to who I am now, a little more unsettled and brazen, typically impulsive. Though, there wasn't all that much room for stupid mistakes."

He reached across his body and ran the pad of his thumb down her temple, the gesture seemingly more to reassure himself than her, as though speaking about the past made him want to prove he was still firmly in the present.

"So, what made you leave the Marines?" She permitted a long silence while his chest rose with another sharp and hissing breath, the reaction and delay another clear sign this wasn't an easy conversation.

"You mean apart from being young but not naive enough to notice that enlisting didn't always mean 'helping' the people you thought you'd be helping?" His gaze left her again, his expression tense and twisted. A frown, but more than a frown.

His pause seemed more about grappling with emotion than thinking of what to say next. "And still, it wasn't my choice to leave. The bad conduct discharge and two months in military jail saw to that."

She shot up onto one elbow and tried, but failed, to slow her racing thoughts. "Whoa. Wait a minute. A bad conduct discharge and two months in jail? How'd that come about?"

He let out a sigh, his attention on the roof unfocused and distant. "By that point, I was just over twenty-three years old. I was in

Afghanistan, and even though my commander was one prickly son-of-a-motherfucker, I was moving up the ranks nicely."

He paused again, his long fingers collecting a lock of her hair fanned across his chest. He wound that lock over his forefinger while she watched the slow and meditative action. "Some of the guys in my squadron decided to go out one night. We wanted to let loose, do something other than work, eat, sleep. We ended up at a bar in Kabul. Nothing glamorous, just some family-run place where no rules applied, including the fact they had minors serving drinks. I had early patrol the next morning, so stopped drinking after a couple of beers, but stayed for a bit to chat with the guys. After a few hours, most were either drunk or had returned to base. I was on my way out too when I heard my staff sergeant slur, *'You gotta learn sometime, honey.'* I turn and he has this girl pinned against a wall to my right. She couldn't have been much more than sixteen—"

She pressed a hand to his chest. "Oh. No."

A cold sensation washed through her, but he nodded all the same. "His hand was pushed under her skirt. She looked downright terrified, while two people who I figured were her parents stood behind the counter, their stares frozen. Probably because they wanted to step in, but figured there'd be a blood-price to pay."

She reached out and ran her thumb over his rough jawline, her heartbeat settling when his gaze joined hers. "And based on your actions with the Chadleys at the nursery, I'm going to take a wild guess here and say you didn't let that one go?"

"No. I pulled him off the girl. Told him to come back to base with me and sober up," he scoffed, and lifted his hand so he clasped her wrist. "Except the sergeant told me to go fuck myself and took a swing at me. Of course, in his drunken state he missed, but he turned for the girl again. By that point she'd started to scream, and she slapped him repeatedly, trying to fight him off. Even her parents found their voices. The scene got loud and ugly fast. He ripped the top buttons on her shirt, still struggling with her. I didn't have time to think, much less weigh up consequences. So, I knocked him out, and me and a couple of the guys dragged him outta there."

"I don't understand." She took his hand and pressed a kiss to his knuckle. In so many ways at work, though never that extreme, she'd been that girl in the bar. Just like her incident with the two college boys earlier tonight, it was rare to have someone stand up and help. "What about any of that would land you in jail?"

"Just the part where the staff sergeant was a sour pissant who used his higher rank to craft some story bad enough to lump me with a court martial. All the rest followed after that."

"But you had so many witnesses. Why didn't anyone vouch for you?"

"Simple. The family refused to talk. I can understand why. They'd already been through so much, and this war-zone was their home. Soon enough, we'd be moving on, they wouldn't. The other guys? They were either too drunk at the time to be a credible witness or too chicken-shit to speak up. By the time we got to court, the staff sergeant spun a story where the roles were reversed. I was the drunk and would-be rapist. He was the one trying to stop me and I assaulted him in the process. Our age and rank difference made it a credible enough tale. There were no guarantees I'd be found innocent, or that anything would happen to the staff sergeant. I guess the other guys figured they'd be stuck working with him, and he'd make their lives hell too if they spoke up. So, the rest is cut and dried. I did the time, then got booted back home."

She shook her head and clasped at his hand, his warmth seeping into her palm and a heavy sadness gripping at her insides. For all the good he'd done, his life had been ruined. "It's hard enough as it is for most returned service people to start over."

"Yeah, and in my case, with five years scrubbed off my resume and a prison record, it was impossible." He held her gaze, his cheeks slack, and his expression pleading for her not to judge him. Not that she would… "I tried LA, figuring it was a big city. Maybe it would be easier to disappear and find work. It wasn't. I tried. I really did try. But the bills kept growing, and I was on the edge of being yet another homeless vet. So, I gave up. I figured, what the hell? I was already guilty. What difference would it make if I got my money from the wrong crowd?"

Thirty-Four

"WRONG CROWD?" Sarah pushed herself up and sat away from Dean, clutching the bedsheet to her chest, as if this man hadn't seen her naked a bunch of times before. But his story. The one about working for "the wrong crowd". She already had feelings for him, but hell, how had she been so ignorant? "You mean crime?"

"Not exactly." He reached for her hand, which she let him hold, but kept her fingers limp. "I never killed anyone or stole anything."

She spat out a laugh and scuttled back even farther, ripping her hand out of his. "Oh, well, that makes everything so much better."

"Sarah, listen." He sat now too, leaning in her direction, pleading that she stay put, though still giving her space. "The crowd I worked for kept me around to look scary and intimidate. Occasionally I'd use my military skills to track someone down. The job paid well, and no one cared about my past. I didn't hurt anyone in any critical way, do you understand?"

"What about your family?" She jutted her chin at him, not sure where to look, her heart aching because she didn't want to believe him to be a bad person. "Couldn't they have helped you?"

"What family, Sarah?" His voice was husky and hurt, a dull cast overtaking his eyes. "I was twelve when my mother ditched me, and eighteen when I aged out of foster care. Just like many kids in that situation, I enlisted the second I could. Serving my country was my ticket to freedom, to being self-sufficient. Except, I blew my chance at having any real sort of life."

She stared at him for a long while, still clutching the sheet to her chest, his line about blowing his chance bouncing around in her head. There'd always been a sense of familiarity with this man. She'd asked him for the truth. He'd given it to her, hadn't he?

She knew about growing up too soon. About paying the price for other people's actions. About needing to survive. And for that he'd been judged and tossed aside time and time again. Yet, he'd never done a thing to hurt her or anyone she knew. At what point did a person get to have a second chance? She could hear him out or at least not slam yet another door in his face.

She held the stand-off a moment longer, the tight tug of her heart telling her to take him in her arms and promise those harsher days were long behind him, but she still had reservations, so she offered acknowledgment instead. "You had no choice."

He gave a small shrug, holding impossibly still, as though he feared any sudden movement might send her away completely. Maybe he wasn't all that wrong. "Choice or not. My past is what it is, and I'm trying to leave it behind."

The musk of his skin still clung to her, drawing her in, even though his story filled her with doubt over what he'd spent his last years doing.

She flicked her gaze back to his, those cobalt eyes holding her, arresting her breath, as if he sensed her emotional step backward and pleaded with her to see the little boy in him. The one who'd already been abandoned and didn't want her to do the same. What that must have been like for him.

Sure, her parents had skipped out in their own ways too. She could relate, except he'd been so much younger and without the support she had here in Harlow. And what about the years prior to his abandonment? How had it all come about? The rest of his adulthood didn't seem any warmer either.

She found her words again, seeking to put at least some of the pieces together. "Are you still with the 'wrong crowd'?"

"No." His fingers curled into the bedsheet, as though he wished to reach for her but stopped himself. "That's why I stayed in Harlow. I needed to start over, Sarah, and you—"

She shook her head, demanding he stop, the heat behind her eyes building again. Her heart pummeled in her chest, taking with it her desire to fight.

The hint that she might have been the reason for his "restart". He'd mentioned something to that effect before, but she hadn't thought much of it, figured he was just talking about the complexities of moving states. Now that information, along with all the rest, was more than she could process.

How many times had she wanted to hit STOP on her life and change course?

More than she could count.

But unlike her, Dean here had actually done it.

"Just tell me it's all over." She focused on him, focused on what it cost him to admit to all that he had been, whilst almost certain she was the first person he'd ever talked this over with. "Promise me."

His gaze searched her face, and for the longest while he said nothing, though the creases between his brow suggested her mistrust hurt him. Still, he reached for her now, his hand cupping her cheek, his thumb stroking her chin and then skimming her lower lip. "I will never go back to that. I will never let any of it hurt you. Do you understand?"

The steadfast hold of his stare, his gentle touch, his resolute tone revealed no doubt, no dishonesty.

She drew a sharp inhalation since she'd barely breathed through this whole interaction, her exhale dulling the strain in her shoulders and across her chest. She'd dropped her entire life to sulk in Harlow, to piece together the irreparable tatters of a dream that looked like her family, but had never been real to begin with.

Not a day passed where she didn't question that decision, and lately, she downright regretted it. So, she nodded and took more breaths, wanting that clean break too.

"I can't do it again, Dean." She reached up to her face and pressed her hand over his, closing her eyes to savor this new calm. "I can't give up my dreams, everything I know and love, for someone else's sake."

"I would never ask you—"

"*Harlow* is everything I know and love, do you understand?"

He nodded and shuffled back, pulling her along with him until they both sat with their backs against his dark wood headboard. "What dreams, Sarah? Tell me what dreams you gave up."

She peered over at him, then down at their hands clasped together in his lap, and one of hers still clutching the sheet to her chest. For someone who didn't do cuddly moments, this was mighty cuddly.

"My mom and dad didn't exactly get on well. They were more high school sweethearts with a tragic ending." She gripped harder at his hand, her knuckles turning white, even though she didn't so much mind this talk right now. "They thought sticking together was for Chip and my benefit, except that just made our home a miserable place to be. So, I turned to escaping outside and hitting a ball with a racket whenever I got the chance."

"You mean tennis?" His eyes narrowed, but his lips turned upward as though she'd given him a pleasant surprise. "You played tennis?"

She nodded, a small smile tugging at her lips because, despite everything, the thought of hitting and chasing a ball still brought her inordinate amounts of joy. "Yeah, I even managed to nag my mom into taking me an hour out of town for weekly lessons. I just loved playing. I got all the way to a training scholarship in Florida at sixteen. They were even talking about swapping me from the junior circuit to the pro-tour."

"And let me guess." The levity in his expression sagged. "That's when your dad up and left, and your mom didn't take it so well?"

"Yep." She peered down, unable to look at him for the next bit. "I got pulled in from practice one day due to a call from Sheriff Marlin. He told me that Mom had been drinking, and my brother had come home to find half the house's stuff broken and on the front lawn. When he found Mom, she was on the bathroom floor harming herself with an old razor blade."

"Whoa, Sarah." Dean shifted again, turning as if he might grab her up and comfort her, but she shook her head, wanting to continue.

"Chip was just thirteen years old, Dean." She swallowed, trying to work past the tension pressing at her throat, but the strain didn't ease. "Call it small-town pride, or maybe Mom's well-to-do upbringing, but she just never coped all that well with life's roadblocks."

"And so little Sarah compensated?"

"I'm that predictable, aren't I?" She pressed her lips together and drew a breath. He *was* right. "Compensate, I did. I quit tennis, came back home, demanded my dad take my brother while I finished school and kept the bar running with Aggie and the sheriff's help. Mom came back for a little bit. She tried to open a window where I might return to playing, but she hit the bottle within a week and didn't hold it together more than two months. It became clear I was never going anywhere. It was the sheriff who came by and took her away. He made the decision I wouldn't. Mom was too much of a danger to herself and me to stay in the house, and once she was gone again, she never came back. She said our house, Chip and I, the memories, was all too much for her."

"Sarah…" Dean's voice dipped low, and the subtle drag held a hint of sympathetic warning. "You took on too much. The sheriff and Aggie, basically anyone in this town, could have maintained the bar while you took some time to grow up and do your thing."

"Maybe." She frowned down at her lap. "I was in denial—or maybe I should call it naive hope—the rationale of a desperate seventeen-year-old not thinking things through. I figured if I just stayed and waited, there might be some big revelation on my parents' part, then we would all be together again. And here I am, years later, still waiting."

A jagged laugh broke from her, and she shook her head.

"You were in shock." His easy tone pulled at her, his plain acceptance shining a light on the rejection of it all. She'd been left behind, isolated. Something Dean had experienced himself. And yet, despite all her stonewalling and bluster, he was far more skilled at moving on than she was.

She shrugged, all while flicking away her deeper thoughts. "By the time everything settled and the desire to play returned, I was nearing nineteen and hadn't picked up a racket in years. My carefree innocence was gone, and I simply didn't have it in me to go back to what I'd lost. To watch all the kids I'd played against thrive while I scratched through the ashes, trying to find some piece of what I'd had. My parents let me keep the house, and I had the bar. It was *something* over having nothing."

Dean stared at her for a long while, his penetrating silence twisting an invisible cord within her, making it hard to simply hold still and accept his attention. "Your parents should never have expected you to look after them that way. You were young, and everything you'd known was destroyed. I'm sure they were probably in over their heads, but I would never let any child of mine take the brunt like you did. Just like I promised I wouldn't let anything hurt you, I would protect them too, Sarah."

Her breath caught in her lungs, and she stared into his eyes, stunned into silence. So much about his words hurt. The reason she never spoke to her dad. Because while her mom fell apart, his new life with his new woman had continued uninterrupted.

And speaking of dads, she could imagine Dean as one. Despite his confession about his checkered past, the inherent good in him meant she could see him doing everything in his power to protect any child. Not just his own.

Then there were the unspoken sentiments. That he would protect her *and* his child, as though the two were connected.

The space beneath her ribcage filled with an overly full sensation, her next breaths hard to take because she hurt for herself and she hurt for him.

She hurt because she *hurt*, after years of shutting every meaningful emotion away.

"You're right." She lifted her chin, once again sweeping away the deeper stuff and relying on bravado. "And maybe it's time I stopped coasting and stopped setting my standards on everything just staying the same. Maybe I should start making some decisions. Ones that will shake things up a little."

He chuckled and so did she, then he pulled her in and captured her lips in one full and meaningful kiss. "You know, the sexiest thing you can ever say to a man is that he's right?"

His smile remained, and he rolled her under him, making it clear what he wanted next. She laughed and accepted his move. The way it made her feel. *Wanted. Unreservedly wanted.*

As if to confirm that *want*, his soulful gaze swept over her face in a way that made time stumble and slow. "As long as all your new decisions include keeping me."

Thirty~Five

"HERE YOU GO, honey. Dry your tears."

Sarah pulled a napkin out from under the bar and passed it to a sobbing Emilia. Blaine's new fiancée pitched forth a wonky smile, an onslaught of patrons milling around at her surprise engagement party.

"Thanks." She grabbed the tissue and dabbed at her eyes. "What a day. If anyone had told me three months ago that I wouldn't be married to Anthony anymore, that I'd be living here in Harlow—a place I'd never even heard of back then—and that I'd find my long-lost first love hiding here." She shook her head and lifted her hand, flashing her engagement ring, a gold band with a pink stone butterfly. "And now *this*. This is just unbelievable."

Sarah smiled back. "It's no more than you deserve, Emilia. I'm happy for you."

For the first time since Emilia set foot in town, Sarah did wholeheartedly mean it. She *was* happy for the woman. If she hadn't reunited with Blaine, then Sarah would never have taken Dean home that soiree night. And that night had changed her. It had given her heartbreak over Blaine a whole new perspective.

Emilia and Blaine were always meant to be. That much was clear now. Sarah could pause her skepticism long enough to acknowledge the universe had different plans for her. Plans for change. Plans with Dean. She could see where her life was headed. Could finally let go of her old fear and could finally dream.

Emilia's warm brown stare pulled Sarah back to the room, with all the clatter and snippets of jovial conversations bouncing around. "You're not upset about this engagement? I was a little horrified when Blaine said he had you organizing this event."

She let out a laugh, her shoulders shaking over the stagnated sound. "I was a little horrified when I offered too, but no, I'm moving on these days and I wish you both well. Just save me a decent spot at the wedding."

Emilia dipped her chin and peered up, the corners of her lips curling skyward. "Moving on? As in, you're seeing someone?"

Sarah paused, not sure she was ready to tell anyone yet, though she'd pondered the idea of going public about Dean since their intimate conversation five days ago. He'd discussed significant details about his past, and she'd shared her fears over having new dreams to pin her already shattered hopes on.

But she peered around, making sure no one stood close enough to hear before leaning across the bar and closer to Emilia. "I haven't told anyone, and I'm only telling you because I don't want you to feel bad about Blaine, okay?"

"Oh Sarah." Emilia pressed both hands to her mouth, her eyes glittering above her concealed grin. "That's the second-best news I've heard today. And yes, I do feel less guilty now. I'm so happy for you too."

Sarah leaned back, a weight slipping off her shoulders and a new lightness taking over. Telling someone felt good, especially when that telling closed the door on what had been a messy and heartbreaking situation.

Emilia turned for a moment to accept a quick congratulations from someone in the party, before refocusing on Sarah. "You have to tell me who it is!"

"Who is what?" Aggie grinned from Emilia's left, the elderly woman's eyes sparkling, never one to shy away from a new adventure.

Sarah grabbed a tall glass and prepared the woman's usual gin and tonic, a distraction more than anything. "Never you mind, Aggie. When there's something to tell, you'll be the first to know."

"Oh, don't you mind, dear." The skin over Aggie's cheekbones wrinkled some more, her grin expanding farther. "Your face tells me all I need to know."

Sarah scoffed and pushed the drink toward Aggie's freckled hand, then pressed both elbows into the bar and eyeballed the older woman. "Oh, yeah? And what exactly does my face say to you?"

The woman took a long sip through her straw and eyeballed Sarah right back, before throwing a wink and replying, "Someone's got your fancy, and by the looks of things, you've fallen hard, too."

Sarah's face turned instantly cold, and her lips slipped open just a bit. "We've only just—"

"*Uff...*" Aggie swatted a hand and turned to Emilia. "I don't know why you kids insist on arguing with me. Sarah here is in love. I'd stake my nursery and the lavender farm right along with it that I'm right."

Love?

Sarah stood silent, not really looking at anyone around her, just staring out into blank space while she clapped a hand over her heart and pondered Aggie's assertion.

Was she in love? She couldn't say for sure.

Or maybe she didn't *want* to say for sure.

But why?

I'll have no choice but to move out of the stasis I've lived in all these years...

I'll have to trust someone...

Things will change and I won't be in control anymore.

And...

A light chuckle tore Sarah from her panic, a chuckle belonging to Emilia, the gleam in her eye rivaling Aggie McKey's. Damn these two women. Damn them and bless them all at once.

Emilia tilted her head, gesturing to Blaine, who stood some yards away over her shoulder. "I should go. Sarah, don't argue with Aggie. I speak from experience when I say she's rarely wrong."

Emilia patted the bar and then swanned away, leaving Sarah with

Aggie and her still-beaming face. "Rarely? The cheek of that girl. I'm *never* wrong."

Sarah laughed but only so long as it took Gordon to call out to her through the kitchen pass. "Sarah, someone back here wants to see you."

She gave Aggie a quick nod goodbye and headed for the kitchen where Gordon, busy frying steaks in a giant pan, pointed to the back door. She pushed through the door, only to find Dean waiting for her.

She drew closer and gave him a quick kiss. "Why are you here? You could have come through the front like a normal person."

His lips inched up, his eyes glinting in that wicked way that made her insides flutter every time. "You wouldn't like me so much if I were a normal person."

He pulled her into him, stunning her with a deep and passionate kiss, as though her quick one wasn't enough. Maybe it wasn't because her whole body melted into him, only finding purchase when he set her free. "You told me Blaine and Emilia had their party at the bar tonight. I wasn't sure I'd be welcome."

She thought back to the day of their fight in the alleyway, her face flushing as a wave of guilt took over. Things had changed since then. "Sorry 'bout that. I'm sure no one will mind if you join. Besides, while the engagement party *is* taking up half the bar, the other half is still open to anyone else who wants a drink."

He gave a soft smile and ran his knuckle over her cheek. She closed her eyes, savoring the tingling sensation overrunning her body. "I'll come by and join you out front in a minute, but since we're here and we're alone…"

He kissed her again, stirring desire until it burst into fully fledged need. She groaned and dragged her arms around his neck, his mouth hard against hers, his hand entangling her hair and pulling her deeper into the embrace, all while he walked her backward into the bar's brick wall.

She laughed, feeling like an impulsive teenager, all the more thrilling because she'd never had a chance to be an impulsive teenager. This whole thing was an exciting risk since she was still at work and anyone could walk by at any time.

Bad enough Blaine and Aggie had already figured things out. So, as much as Sarah wanted this to continue, she pried her lips from his and vowed to finish this when she didn't have a job to do. "Whoa, there tiger. Seems I might need to get you a cold beer to cool down."

"One beer won't help." He offered another irresistible smile, his intent stare dancing about her face. "But you got yourself a deal, princess."

He dropped a lighter kiss on her cheek, his gaze lingering even as he took a few slow backward steps, then disappeared around the corner.

She re-entered the kitchen and slipped behind the bar again, regretting making him walk around Maynard's to continue the charade of their active rivalry, or at least, barely knowing each other. Then again, Blaine and Emilia's engagement party wasn't the time to let loose with her new relationship. Also, she wanted to talk things over with Dean before going public.

The bar's front door swung open, and she smiled as he strolled in, his stare searching her out and his own instant grin taking over. She schooled her usual stony-faced expression, the one she used just for him, only for a bloodcurdling scream to rip through Maynard's.

The entire venue fell silent. Everyone turned to Emilia in the restaurant's far right corner—her hands clapped over her mouth, her eyes impossibly wide. She stumbled back, fell into Frank's arms, her screams changing to loud sobs.

Blaine stood just yards away, his face pale and frozen. Both he and Emilia stared at Dean.

Sarah's attention darted between the three people. No matter where her thoughts went, nothing about this scene made any sense.

"What's all this?" The sheriff rose from his table, not in uniform since he'd taken the night off, and had been having a quiet conversation with his three lifelong buddies—enjoying the engagement party like everyone else. From the stiff look on his face, he'd slipped into sheriff mode. *But why?*

"It's him." Fat tears rolled down Emilia's cheeks and her fingers, still pressed to her mouth, trembled. "Oh my God, it's him."

Dean's gaze bounced between Blaine and Emilia, his jaw sagging in a look of recognition, his hollow expression akin to a lion trapped in a cage. She didn't understand. So many here seemed to know what was happening, but she didn't.

He turned to her, and his name fell from her lips in the form of a question. "Dean?"

"Dean?" Blaine's voice held a firm edge, and he turned to her, his cheeks easing as though some vague realization took over. "You know him?" He spun around to Dean, expression suddenly hard. "You son-of-a—"

He launched forward and slammed a shoulder into Dean's chest. Dean's back slammed into the bolted door, the side latched shut. A thunderous boom split the air. Bolts ripped from the door frame, wood splinters exploding everywhere.

Something indiscernible snapped within her, and before she could think, her legs propelled her forward and toward the grappling men.

"Let him go." The words flew from her mouth. "You're hurting him. Let go."

Blaine's fist slammed into Dean's face. She screamed, a sound so utterly unlike her, so wild and heartsick—all while blood welled and spilled from the new split above his left brow.

Sheriff Marlin pushed between the men while Blaine shoved back. Dean merely stared, not defending himself, a man all too accepting over what unfolded.

Why? Why wasn't he fighting?

She threw herself at him and latched onto his arm. He moved to shove her behind him, clearly not eager to have her defense. Amongst the fray, someone's elbow connected with her cheek, the forceful impact sending her to the ground.

She slapped a palm over the searing pain of her face—her eyes stinging, warm liquid coating her fingers. Not tears. Blood.

Stunned, she mused at the glossy red on her hand.

"Sarah." Blaine's voice tore her focus to his pinched stare, his drawn expression hinting something akin to regret. Maybe his elbow had struck her?

Dean pushed forward, as though he'd finally found his fight and meant to go to her, but Blaine swung around and shoved him into the already splintered door. "Don't you fucking talk to her. Don't you fucking dare."

Blaine's voice was a low growl, even the obscenities so unlike him. She'd known this man for years. Never would she have guessed him capable of so much anger and resentment.

"Blaine." A sharp pain twisted and dug at her heart. She just wanted to understand. She wanted this to stop. "Let him go."

He grabbed the front of Dean's dark blue shirt and shoved at him again. "Let him go?" The door groaned, suggesting the wood frame might shatter completely. "This man deserves to rot in prison."

Why would he say something like that? To a man he'd never met?

Blaine didn't understand. Dean had come to mean the world to her and right now her world was imploding.

"Please." She lifted her voice, wanting nothing more than for all the violence and hatred to stop. "Please, I love—"

"No." Dean's voice boomed over hers, harsh and commanding, enough to fracture her delirium. "Don't!"

Don't?

Hot blood trickled down her neck, and pain still cracked her focus. She hadn't admitted to those feelings yet—not to herself, not to Dean, not to anyone—but she'd been ready to declare her love for him to a room filled with everyone she knew. All to defend him.

Don't?

Dean's response was... *don't?*

She glared up at him and shook her head. How could he be so cold?

"Now, you boys break this up." Once more, the sheriff squeezed between Blaine and Dean. "Or by God, I won't hesitate to stick the both of you in my holding cell tonight."

Blaine released his hold on the front of Dean's shirt, only to give him one small and final push.

Blaine turned to her, shoulders dropping as though he'd cooled down some, his gaze soft and suspended somewhere between surprise and pity. Meanwhile, Emilia's muffled sob overpowered any silence, her reaction to Dean having been nothing short of terrified. *Why?*

Sarah refocused on Dean. His eyes creased at the corners, his taut stare on her expressing intense sorrow. Or maybe an *apology.* She'd always considered herself a strong judge of character. Had she read this man completely wrong?

"What did you do?" Her question poured out on an unrecognizable rasp, so hollow and grave.

His gaze fell to the ground, and he said nothing.

Blaine stabbed his thumb over his shoulder in Dean's direction, the sheriff holding him back from instigating another fight. "This piece of shit helped Anthony take Emilia from me ten years ago. Dean here attacked me. He split us up. That's how I wound up back here in Harlow, instead of staying in LA. Sarah"—he paused, shaking his head in a slow and pleading sort of gesture—"please don't tell me *this* is the guy you've been seeing?"

Her mouth fell open, an instinctive move to answer the question, though no sound came out. She turned to Dean, seeking denial, but his attention on her stayed hollow and unreadable.

The sheriff turned to Dean. "Is all that true?"

He pulled his focus from her and nodded, his gaze falling to the ground. She gaped at him, the denial coming from her, not him. A surge of bitter bile pushed past her throat and coated her tongue while her whole world froze.

Or maybe her heart froze.

If only that were possible, death would yank her right out of this moment. Out of this excruciating intersection of lives. Her. Blaine. Emilia. Dean... She didn't want any of it to be true. That love could fool her twice. This second time was even worse. This man she loved, so rotten to the core.

The sheriff stepped closer to Dean. "I'll spare you the handcuffs if you come quietly now."

Dean nodded again, and the sheriff cupped his palm over Dean's shoulder, turning him through the door.

Save for the door's dull *thwack,* the room maintained its long and shocked silence, the hiss of low whispers developing a slow, but distinct build. Those whispers. All about her. Her failure. Her life once again on display.

She stared at the ground, trying to block it all out, only for a pair of red suede shoes to step into view. She peered up. Blinked against the lights. At Ally frowning down. She didn't so much as reach out a hand to help Sarah stand.

"Good for you." Despite the seeming praise, Ally's voice spun a flat delivery, her expression just as cold. "Maybe it's not so bad that I'm a wallflower, after all."

Thirty-Six

THE HOLDING cell at the sheriff's office was the smallest one Dean had ever been in. A narrow cot sat sandwiched, end to end, between two brick walls, the cell's metal bars less than a few yards ahead. There were no clocks, but if he had to guess, he'd been in this steel cage for close to two hours.

He lay his half-beaten body on the sheetless cot, nothing but the mattress with its cold blue plastic cover pressed against his skin. The tiny, bare room shouldn't have been a surprise. In a town like Harlow, filled with good people who probably did little wrong, chances were, this cell didn't get much use.

This town and those people, they served up a stark contrast to him and his current predicament. The cell's unwelcoming metal toilet and soulless gray walls were an apt reflection of where his life sat. But hadn't that always been the way?

Except for those blissful few weeks.

Sarah.

The look on her face when she realized the truth.

What I've done… Who I am… I deserve this misery and more.

He dabbed at the weeping gash above his brow with a ball of scrunched-up tissues. Blaine Callahan, for all his injuries, packed a mean right hook. No doubt being a carpenter gave the man's hands an unusual amount of strength.

Where was the sheriff? This room was all too quiet and unfamiliar, though perhaps this was his way of biding time for Dean's thoughts, and thus nerves, to run wild. Deprive him of human contact. Get more information.

Well, at least this time he *was* guilty, but never had he guessed how gut-wrenching real guilt was.

His body ached, but that pain paled in comparison to the crushing agony clutching at his heart. Then there was the sickening churn of his stomach and the hollow growing within his ribcage. What had he done? To Emilia. To Blaine. To Sarah. He'd always told himself that his actions boiled down to mere survival. The world was a cruel place that had never been kind to him, so why should he care?

But he'd come to care all the same. And he was just one man, whose survival had hurt many. Unintended or not, he'd taken his sore lot in life and inflicted his *screw the world* attitude on innocent people.

And the irony, that of all the fucked-up things that had happened to him, *he* was the cause of his greatest downfall. The loss of his second chance. Once more in a cell, his freedom gone.

He'd entered Maynard's believing Blaine and Emilia wouldn't connect him with Anthony's appearance in town. The mutual recognition based on an incident from ten years ago—the details of which he'd mostly forgotten—came as a shocking sore statement on the damage he'd caused.

This end was inevitable. Sooner or later, he would have landed in this cell. In no time at all, he'd be logged into the prison system and Luciano would know. When that happened, some connection or another would find Dean and take him out of this hellhole world altogether.

So be it. He should never have stayed here in town, allowed his feelings for Sarah to grow or take over. Not because those feelings brought about his downfall. No. His broken heart and his incarceration he could handle, but the truth had broken her. Truly broken her. After he'd spent weeks pretending he was someone worth trusting…

Why? Why did I do that?

Because I took one look at her and lost my fucking mind. That's why.

I lost my mind and fell in love.

And everything he'd ever loved had ceased to be. He should never have expected anything different.

Because of love and hope, I didn't have the strength to walk away. I should have walked away.

A derisive scoff burst from his lips. His weakness hid behind a facade of strength. A man everyone looked at as some big and all-encompassing monolith. An intimidating model of masculine control.

But he was just as breakable as any other.

He'd had dreams and deficits. A little boy palmed off so his mom could keep the peace and his dad could keep drinking, a little boy who grew into a railroaded young man, one imprisoned for his naivety. And now to the man he'd become…

He'd needed love. Always needed love. Just like everyone else. And time and time again, he got the same result. Rejection. And each rejection left him more and more alone.

I should just take the hint…

A sharp, metallic screech came from his cell door.

The sheriff pushed the metal bars open. "Follow me."

The sheriff had changed into his uniform, his face now pale and drawn. He stood aside, making room for Dean to pass, once again not using the handcuffs, as if he grasped Dean's lack of will to fight.

He dipped his chin, and followed the sheriff toward his office, an office Dean knew well since he'd carried out repairs there not that long ago.

"Take a seat." The sheriff pointed to a wooden chair before his small metal desk, and Dean sat.

"That was a pretty impressive showdown at Maynard's tonight." The sheriff groaned and took a seat at his desk, a couple of tall metal filing cabinets behind him, all with locks to secure whatever hid inside. "I've talked to Blaine and searched some records pertaining to his version of events. Now I want to hear yours."

The sheriff picked up a cheap plastic pen, ready to record whatever Dean had to say.

Dean didn't meet the sheriff's gaze, instead choosing to stare at the pen. "I'm sure whatever Blaine told you would be close to the truth."

The sheriff let out a sigh. When Dean peered up, the man's brow formed a hard line. "He says you and Anthony ran him out of LA ten years ago in an unprovoked attack. While he confirmed you didn't hit him, he says you pushed him into a car window and prevented his escape. Is that correct?"

Dean bowed his head and nodded, the churn in his belly intensifying. "Yes."

A tide of memories swept through his mind. *That night.* Emilia and Blaine were not much younger than himself. A supposedly non-violent intervention instigated by Anthony, which had ended in blood. The screams still rang vivid in his ear.

"And Anthony Stucco." The sheriff's voice drew Dean's attention. "He wasn't married to Emilia at the time, but he attacked Blaine with a knife and proceeded to kidnap her?"

Dean squeezed his eyes shut and pulled a quiet breath, centering himself, before nodding. He'd known the situation was unfair but was new to the job. New to working with Luciano. Needed the work and knew he had little room to protest. Frankly, he'd also become numb to helping in a crisis.

On the surface, in light of his years in the service, the whole event seemed insignificant. Two little boys, inexperienced with true misery, scuffling over a girl. Even if he *had* intervened, by that point, he had more to lose than his job and freedom. Chances were, he'd end up with a bullet in the head and a shallow grave in some deserted part of town. Luciano would have made sure of it.

The sheriff leaned back, his chair creaking while he blew out a hard breath, his narrowed glare sweeping over Dean. "How did you know Mr. Stucco?"

"I didn't. I was hired to help him."

The sheriff's expression dropped. "Hired?"

"Yes, hired. I did what I was told and within my limits."

The sheriff leaned in, his elbow propped into the desk, his stare hyper-focused. "What limits were they?"

"I never murdered anyone if that's what you're looking for." Dean returned the sheriff's stiff stare.

The sheriff responded by pressing his back into his seat again. "So that's what you meant when you said your time after the military involved doing 'odd jobs'. You weren't fixing leaking roofs and broken mail boxes. You were muscle for hire. Is that right?"

Dean shrugged. "I had a special knack for finding people. It's just a bonus that I look like I might hurt them while I'm at it. But I never went out of my way to hurt anyone, certainly not on command."

"And that's what brought you to Emilia and Blaine's doorstep ten years ago, and again more recently? Money for *finding* people?" The sheriff's gaze searched Dean's face as though he saw him in a whole new light. Not a surprise, really, but Dean had never learned to dull the sting of *that* look.

He peered around the desk, trying to escape the sense of judgment, a sense he deserved, but coming from the sheriff, it hurt even more. Dean could handle disgust and indignation, but the sheriff—in all his fatherly and good-natured glory—gave none of that.

He peered up, wanting to end the aching silence. "Aren't you going to ask who I was working for?"

The sheriff didn't answer right away, though his brow dipped and formed a stiff line, suggesting thought. "I guess a more important question would be whether you're on the job right now?"

An impulsive laugh escaped Dean. Maybe because working for the syndicate felt like a million years ago, like he was a different man after just mere weeks away from it all. But he shook his head anyway, answering the sheriff's question. "Would it make you feel safer to hear I quit the job the night Anthony went rogue on me?"

"Rogue?" The sheriff lifted a brow, though the rest of his face didn't move.

"I had no clue Mr. Stucco had a gun that night, much less that he would use it. As you recall, I wasn't even there."

The sheriff continued his stillness, though he offered a slight and repeated nod. "I'm less convinced with what you're saying, Mr. Holloway, so much as your actions, thus far. Your intervention with the Chadleys, maybe I could figure was just you playing the part to fit in.

But your reaction tonight, not retaliating against Blaine, and your interaction with Sarah"—he shook his head through a long pause, his stare unwavering—"that was something else, now, wasn't it?"

"Why?" Dean lifted his chin, trying to escape the swelling pain from within at hearing Sarah's name. "Because I didn't beat the shit outta Blaine Callaghan?"

The sheriff shot out a short laugh. "Less that, more the look on your face when you had to tell Sarah the truth. That look was more than guilt over getting caught. It was something less easy to fake. Frankly, I'm starting to think it wasn't Anthony's off-script behavior that had you looking for a different life. It would have been a million times smarter to disappear somewhere far away from Harlow, now wouldn't it, Mr. Holloway?"

Dean held the sheriff's gaze, his insides stiff and buckling that he was so easy to read. So openly pathetic. So unrecognizable to the man he'd been. Not a bad thing, maybe. But to what benefit? He would be in prison within hours.

"That's mighty trusting of you, Sheriff." His tone came out flat and lacking in life, so not all that removed from him after all.

The sheriff shook his head, as if somehow disappointed, all while he tapped the end of his pen against the mostly blank page before him. "Cut the bullshit, Holloway, and while you're at it, maybe tell me who you were working—"

"His name is Luciano Conti."

The sheriff's face turned still and pale, as though he hadn't expected to get the answer so easily, or maybe because he recognized the name. Still, just to be sure, Dean added, "He's the ringleader for a West Coast crime syndicate. Though believe me, any kind of half-hearted digging will show that syndicate is much bigger than just Luciano."

"Why are you telling me this?" The sheriff's expression hardened again. "I would have thought you'd bargain for some kind of legal leniency before you offered that information."

"You think one name is *all* the information I have?" Dean drew his jaw tight, a dull pain radiating through his teeth.

Even if he was unlikely to survive his next prison stint, he wasn't about to take any extra hits protecting an asshole like Luciano, not when he could take the man down with him. The man had knowingly put him in an unstable situation with Anthony. *Twice.* All for greed. All to add more money to his already ludicrous pile. And then the audacity to hurt anyone who no longer wanted a piece of that action… Luciano was spineless. A bully.

Dean relaxed his jaw, resigned to explaining further. "I've seen eight men try to leave the syndicate and die for their trouble. Luciano can rot in hell as far as I care, but a prison cell will have to do. If it makes more sense to you, then call this my last chance to make the world better for having had me in it."

The sheriff held a pensive stare before peering down and scribbling in his book. "Seems Mr. Stucco did most of the dirty work in both your interactions. I'd also say there's a statute of limitations that's probably lapsed from your work with him from ten years ago…"

Dean sat quiet for a while again, this conversation far too polite for his comfort. "Is this you trying to help me?"

If so, why?

The sheriff put his pen down and peered up again. "Let's just say I didn't trust your first story weeks ago, so I did a little research."

Dean scoffed. "You must have found something glowing in that research that I don't know about."

"Not glowing, Mr. Holloway. Inconsistent." The sheriff narrowed his eyes, his attention sweeping over Dean again, as though he questioned whatever he had to say next. "Don't fool yourself into thinking you're not in trouble here, son. You're in a whole heap of it, and a prison van will be here within the hour to take you far from Harlow."

He leaned in and pointed Dean's way, the man's focus zeroing in. "But you're also one lucky son-of-a-gun, because in all of this, there's one person who's defied all common sense and done something to help you."

Thirty-Seven

"Seems strange to me, Mr. Holloway, that you would be a Marine on the rise one minute, only to go uncharacteristically postal on your staff sergeant the next."

The sheriff settled back in his seat, his expression relaxing like he'd been waiting a long while to let loose with that observation.

"Isn't going postal meant to be standard army guy behavior?" Dean narrowed his stare, not sure what the sheriff's point was, which further bolstered his decision to match that point with his own brand of sarcasm. "You know, gun-slinging meathead who just saw too much misery and hit his limit?"

"I looked up your court documents." The sheriff shrugged, hinting he didn't buy Dean's explanation. Even the sheriff's reply didn't clarify his earlier comment about some mystery person "defying all logic" to help him.

Given the sheriff's change of subject, maybe that person was Ramos —Dean's only friend and from his army days at that—though Ramos connecting with the sheriff seemed hugely unlikely. Things had escalated at Maynard's only hours earlier, and not even Ramos was that quick to find shit out.

"Good for you, Sheriff, but my memory of my legal woes isn't so damaged that I need the recap."

"You were in Afghanistan." The sheriff's brow crinkled, the corners of his mouth tensing like he edged on annoyance. "You claimed you attacked your sergeant in an attempt to stop a sexual assault. He, on the other hand, claimed the same about you. No witnesses backed either story, but you took the hit all the same. Now, I've been around long enough to know that what happens in a court doesn't aways reflect the truth—"

Dean laughed, a quick and barking sound. "Nice theory. I should have hired you as my lawyer."

Despite the joke, the sheriff's hard expression remained. "Tell me what happened to get you kicked from the Marines."

"I don't have to." A slow realization took shape in his brain, that realization stealing his breath and rocking his belly with instant sickness. "Sarah told you, didn't she?"

There's been one person who's defied all common sense and done something to help you.

That's who the sheriff had been talking about.

Why? Why would she still help when she needed to focus on getting as far from him as possible?

Don't start getting hopeful, asshole. You're still going to prison.

The sheriff's silence, coupled with the slow drop of his shoulders, confirmed Dean's theory, even if the man didn't say anything more than, "I imagine time in prison and a Bad Conduct Discharge, didn't seem fair at the time."

"It wasn't, but shit happens." Dean fought an urge to look away, but he wanted to see where all this went.

"Sometimes, yes." The sheriff nodded as though, as someone somewhat older than Dean, life and his profession might have given him first-hand knowledge on the subject of injustice. "No one spoke for you, though it seems as though there should have been plenty who could. I wouldn't wholly blame a man for abandoning his care for the law after that."

The sheriff's brown eyes mellowed, conveying an unshakeable sort of understanding. Still, any sign of compassion rubbed against Dean's years of warranted mistrust, so he laughed and offered, "Is this your way of saying you're letting me go?"

The sheriff threw back his head and let out a genuine but unexpected laugh. "You know I can't do that. Heck, I'd be grilling you for all sorts of information if it weren't for the fact that you've already given me Luciano Conti's name. Besides, I'm sure you'll get more grilling from far more qualified detectives once I pass you onto the state prison system."

The sheriff paused, his focus remaining forward as he rolled up one of his shirt sleeves, revealing a faded tattoo of an American flag on his inner forearm. Dean had to squint. There was a picture of military dog tags underneath, but he couldn't make out the numbers. Meanwhile, he grappled against the idea that someone as straightlaced as the sheriff even had a tattoo.

The sheriff used the end of his pen to tap at the ink on his skin. "First Gulf War. I have some idea what it's like, putting your life and sanity on the line. And for all your trouble, Mr. Holloway, you got sent home and your name smeared."

Dean stared across the desk, still not too sure of what to make of all this or why the sheriff even believed his story. "You're telling me this because…?"

"Because, besides myself, if there's anyone in this town who's a decent judge of character, it's Sarah Overton, even if she doesn't think so lately. I've never seen her trust someone who was wholly untrustworthy. Reckless, maybe, but not untrustworthy. I also never let go of my suspicions over your link to Anthony Stucco, so I can't say I do outright believe you, but I believe Sarah. She says you're not a bad person, even though you've had a whole lot of bad come your way. All the evidence since your arrival in town points to you trying to, as you say, change. To make the most of the nothing that life gave you."

"Why would she vouch for me?"

The sheriff put down his pen, his face holding a blank expression as his head did a small, wobbly sort of shake. "Are you really that empty in the skull?"

Dean frowned. "What?"

The sheriff pressed his eyes shut and swore under his breath before addressing Dean again. "Never mind. Anyway, Miss Overton wants a few words with you. I'll need you in your cell before I can allow that."

Dean nodded and the sheriff stood, heading for the door. "You never know, Mr. Holloway, you might be in some kind of luck. If what you say about Luciano Conti is provable, perhaps any half-baked lawyer might argue your actions were performed under extreme duress."

The sheriff held the door open, and Dean followed in silence, not mentioning the evidence he'd collected over the years. Frankly, he needed a break from talking about Luciano and the syndicate. In no time at all, his whole life would no doubt be consumed with talking about little more than that.

The sheriff held Dean's cell door open, the heavy metal gate soon clinking shut behind him. He sank down onto the plastic mattress against the wall and buried his face in his hands. He'd expected anger and disregard, not the sheriff's compassion, much less his attempts to understand. And somehow, compassion and understanding hurt more—seemingly soft emotions—with enough aching precision to cut him to the core.

His thoughts slipped back to that little boy. *Him.* A black trash bag heavy in his hands, a bag containing a few sets of clothes and not much else. He'd needed compassion then, and decades on, compassion continued to duck away from him, leaving him on the losing side of any change he tried to enact.

The door outside his cell clicked open. He understood who likely stood across from him now. Watching. Waiting. His mind caught on the heat behind his eyes and his time "keeping peace" overseas.

Little girls, some babies, sold to older men. Some said to help with "domestic duties," but everyone knew different. The women. The children. They always suffered the most. And that night with his staff sergeant? Dean had only tried to intercept one moment of misery, but he'd fought an unwinnable war on more than one front.

An intense pain gripped his chest, and he sucked in a sharp breath, the wall he'd built to lock away his nightmares had a giant fucking crack in it. Nothing could stop the darkness from filtering through.

He lifted his head out of his hands, his gaze slamming into Sarah.

She stood some yards away, still watching, still waiting outside the metal bars.

"Why?" The question fell from her pale lips, the skin around her eyes red and splotchy. Blaine was beside her, his arm around her shoulder.

For one brief moment, he'd wanted life to be simple, and his brief moment had come at her expense. Of all the shitty things he'd done over the years, this was the worst, but all he could offer was a useless, "I don't know."

His husky voice scraped at his throat, dry and brittle. He wanted to give her a better answer, but it all sounded so selfish now.

He'd gotten what he wanted, what he'd *always* wanted—someone to give a damn about him. Somewhere he belonged…

She shook Blaine off and strode forward, the first signs of her innate inner strength bursting through. "Dean, just tell me why."

But he couldn't speak and his focus rose to her ruffled hair and down to the dried blood over her cheekbone. A wound she had sustained trying to defend him.

What an asshole. I'm such a selfish fucking asshole.

"Don't torture yourself here." Blaine padded to just behind Sarah, and he wrapped his arm around her shoulder again. "He's got nothing good to say. Let's go."

Blaine shot Dean a tight look, one that was deserved and spoke volumes about how little he thought of him.

Still, Sarah pushed him away again.

"No. Despite what you all seem to think of me, I'm not crazy. I know this man." She lashed her glare at Dean, one that once again commanded him to speak. "Go ahead. Tell me I'm not crazy."

But her sanity wasn't what she really wanted him to endorse.

What she really wanted to hear was that she hadn't imagined the goodness in him.

But he saw nothing good here. Not *in* him. Not *for* her. Even if his time in Harlow had briefly convinced him otherwise, the ordeal at Maynard's only verified he'd lost sight of who he was years ago. All he'd ever done was pretend. Until, of course, reality inevitably caught him.

"I'm sorry." His apology fell from his lips, habitual, low, and weak. What more could he give her? So, he turned to Blaine. "I'm sorry to you too, and I'm glad you got your woman in the end. I guess, good or bad, the past finds us all, eventually."

His attention stayed on Blaine long enough to see the man's expression fall, his posture turning slack like he hadn't expected any kind of remorse. At least that was one absolution to all this.

Meanwhile, Sarah shook her head, and her eyes glistened again, like she didn't want to hear him confirm the truth of who he was and what he'd done. Or maybe that this really was the lackluster ending they would get.

She shuffled forward some more and clutched her fingers to the steel of his cell, her knees collapsing beneath her, as she slid to a defeated crouch on the floor. A once strong woman, *broken*.

Yet another thing to haunt him through the years.

For the longest time she said nothing. Her tears fell from her eyes, those eyes squeezed shut while she pressed her forehead to the bars, her sobs mostly muffled. She tapped her forehead against the metal, as though that might end the pain or the reality, ripping him to shreds in the passing minutes.

He'd wanted her. Wanted the life she'd offered. Blinkered himself to the consequences of what loving him entailed.

Love?

He scrubbed his hand over his face. The sheriff had called him empty in the skull, and now Dean knew why. As always, he sat ignorant to what went on within. Within him. Within Sarah.

She'd vouched for him, publicly, when she'd expended so much energy making it clear she wasn't the type to fall easily. Though nothing about this relationship was easy, he'd fallen too, and almost certainly first.

Blaine hunched over her and hooked his hands under her armpits, helping her stand. "Come on. Don't cry."

His third attempted exit held far less vitriol than the others, like maybe he'd twigged there was so much more here than a bad guy taking advantage.

This time, Sarah did as she was told, even though she shook him off so she could walk on her own. "I'm not crying. I don't cry."

Her gaze hit Dean, and she stopped just before the door. The scrunched heartache was gone from her face, replaced with something harder and more unreadable, her old and familiar defenses seemingly restored.

"I hope you stay in a cell forever." She pressed her trembling lips together for a moment, as though her harsh words hurt her as much as they did him, evoking more pain than he'd experienced in years—not since that little boy pushed alone into the world by a mother who'd perhaps never cared.

But Sarah did care.

So maybe the hurt here was worse.

She released the tension in her lips and drew a slow and shaky breath. "I didn't want to love you, but you let me, anyway. So, for that —for the years of hurt you've lumped on me—I hope you stay in a cell forever, and I hope my face haunts you for just as long."

Thirty-Eight

"Oh dear, no one expected you'd come in tonight."

Sarah ground her teeth together and blinked in silence at Maureen. The *no one* in her statement suggested *everyone* had been talking about the fight between Dean and Blaine, with her thrown in the middle. She shouldn't have expected any different, but four days had passed, and she'd hoped some of the frenzy might have died down.

The misery of being at home alone, bored, with too much time to think, had gotten to her. So, she'd come to work seeking an escape. But an hour into her shift, everyone still kept staring at her. The incessant whispers laid the sympathy and speculation on her far too thick, each person stuck somewhere between pity and fear.

A wash cloth still lay clasped between her fingers, and she slapped it down onto the bar top, leaning a hip against the counter's edge. At least Maureen here dared to speak to her. "Did you all think I'd hide forever?"

Then again, she'd given a criminal a reason to stay in town. *How fucking embarrassing.* Everyone's fear wasn't unfounded.

"No, of course not, dear." Maureen patted her hand over the bar, perhaps because Sarah didn't get close enough to let the woman touch her. "Work can be one way to heal a broken heart."

Sarah took her gaze away and stared down at her hand over the cloth. Words of sympathy were hard enough; words about her broken heart were unbearable.

I wish Dean never happened.

An all-too-familiar swelling took up space in her throat, and she swallowed at the permanent lump there—the discomfort, as always, refusing to budge. In the wake of her break up with Blaine, she'd been adamant about never wanting to fall in love again. The problem with Dean, there'd been no choice. Love had just happened. It had dragged her, kicking and screaming, into happiness and misery unlike anything she'd experienced before.

Frank sat beside Maureen, Aggie on the other side, the next to speak. "I for one don't blame you."

Sarah scoffed. Blame her for what? Falling for Dean? Or just for entangling the whole town in his trouble? As much as the old woman attempted to comfort, her statement only confirmed that some people *did* blame Sarah for *something*.

"That's right. We were all wrong." Frank spoke, though Sarah kept her gaze lowered and couldn't see him. "We all assumed Dean was a good guy, and ouch—"

She flicked her gaze up to Aggie glaring at Frank and Frank rubbing his arm, the action suggesting Aggie had pinched him into shutting up.

Aggie's words, and her intervention now, left Sarah wondering. Did Aggie know about Sarah's doubts? That, as much as everyone here, including her, wanted to paint Dean as an out-and-out evil person, a gentler internal voice kept reminding her that she knew his story. That he'd tried, in a roundabout way, to tell her who he was.

Like a naive fool, she'd ignored all signs. And *still* like a naive fool, she wanted to believe she knew the man. That some of what they'd shared had to be real.

Her stomach roiled and a good portion of her energy left her body. That she still felt *anything* for him even though he'd hurt people close to her. He was a monster and now he was turning her into one too.

And even as that harsh sentiment worked its way through her brain, another part of her still clung to the sheriff's kernel of hope. That

Dean might bargain his way to freedom, that he still had the potential to turn into the man he'd claimed to be.

What a mess.

How could she pin her hopes on potential?

How could she ever want him near her or anyone she cared about again?

She rubbed her cloth against the already clean counter, her movements jerky, uninterested in speaking about what had happened. Even if no one here did blame her, she blamed herself. For all her caution, she'd let yet another disastrous relationship become far more than it ever should have.

She growled under her breath and pushed the cloth away, unwilling to answer why she'd done any of what she'd done. Shared a bed with him. Shared intimate details of her life. Shared a giant piece of her heart that she would never get back. It was far easier to tell herself over and over again that Dean was a bad person with no redeeming traits.

She turned from the group, not offering so much as a final glance or goodbye, unable to voice any words as she headed for the kitchen and bolted for the back door. Outside, an aptly empty field stretched into the darkness ahead, the night lonely and hollow.

She pressed her back to the brick wall and slid down to the step. She pressed a hand over her eyes and tried to escape from the fact that she, Sarah Overton, had devolved into a cowering and emotional mess.

Where once she took pride in her inability to shed tears, now, she simply couldn't stop. Sleep evaded her. A perpetually crushed feeling surrounded her heart. All this over a man—a man she'd met just weeks earlier. A man who'd left her, alone, humiliated, her world forever changed and not for the better.

And despite all the evidence, what she hated most was that she still cared. Still wanted to know he was okay.

She rummaged through her tight jeans pocket for a tissue only to come out empty-handed, so she swiped at her eyes with the back of her hand. It didn't matter what her heart wanted. The fact was Dean had lied to her. He was in prison. There was no reclaiming what she'd lost.

Best to get that in my stubborn head. Stop sniveling. Get up and get on with life.

If only getting on was that simple.

"Frank told me I'd find you here."

She jolted and peered up at Blaine standing over her, his lips pressed in a tight and lopsided smile, his hand outstretched in an offer to help her up. She swiped at her eyes again and reached for his hand. "I can't believe I fell for it."

"You didn't fall for anything." Blaine squeezed her shoulder and made a shooshing sound, his attempt at helping her find some calm. "You took a risk, and it didn't pay off. It happens to the best of us."

"No, no. I'm sure this stuff only happens to me." Tension pulled the muscles on her face, probably making it obvious she included him in *the stuff that only happened to her.* "I was sure he cared for me too. The fact I even care—"

Blaine pulled her in, allowing her to bury her face in the soft fibers of his gray flannel shirt. "Shoosh now. From the looks of things, he did care about you."

She shook her head and mumbled into his shoulder. "So now you're on his side? How can someone who did all those things really care about anyone else?"

"I don't know." He drew a slow, tense breath and patted her between the shoulder blades. "You spent a heck of a lot more time with the man than I did and have a better sense of his nature. Don't get me wrong, I'd kick his ass all over again if I could, but you know, I guess it's possible for a person to be two things at once?"

She stepped out of his hold and nodded to the ground, just as Blaine gave her shoulder a gentle squeeze. "Sheriff Marlin stopped by my house earlier."

She peered up now, at his mouth pulled into a tense smile, his spare hand jammed into his jeans pocket. "He wanted to check if Emilia was holding up okay. And she is. After all that's happened, she's developed a pretty thick skin, but the sheriff dropped by for another reason too... He wanted to tell us Dean's been released."

"What? How?" Her pitch slipped from her control, and she

stumbled back a little. "It's not even been a week and all those things he did…"

Both hands now shoved into his pockets, Blaine scrubbed the toe of his boot into the dry dirt. "Turns out he had quite a story and a whole bunch of information to turn in about some criminal kingpin. That information checked out, and he cut a deal. As long as he continues being helpful throughout the investigations and trials to come, he gets to keep his freedom."

Sarah frowned, struggling to believe what she heard. "And what's to stop him from simply disappearing?"

"No idea. Seems you're not the only one he made a good impression on." Blaine's lips curled in a sign of jest, and for the first time in days, she mirrored the humor. "Sarah, if he comes back to town, do you plan on reconnecting with him? I'm only asking for safety's sake."

"No." She shook her head at the ground again. "No. There's just too many lies to sift through. Too much I'd have to overlook."

"Okay." He gripped her shoulder again. Another undeserved show of support. "In case you start having doubts, just remember Emilia and I are here for you. Believe it or not, we might find it in us to be objective. From what the sheriff had to say about Dean, I kind of feel sorry for the guy."

Sarah snapped her attention back to Blaine's face, his expression unexpectedly open and relaxed. "He attacked you and played a part in taking Emilia away ten years ago, then came back to Harlow to finish the job." A manic sort of laugh tore through her. "Meanwhile, I'm drowning in guilt over being the reason he stayed in Harlow."

"Hey." Blaine held both hands up as if to profess innocence. "All I'm saying is I know what it's like to be a victim of circumstance. Dean might have played a part in me being forced out of LA, but he wasn't *the* reason. If it hadn't been for him that night, Anthony would have found someone else. And don't get me wrong, I'll probably always be suspicious of the man, but if you think about it, his lot in life has been horrendous. I can't begrudge him that."

She held a long silence while she stared Blaine down. How was it that he could dredge up forgiveness so much easier than her? Was it that he'd had ten years to process the worst of what Dean had done, while she'd had mere days? She couldn't say her gripe with Dean was more personal than Blaine's. The man had literally pulled him away from the love of his life.

"You're being awfully forgiving here."

One corner of his lip rose. "All for selfish reasons. Emilia and I have wasted enough years holding on to anger and what-ifs. At some point, it's impossible to hold on without turning that hurt onto yourself. Sarah, you should try letting go a little too sometime. Even if you do decide to justifiably keep your distance from Dean."

She held his gaze for a moment more, a man she'd loved, but perhaps in the wrong way—a love that still existed, even though it had changed to an extreme degree. She gave another small nod, still confused but a little lighter. Who'd have guessed that a man who'd broken her heart could also help soothe it?

He stepped into her now. She wrapped her arms around him, comforted that at least someone else in this town saw the man behind the crime, even if she had no intention of forgiving Dean. Not for what he'd done to her, anyway.

Blaine had the biggest reason, other than her, to hold a grudge. The fact he didn't, meant maybe she hadn't been completely irrational for falling for someone so critically flawed. Maybe she too would get to a point where her heart didn't hurt so much—where she could trust her judgment once more.

They pulled apart, and Blaine followed her inside where she bought him a drink and finally settled into the rest of her shift. Though he didn't stay long, her next few hours passed quickly, and she even stayed back to close up.

With the venue cleared, she wandered about the dining area lifting chairs onto the tables, making room for the morning cleaners to access the floors. A dull click cut through the space. The sound emanated from a far-off point toward the back door, as though someone had entered, even though Gordon had left over half an hour ago, and she *should* have been alone.

Thirty-Nine

In less than an hour, Dean had gathered his few belongings into a pile beside his front door. What little furniture he owned would be delivered to a local charity within the week since the time had come for him to truly disappear. Properly this time. He couldn't leave any clues to connect this life with his next, and only the detectives investigating the syndicate knew how to contact him and where his next stop would be.

The message he'd received from Ramos to get the hell out of Harlow only solidified the decision to leave. The fact that the message had been sent two days ago, before he'd gotten access to his phone, meant he needed to hurry his exit along. Hell, he'd been damn lucky to survive his short but protected stint in prison as it was.

He stood before his couch now and zipped his last bag of belongings closed, ferrying it over to join the others, where he paused at his door to take one final look around. This house and Harlow had given him so many memories in a short amount of time—good *and* bad memories—the bad stuff all his fault. And Harlow could have been any other middle-of-nowhere town, except Sarah had made it so much more.

He wouldn't have cared about leaving if not for her. That's what hurt most about all of this. More than getting caught. More than having a target on his back. He'd hurt *her*. Was leaving her. She no longer wanted him and was safer and better off without him.

And then there were her parting words…

"I hope you stay in a cell forever, and I hope my face haunts you for just as long."

No doubt his face would damn her for all the wrong reasons. Not because she loved him but because she rightfully hated him.

He squeezed his eyes shut at the assault of emotions bringing an ache to every breath. Best to get this over with. Best just to leave. He picked up two bags and made his way out the front door. His car waited just ahead on the drive when the thud of footfalls brought Ramos's message screaming back to life.

Get the hell out…

A heavy weight slammed into his back. *Too late.* He crashed forward, his chin striking the hard ground covered in spiky grass. He groaned at the air forced from his lungs. At the sharp pain of his teeth smashing together. At the heaviness still pressing on him.

Get the hell out…

Yes, he had to fight. Had to escape.

So, he released the two bags still in his hands and kicked and rolled, slamming an elbow up as he did.

Another grunt. Not his this time. He flipped fully to his back, his gaze slamming into Andre Ivanov. One of Luciano's guys.

Fire burst in the pit of Dean's stomach. Revenge had come to his doorstep. The angry glow to Andre's eyes said as much.

Dean struck out, his fist connecting with Andre's ear. "You've come a long way to fight a rich fucker's war."

The man reeled but remained on top of Dean. Andre recovered quickly and flung his weight forward, using his forearm to crush Dean's neck. Dean coughed and spluttered. Andre's sneering face drew nearer. "And of us two poor fuckers, one must die, yes?"

Andre's thick Russian accent filled Dean's ears, and he wanted to shake his head, but he managed nothing more than to gasp for air. Air that didn't come. His face turned inordinately hot. His skin and lungs burned in the effort for breath. He would die right here on his lawn.

He bucked, sending Andre off-kilter, bringing the man's face even closer. Dean threw all his effort into thrusting his head upward, sending his forehead into Andre's already crooked nose.

The man flailed backward, his arm disconnecting from Dean's neck. Loud gasps of air filled Dean's lungs. He coughed against the discomfort in his throat, all the while fighting to stay focused on Andre, who still remained seated on his belly, the fucker's nose now pissing out blood.

They'd worked together a handful of times. Dean had nothing against Andre, except that Andre stood in the way of Dean's refusal to let Luciano snuff him out like every other sucker in the past.

As if the others didn't fight back too?

Sure they had. But he was done being a stepping stone in other people's rivers, collateral damage on the way to getting what they wanted. Usually inane things like more booze, money, a shitty relationship… There'd been his parents. The sergeant. Then Luciano. Dean wouldn't take anymore, so screw them all, including Andre here.

He swung a right hook at Andre's head, flinging the asshole sideways long enough for Dean to shuffle out. He scrambled onto his elbows on his way to standing, only for Andre's heavily booted foot to sweep the ground from under him.

He hit the lawn again, though at least he had his hands free to catch him this time, and he kicked a leg out, hoping that blind kick would land somewhere in Andre's vicinity. A low scream validated his hope. He rolled onto his back and sat, grimacing at the sight of Andre clutching his nose again. Hit twice in the same spot, likely on a bone that was already broken…

Andre's warning about one of them having to die had Dean scrambling to his feet. He couldn't waste time. So, he ran for his car. Like a man on fire. Like his life depended on this escape. Which it did.

Not just his life.

A whole host of lives.

Even Andre's.

All the people Luciano and the syndicate would hurt if Dean failed to survive. If he could just get to his car and away from Harlow. If he could just live long enough to attest to all the evil he'd recorded and witnessed over the years…

He lunged for his car and pried the door open, throwing himself into the front seat and then gunning the engine. He jammed the gearstick into reverse, his front door still open and now forgotten.

Even as he roared out of his driveway and his house faded around a corner, even as he escaped Andre alive, one glance through his rearview mirror revealed a white sedan trailing a block behind.

This ordeal was far from over.

———

"Gordon?"

Sarah turned toward the kitchen and glanced through the pass to see who had entered the back door. Gordon had clocked-off ages ago, but maybe he'd come back. Maybe he or one of her other staff had returned to grab something they'd left behind. Maybe the cold nerves rippling under her skin and bringing a weakness to her muscles was all for nothing.

And still, I have a bad feeling about this…

She paused in her tracks and listened. Nothing. Even though she'd definitely heard the door click shut, followed by footsteps, not all that long ago. She took a deep breath and shook her head. Time to stop overthinking this.

A set of swinging doors separated the patron area from the kitchen, and she strode through, determined to get on with closing the bar. While the back door sat slightly ajar, no one else was there. Maybe her panicked mind had imagined the footsteps. Recent events meant she wasn't thinking straight, so maybe someone simply hadn't shut the back door properly, and the wind had blown it open.

She crossed the kitchen, grumbling to herself to get a grip, only to pause at the night air blowing through the door. An eerie chill crept over her skin, followed by an inexplicable warmth, like someone stood beside her, so close their body heat touched her skin.

Wait. Didn't I check the door not ten minutes ago?

She froze. She could turn—confirm that this feeling was once again her mind playing tricks on her—but what if she was wrong? She trekked her gaze up the wall to her left, to the change in light and a diffused shadow looming over her shoulder. *Holy shit. Run!*

She gasped and stumbled forward, pushing the door wide. Not fast enough.

An arm latched around her shoulders and lifted her off the floor, but she swung at the space behind her head, her knuckles connecting with the edge of someone's jaw.

"Fuck!"

For a moment, she thought maybe Dean had come for her, but the male voice didn't belong to him, and this guy smelled of cigarettes. Dean didn't smoke. An instant pain cut into her knuckles, but she didn't have time to ponder the ache.

Another hard arm hooked around her waist. She was dragged backwards and wild screams tore from her throat, tears streaming down her cheeks as she caved to her panic.

The crushing grip around her body established an intent to hurt her, so she swatted out toward the stocked shelves, trying to gain purchase on something—*anything*. Her hands connected with cans and glass bottles, many of which crashed and shattered on the brown tile floor until she ran out of shelves altogether.

An almighty shove came at her back, and she found herself tumbling through the open freezer room doors, her hands and knees hitting the cold, hard floor before she scuttled forward, but not in time to stop the heavy metal doors from slamming shut, locking her in.

Forty

DEAN PEERED at his rearview mirror again, the white sedan, an Alfa Romeo, roaring behind him and incrementally gaining. He clutched his steering wheel with one hand and used his other to pat the pockets of his cargo pants, thanking fuck he hadn't lost his phone in the scuffle with Andre.

He switched his gaze between the Alfa and the road, making sure the Alfa stayed behind him while he used the voice command to make a call.

"Hello?" Peter Marlin's voice held a confused note.

"Luciano's in town."

"Dean?" The confused note deepened, maybe because Dean was the last person the sheriff expected to receive a call from. "Wait? What?" A shuffling sound took over, denoting movement, like the sheriff already sprang into action. *Good.* "Where are you? Where is he?"

Dean glanced at his mirror again. "He's here. As in, trailing me at speed down Sherwood Road. I'm leading him to Mirabelle Falls, but he's not working alone. So if you've got anyone else on duty tonight, call in all the help you can."

"Got it. Where exactly at Mirabelle can I find you?"

"The bend, just after the picnic grounds. We're on the move, but I have an idea on how to stop him, so you need to get here fast."

"Right." The slam of a car door cut over the sheriff's voice, followed by a siren. "On my way."

Dean hung up and tossed his phone to the console. From his glimpses through the mirror, he'd gleaned Luciano had a driver, some guy with a mean-as-fuck glare. Meanwhile, Luciano's expression remained generally unaffected. Maybe because he'd been in the crime business forever and had seen and done everything there was to do. Maybe because, unlike his driver, this night didn't necessarily have a live-or-die price tag attached. Maybe Luciano was just an arrogant, ignorant fuck, who could only envision an end where Dean died with a bullet between his eyes.

Maybe the man's not wrong.

Two against one. And Luciano's car was built for speed, unlike Dean's.

The road straightened and now ran parallel to Mirabelle Falls. He planted his foot hard on the accelerator, trees flickering past his driver's side window, the glow of bugs catching his headlights in the dark while he waited for the river to come into view.

Luciano's car grew louder, the sedan eating up the distance on his right. His heart raced, the breakneck speed stoking a knowledge of just how this could all go wrong.

The river glinted against the moonlight to his left—his approaching destination a small win in a near impossible setup. The mob boss himself had traveled across the country, which meant the mission to kill Dean had long turned personal.

Luciano likely didn't know about Dean's arrest. That information had been suppressed, so why was he so invested? Because Dean had tried to break away? Because he hadn't followed orders and served himself up for literal termination? Because Luciano's fragile ego couldn't allow for others to go their own way?

I guess his suspicions are right. I've already sold him for my freedom and to spare any other poor soul that might cross his path.

Not that Dean had any regrets. Any moment now, the cars would be level. Though he tried to take up as much road as possible, Luciano's car would gain, and that's when he would start shooting.

A sudden jolt ripped Dean's attention to his side mirror and Luciano's car ramming the SUV's back quarter panel. The active part of this attack had started. Dean's car fishtailed along the road, and he fought his steering wheel to gain control.

The swerving caused his car to lose ground, and he turned to his left to find the sedan's front windows at his own.

Fuck!

He swung his wheel hard, a dull thud came, and the sedan wobbled and fell behind, the two men getting a taste of their own bitter medicine. *Just what he needed.* If he could hold them off, if he survived the next couple of minutes, he might survive altogether.

The Alfa roared again, inciting him to stomp the accelerator. Both cars hurtled on, the unfinished and bumpy road sending rocks and dirt pinging into the body of his car. Within seconds, Luciano's car came level with his.

Dean's passenger window exploded. He swore and ducked, a bullet hole appearing in his windshield about ten inches from his head. A lucky miss. Or unlucky, for Luciano. So, Dean took that luck and swerved his car again, ramming the Alfa until its tires edged the ditch on the other side of the road.

Within seconds, the Alfa righted and caught up to Dean once more.

"Pull over." Luciano's muffled voice crossed over his driver and through Dean's shattered window. "Holloway, you're gonna wanna pull over."

He could have laughed at that. As if he'd ever stop. But Luciano called out again. "We've got your woman. Pull over."

The muscles over Dean's chest bunched, and an instant sickness kicked him in the gut.

How would Luciano know about Sarah?

Maybe he was bullshitting, gambling on the off-chance Dean *did* have a woman.

Then again, Harlow people loved to talk. A couple of hours in this town, and Dean had learned about the soiree, about Emilia having

Blaine… Given recent events and the scene at Maynard's, it wouldn't be hard to find someone willing to share gossip.

"Let me see." Luciano's raised voice battled against the rumbling wind. "Green eyes. Pretty blond. A feisty one, that's for sure. I'm told she put up a good fight."

Dean clenched his jaw and swung his car into Luciano's again. The fucker was lying. He had to be. Hell, one trip to Maynard's and any fool could have figured all those details out with just one tiny interaction.

"Give in now, Holloway. Or I'll have Sarah pay the price."

Sarah.

He said her name. That name from his mouth brought a higher panic, and Dean's body turned cold all over. He couldn't assume anything. Couldn't continue as though Sarah was safe. Not until he saw her again with his own eyes. Free and alive. And yes, his survival would save lives, but *right now* one life lay at imminent risk.

But even Luciano's request for Dean to give up wouldn't fly. Giving up wouldn't stop anyone from putting a bullet in his head, much less Sarah's, with death by bullets the nicer outcome. First there would be torture—hours and hours of soul-crushing pain.

He swore again and slammed a fist into the steering wheel. As much as it seemed he should mull through the options, there was only one way out of this. He *had* to escape. Had to hope the universe bucked its trend of screwing him over. Maybe then he might live long enough to confirm Sarah was okay.

Between the engine sounds and rushing wind, a relative silence filled the space, so he turned to Luciano's car and finally addressed the man.

"Don't hurt her." He jutted his chin toward a structure up ahead. "I'll turn myself in. Just stop by the bridge up there, okay?"

Luciano gave a small nod and flicked a hand onward. The bridge, a small wooden structure, had room for only one car at a time. Luciano's driver did the logical thing and slowed, allowing Dean to inch ahead, so Luciano could eventually stay behind and keep track of his new hostage.

Dean kept the SUV at speed and waited for the nose of Luciano's car to slip back to the half way point of his. That's when he slammed his foot to the brake and swung his steering wheel hard to the left, clenching his eyes shut as the tail end of his car slammed into the Alfa.

Both cars spun in opposite directions. The SUV crashed into the bridge's thick end pillars, a loud *crack* a testament to the damaged wood. Dean's chest bounced into the steering wheel and then ricocheted him into his seat, his back smashing into the leather and his mind swimming before he swung around to track the trajectory of Luciano's car.

The sedan still skidded across a grass patch, the side soon slamming into a giant oak. Just like Dean's car, Luciano's bounced, but no bridge caught him, and the Alfa Romeo did a quick slide down the river's embankment.

A heavy and quiet moment passed—Dean's body turned numb through a clash of adrenaline and relief. Maybe he *would* live. But his life meant little if Sarah didn't live too. And if they *hurt* her…

He had no idea where she was or if she was even still alive, but he couldn't think on that, or he'd fail to be any use to anyone. So, he leaned across the middle console and pulled the glove box open, his Glock quick to slip out and greet him.

He might have made a vow to never kill again, but there were special circumstances for everything, and if he had to put a bullet in Luciano's head to end all this, he would.

But first, find out about Sarah.

He kicked his door open and ran to the embankment. The Alfa Romeo's hood lay submerged under the river's murky water, the entire front end sinking fast. Luciano had somehow made it to the back seat, and he struggled with the back door. His driver lay slumped over the steering wheel, dead or passed out.

Dean held up the Glock and called out, "Don't move."

Luciano ceased with his frenzied movements, his wide stare colliding into Dean.

"Please." Luciano darted his gaze about, the car sinking and sinking fast. Still, he didn't move. Even this idiot could see a bullet would kill him before the water ever did. "We'll call it even. Just get me out."

Dean's focus caught on the end of his Glock, Luciano still in his periphery. For the first time ever, he was alone with this fucker, a loaded gun pointed at his head. "Where's Sarah?"

"One of the newbies has her down at her bar." Luciano's breaths were rugged and rushed. Meanwhile, Dean's had turned shallow and near non-existent.

"She's still alive?"

Luciano nodded.

A new silence took over. A frightening kind of calm.

Dean had the information he needed. He could kill Luciano—just wipe him off the face of the earth, never to bother anyone again. Luciano had chased *him* after all. So, a classic case of self-defense.

Faint sirens wailed in the background, likely the sheriff. Meanwhile, Luciano held stock-still, his gaze clinging to Dean as though he read what went through his head. As though he too had been in this position—with the unfettered chance to take out an adversary, once and forever—all Dean had to do was squeeze the trigger.

Then again, the only difference between him and Luciano was he had never crossed that line.

Being in Harlow, meeting Sarah, he'd seen a world so far from the one he'd known. Killing this man, however evil, would be a backward step away from everything he'd escaped the day he decided to stay in this town.

The sirens grew louder. The sheriff was less than a minute away.

Dean stepped back but kept the Glock in position, his retreat a sign that Luciano could exit the car. The man shoved his door open and a flood of water rushed in; he waited, then battled the current and mud until he fell to his knees on the banks.

Luciano pressed a hand over his black pants pocket.

"Hold still." Dean stepped closer. "Or I'll put a bullet in your head."

"Calm down, you fucking maniac." Luciano shook his pocket until a water-logged cell phone fell out onto the wet grass beside him. He peered up at Dean and gave a crooked smile. "Looks like I can't call off the dogs. You'll have to go to the bar and get her yourself."

Dean ground his teeth together just in time for a flood of light to hit him from behind, the sheriff's siren now blaring in his ears. His own car might have been banged up, but it was at least still drivable. "You never should have dropped Sarah into this mess. If something has happened to her, sheriff or not, I'll come back here and put a bullet in each one of your vital organs."

Sensing the sheriff behind him, he stepped back, but in typical Luciano style, the man couldn't help but get in the last word. "You gotta be quick, Mr. Holloway. I hear they're keeping her in a freezer."

Forty-One

SARAH HELD a huddled position next to the freezer's door, as far from the shelves of frozen goods at the back where the temperature was perceptibly colder. Her breaths puffed in thick clouds around her, and the icy air made each of those breaths sting, each inhalation a testament to her new goal of staying alive as long as possible.

If only she hadn't left her phone in its hiding place under the bar's counter. *Stupid woman.*

Then again, she'd never tested the reception inside the freezer, so maybe the thick metal walls would block her from calling for help. Though, at least having a phone could have told her how long she'd been locked in here, or maybe she might have found some game on the device. Something to distract from the pain of wearing little more than a white work shirt and black jeans. She was cold, so very cold. And the psychotic man who'd shoved her in here likely waited just outside. So really, she was doomed no matter what she did.

How long could a person survive sub-zero temperatures like this? Was she here because of Dean? Had his past come looking for him and claimed her too? Maybe the guy outside intended to use her as a bargaining chip to get him. Or maybe they'd just slowly torture her to torture him…

She slammed her eyes shut at that thought and tapped her forehead against her bent knees. Chances were, the guy who'd shoved her in here, just like her, didn't know how long she'd stay alive in this freezer. He just trusted luck that when he finally did open this door, she wouldn't fall out in the form of a human popsicle.

An icy cracking sound came from one of the food products on a shelf, once again reminding her of where she was and the harsh conditions that would likely claim her. A tear trickled down her cheek. She'd planned to upgrade the freezer. To get one with an internal safety release so that getting trapped inside would be impossible. But things like that weren't a huge priority among all the other costs of running the bar. She'd simply never gotten around to it.

Did a different freezer even matter, though? If she didn't die from hyperthermia, the freak outside would have gotten her some other way.

She used her sleeve to wipe her tears. Extra moisture was the last thing she needed in these icy conditions, and why she didn't jump on the spot to keep warm. Growing up in Minnesota, she'd learned a few things about handling the cold, like that people could die simply from perspiration speeding up the freezing process…

Freezing process?

Oh hell. This was really happening.

A panicked sob wrenched up her throat, just as a new and terrifying thought struck her.

What if the man outside had nothing to do with Dean?

What if this was just a run-of-the-mill robbery?

One where the guy who'd put her in here had already left?

She turned around, her knees digging into the unforgiving concrete, as she slammed her fists against the hard metal door. The dull *thunk* confirmed its immovable hold and for what felt like the hundredth time, she cried out.

First came anger, that someone could be so callous with her life. Next came hopelessness, a drowning emotion that left her sagging against the door, her forehead tipped to the glacial steel as more tears came. Within this echoey and bleak chamber came the realization that she really did have nothing left to do now but wait to die.

Dean pushed against Maynard's back door, only slightly relieved that, unlike the front, this one moved. If one of Luciano's cronies waited inside, a new one at that—there was no knowing how the next few minutes would play out, and he needed a silent entry.

Gun in hand and positioned to use, he nudged the door a fraction wider, the hinges creaking and forcing him to hold still. A first glance inside revealed a man pacing the kitchen, his back turned and his black leather jacket marking him as not someone from around Harlow.

The man began to turn, and Dean's heart beat pounded loud in his ears. Maybe the guy had heard the hinges creak because he lifted his hand, his fingers curled around the grip of a gun. Dean didn't think. Didn't need to. He aimed and shot.

The air filled with an explosion, followed by a crimson mist.

"Ahh. Fuck!" The crony clutched at his upper arm and swung around fully.

His dark stare hit Dean, his face scrunched in angry pain. "What the hell did you do that for?"

Dean lowered his weapon, his muscles suddenly weak. "Ramos?"

Adrian Ramos pulled his palm away from his arm, his hand covered in blood. "Thank fuck you're a shit shot, Holloway."

Dean strolled in and peered around the room. "Anyone else here?"

Ramos shook his head, striding toward a roll of paper towel on a bench. Meanwhile, Dean clapped his friend on the back, his form of an unspoken apology.

As bad as he felt about shooting the guy, Ramos would survive, and the wound was nothing more than a deep graze. They both knew the shot could have ended a whole lot worse, one major positive in the whole shit-show that had followed Dean to Harlow. "You're Luciano's newbie?"

Ramos pressed a ball of paper towel to his shoulder and nodded. "How else do you think I got that warning to you? Getting hired was the best way to keep track on his vendetta against you, and I figured, with you gone, the low-life scumbag would jump at extra help. Hell, I even lied about being a private detective and a cold-blooded killer to get the gig, and it's just blind fucking luck I could wrangle my way into this job. So, I'd say I deserve more than a freakin' bullet in the shoulder for my trouble, don't you?"

"I'd offer to shout you a beer sometime, but I think, at the moment, I'm about as unwelcome in this bar as you are." Dean pulled his attention from Ramos and onto the freezer. "Is she really in there?"

Ramos nodded. Dean swore under his breath and stormed toward the freezer door. "Why the fuck did you put her in there?"

"Relax. I meddled with the temperature. She won't freeze." Ramos's footsteps pounded behind Dean. "Besides, your woman is a fighter, and in case Luciano came back, I figured it was safer to contain her than expect her to play along. I always planned on helping her escape. And if all this went pear-shaped, the last thing I needed was your old lady identifying me as part of the syndicate."

"Ever heard of blindfolds and ropes, dumbass?" Dean held his hand to the freezer.

Ramos kept his mouth shut long enough for a muffled scream to come into focus. *Sarah's scream.* Pitchy. Broken. Desperate.

For all the savagery she'd encountered today. For everything he'd put her through in the days and weeks prior. He'd always banked on being able to simply slip out of town and out of her life. That she'd be just fine without him. But trouble followed him, and nothing he touched escaped unscathed.

She wasn't dead, but her cry belonged to someone who thought they would die soon enough. A cry he'd heard before, all those years ago in the service. A cry that sank metal claws into his heart and pointed blame at him for all her trauma.

This wasn't how he'd wanted any reunion to go.

There was no telling what awaited him on the other side of this door.

Forty-Two

SARAH PRESSED herself deeper into the wall behind her, her breaths exploding and her already chilled skin prickling into goosebumps all over. She'd heard the bang. A gun. Followed by a male scream. Now, the fear of being left in this freezer faded, and a wilder terror took over.

She squeezed her hand over her mouth, stifling another sob, doing all she could to remain silent. *Undiscovered.* To listen. To remain forgotten. All while her every regret played on her mind.

Why had she used her mother's breakdown as an excuse not to get on with her own life? She'd stepped right into her mom's empty shoes. Seen so little of the world. Kept people at arm's length. Made them jump through so many hoops just to get to know her, installed so many obstacles that most gave up. Except Dean hadn't.

What a fucking mess.

She held her breath and listened closer to the two voices outside the freezer. Despite all instincts to run, because there *was* nowhere to run, she stepped back and stood her ground, attempting one final chance at freedom.

If the nut-jobs out there want to shoot, I won't make murdering me easy.

The freezer creaked, a low suction noise breaking through as the door shifted just a fraction open. She didn't wait for whoever tried to enter. *No.* She bolted full-pelt toward the door and slammed her weight into the heavy metal—that heavy metal swinging hard into whoever stood outside.

A torrent of swears filled the air, but she ignored everything and focused on slipping past. She kept her head down, didn't see anyone or anything but the open back door across the kitchen, offering escape. She barreled toward it, only for a large hand to lash out across her waist and halt her exit.

She grunted and kicked, her heel hitting a man's shins while his scent of leather and spice assaulted her senses.

"Ouch." He swung her around and sent her back into the freezer. "Calm down already."

Not the freezer again. Her voice broke on an unplanned cry, and she flicked her chin higher, determined to stare down her would-be murderer before she died.

"You?" She stumbled back, almost tripping. "You did this?"

Her cheeks trembled, and hot tears gushed down her face. Dean stood before her, gun in hand, her former lover blocking her escape. She'd loved him. Hadn't she loved him?

Her shoulders rolled forward and a sense of defeat engulfed her. How had it come to this?

There's no hate greater than a lover scorned...

But *he'd* lied to *her.* Lived his double life.

So maybe Dean, her captor, had been this gun-carrying monster all along.

"Please." She held a hand out, her attention falling to the gun while the angry stage of her grief bled into bargaining. "Please don't."

His heavy brow dragged even lower, a cross-hatch of lines forming in the middle. Rage or confusion? Her legs didn't wait to find out, folding and introducing her knees to the floor as she fell to a pleading position before him.

His cheeks turned slack, and his gaze trekked down to the gun in his hand, his attention soon flicking back to her. "Sarah, get up."

He crouched to the ground and laid the gun down, pushing it away so it slid far from easy reach. Meanwhile, her mouth slid open and her muscles softened, less high-alert, more bone-tired from adrenaline.

He held an outstretched hand to her and his fingers shook, his pupils wide, like her trusting him now actually meant something.

"No." She shook her head, her focus lifting to the blood over his chin. Oh, that's right, she'd smacked him in the face with the freezer door. *Well, good!* She had no idea what was happening here, but she knew she hadn't inflicted a fraction of the pain he had on her. "You're the reason I'm in here."

She stood, rejecting his help.

"Sarah." Her name was a raspy whisper from his lips, and now she was the one standing over him.

But she refused to even look his way, so she brushed past him and stormed out of the claustrophobic freezer, into the kitchen's blinding brightness, and toward the back door with its fresh night air and freedom.

On her way past, she snatched her wool coat from a nearby wall hook and jammed it on, her legs picking up pace and taking her outside, past the back steps, and through the long stretch of grass leading to the parking lot.

She greedily gulped at the fresh air. For so long, she figured she'd never see the stars or even Harlow again. Tears fell and new panic set in. A woman who could taste freedom but wasn't there yet.

I never used to cry. I never used to cry. Not until him…

"Sarah. Stop. It's over." Dean followed after her, his longer stride swallowing her lead.

"No." She continued to run. "You sick fucking bastard."

"Sarah, you weren't—"

She didn't want to hear it. Just shut him out. But the panic. Oh, the panic had other plans. Plans she couldn't control. She wanted to keep running, but the tears kept coming, and a new sickness rocked her belly.

No matter how much air she drew, her body took over, and she had no choice but to stop running, her hands landing on her knees while her tummy convulsed.

Before she knew it, she was vomiting onto the dry grass at her feet. Vomiting and crying. Not a pretty sight by any means, but screw *pretty*. Screw Dean. He deserved to see what he'd done to her.

The sickness stopped, but she stayed doubled over, the only thing to straighten her being the growing sound of Dean's footsteps. She flicked her gaze to him and the same hollow-cheeked expression he'd given her inside the freezer and shook her head for him to leave her alone.

She marched on, digging through her coat pockets for a tissue and swiping at her mouth when she found one. The parking lot felt a million miles away, and none more so than when the fast thunder of footfalls raced behind her once more.

She turned to tell him to go to hell—even that place too nice for him—but she found herself encased in a wall of immoveable muscle. It took a moment to realize he wasn't fighting her, he was hugging her. In that time, she was the one to fight, wanting to break free.

"I hate you." She pounded her fists into his chest, a series of movements that exhausted her while seeming to have no impact on him. "Do you understand? I hate you." She punched at him again, one stinging blow after another. Not once did he move or stop her. "That whole time, I thought I would die."

Her endless tears. Her face felt on fire. The sort of fire that burned no matter her efforts to douse it. Then again, Dean deserved her anger, even though her tirade now grew weaker and weaker.

She swung at him all the same, his arms still locked around her but with enough space to let her lash out until she tired completely.

"I'm sorry." He lifted one hand and cradled the back of her head, his apology a mild murmur as he pulled her closer. "I'm sorry." His light whisper disappeared into her hair, and something about that softness, coupled with her sheer exhaustion, had her body sagging into him. "I'm sorry. I'm sorry. I'm sorry…"

She gave a final half-hearted struggle, and he dropped a gentle kiss to the top of her head, each apology stealing her will to fight until she gave him all her weight and an altered cry took over—one so broken and lost and ripping from a place deep within her.

"It's over. I promise, it's over. I don't ever want to give you a reason to look at me like that again." He stroked a hand over the back of her head, gentle, as though she might break in his hold, even if she did consider herself already broken. "Like I might hurt you."

His familiar masculine scent and strong embrace, the forlorn look in those cobalt eyes—each detail was a reminder of what she'd had— that reminder pushing her toward what she wanted most. The path of least resistance. *To forgive him.* As if forgiveness could make all the pain mean something. To have *been* for something.

But not every argument needed a resolution. Not every misdeed deserved her forgiveness. And the restlessness that had poisoned her life of late, would not settle until she shared her bitter truth with the man who'd upended her quiet existence.

"You've already hurt me." She stepped back and ran her palms over her eyes, eyes that stung in their raw and swollen state. "And now, I don't want to look at you at all."

Forty-Three

DEAN HAD RETURNED to Harlow to pack up his life and let Sarah go—but seeing her now, seeing what he'd put her through—he couldn't just leave. His future quite literally backed away from him, her jaw trembling and skin flushed from her tears. Even as his conscience screamed that he didn't deserve another chance, he would grasp at one, anyway. *Because he loved her.* Because she was the culmination of what he'd been headed toward his entire, miserable life.

I don't want to look at you at all.

Those words latched to his soul like rusty old hooks, a long-worn ache drawing him to her with the knowledge that backing away would only intensify his pain. She never wanted to see him again. Frankly, why would she? Yet, she didn't turn away. Didn't run through the night to throw herself into her car and leave him in the dust of Maynard's nearby parking lot.

"We don't need to do this." His voice took on a life of its own. Despite all her justified anger, she'd softened in his arms just seconds ago. That meant *something*, didn't it?

He spoke some more, hoping to get through to her. "Please, Sarah."

"Let it go, Dean." Her voice came out weak and husky, and her halting retreat betrayed her words. "Just let it go."

"I can't." The buckling resignation in his tone surprised him, but then of all the things that had happened in his life, *this* one left him the most helpless.

He strode closer. She jolted and blinked, then shook her head as if coming to her senses and turned away.

"No one here will ever forget what you did." She stalked away, and he trekked the several yards to her car where she wrenched her driver's side door open and played out his worst nightmare. "They'll hate me even more if I stick by your side."

She pulled a water bottle from the holder in her door and took a swig, swishing the water about in her mouth before spitting it to the ground. The action doused his moment of panic that she might leave, all whilst igniting a light within him, one that made the corners of his lips twitch. Her water swigging and spitting wasn't exactly ladylike, but he didn't want ladylike, he wanted *her*. *Her* with all her brash and fragile confidence. The strength and beauty he'd rightly gleaned off her that first night.

She paused, staring at him, her brows knitting together while she took a slow and proper drink from her bottle. "I can't believe I just puked in front of you."

A small laugh escaped him, her comment another sliver of hope, even though his heart clenched at what he'd done. He'd put her in a dangerous situation. Failed to live up to his promise to keep her safe. The puking and crying and unmissable fear... he'd put her in a position where she'd genuinely believed she would die. And if Ramos hadn't intervened, maybe she *would* have died.

She stared at him, her eyes narrowed as though she read what went on in his head. "You're asking for the impossible."

Despite the sinking feeling opening up in his chest, he drew closer and pulled the water bottle from her hands, tossing it into the car, before putting his finger under her chin, and forcing her to look at him. "You took me home that night at the soiree thinking there was no way we would become more. You were sure we wouldn't work. But we *do* work, Sarah. When there are no external forces in our way, we work damn well. Isn't that what all this has been about all along? Doing the impossible?"

She shook her head. "Not like this."

"No. I understand that. And I will spend the rest of my life apologizing to you and the rest of this town for what happened, but Sarah…" He shifted his hand from her chin and cupped her face. "Do you really want our lives to go back to what they were before we met?"

Her posture sank and she broke eye contact, her gaze drifting to some lower point. "I honestly don't know. Maybe?"

A small scoff escaped him, though not at her indecision so much as his reaction to the inescapable truth. "You know, there's not a damn thing either of us can do to return to who we were before. Both of us, we're changed, though maybe that's not such a bad thing. I can't speak for you, but I don't want to go back. Not for anything. Especially not without you."

Her expression dropped, but the tension around her eyes suggested an element of internal conflict. He knew this woman, could feel the defiance flowing from her.

"You don't know me as well as you think."

But just as Ramos had learned, she was a fighter, and she didn't give up or take the easy way out of difficult moments, and Dean honed in on that trait.

"I know you were lonely." He stroked his thumb over her cheekbone, trying to smooth out the strain. "Just as I was lonely. As bad as this all is, we match. In some crazy, unexplainable way, we match."

She shook her head. "I don't know if it's enough."

Even with that denial, she leaned her cheek into him, hinting that she wanted him to convince her. "Sarah, tell me what I have to say to get you back."

"What can you say that will make everyone in Harlow, much less me, accept your apology or forget?" Her expression crumpled, and she tore her focus off him once again. "And the worst part is, I still want to. I still want to believe you're a good man, that your past never came out to hurt me and the people I love. How am I supposed to forget any of that?"

Her question cut him like a knife to the heart, the sharp sting eclipsing the miracle that she even still spoke to him. "You won't forget. Neither will they. I sure as hell never will." He paused, questioning whether he did the right thing, but there seemed no other future than the one he wanted with her, that future the only thing he'd ever truly wanted. "But there is something you've always known."

She tilted her head and gave him a sidelong stare. "What's that?"

"That even before my past came back for revenge, that past is mostly all stuff that happened to me, not who I am. I was never anyone other than the man you met. The man you fell in love with."

Her expression stilled, only to widen in a suggestion of shock. "I'm not—"

He shook his head. She didn't want to admit to loving him. He even understood why. But she'd refused to deny their relationship in the wake of his arrest and gone out of her way to vouch for him. Now she stood here, in her roundabout way, begging him to persuade her to stay. She'd fought for him, and he'd be damned if he didn't return the favor and fight for her right back.

"I've spent ten years being an outcast. If I have to, I can deal with people in this town not liking me." He dared to press his forehead to hers, fulfilling his unspoken duty to persuade her. "There's only one person's opinion that matters all that much to me."

She raised a brow, though her face took on an element of levity. "You know it's not that simple. People's opinions do matter. I still need to run a business in this town, much less live here."

His lips curled into his first heartfelt smile in this whole encounter. "Fine, we start with a little market research, then take things from there."

She narrowed her eyes at him again, rightfully skeptical of his obtuse reply, though the slightest grin lifted her cheeks and made her scowl more playful than critical. "What are you suggesting now?"

"You. I start with *you*."

The low rumble of Dean's voice crossed the thin space between them, his intimate tone melting yet more of her defenses, even as logic screamed at her to jump into her car and drive away. As much as she wanted to, as much as she tried, he held impossibly close, the warmth of his body a welcome comfort against the night's cold wind.

He drew in and touched his nose to hers, flooring her with just how much she wanted him near. How much she wanted to stay.

Hope. A poisonous thing. Something she'd tossed aside a million times before, but not today. Why? Because this night, the moon and the stars, all reminded her of the *other* nights they'd shared, the good nights far outweighing the bad. And his words…

I was never anyone other than the man you met. The man you fell in love with.

She slammed her eyes shut at the haunting statement and hope once again prodded her, made her feel like maybe, just maybe, things would work out.

"I'll start with you, Sarah." His voice called for her to open her eyes, and she did, near drowning in his beautiful blue gaze as he spoke again. "I won't stop giving you reasons to trust me until the day you wake up and realize you believe me. That everything about this last week is an old and tired memory, and the best choice you ever made was to stand with me while everyone in Harlow learns they can trust me, too."

"I don't know if—"

He dipped his chin and deepened his stare, a stare that demanded she take a moment to truly absorb his words rather than blindly react.

New water pooled in her eyes and she nodded, really weighing up what she might lose if she didn't at least try to reroute her habitual tendency to shut down any type of potential disappointment. "You seem so confident you can pull this off."

"Maybe I shouldn't be." He paused to wipe a fallen tear from her cheek, his gaze still holding hers, melting her doubt into a cool puddle at her feet. "But the way I see it, the rest of my life is one long chance to get it right."

Her lip trembled, and she bit down on it to keep from devolving into more tears. That sentiment tweaked at the week she'd had, coupled with all her rejection and years alone, holding together a life no one else in her family wanted.

"What we have, it's intense and uncontrollable." She paused, trying to get her head around all the complexities before she committed to anything. "You know I don't do so well with uncontrollable."

"Yeah, I know." His gaze bounced about her face, as though he sought a sign, any sign that she might say yes, those full lips of his holding an unrestrained smile. "But I'm clearly not so perfect either, so maybe we could cut each other some slack?"

A spontaneous laugh burst from her, and she shook in his hold. The adrenaline from tonight's ordeal, and her nerves over what he asked, got to her. And then there was the prod of what *she* wanted. *Him.* "This is going to end so badly."

He returned a quick nod and laughed too, the breeze ruffling at his dark hair. "Oh yeah, it really is. We're two walking, talking disasters, and the people of this town are probably sharpening their pitchforks as we speak. But you were the one to make me okay with letting my old life go, remember? The price of change I was willing to pay. Though I never wanted you to pay, too. So, let me make it up to you. Let me help you let go, as well."

For the longest time, she did nothing but frown back at him, his pupils wide and hope-filled, while she weighed up how to say no.

But then she imagined her life as it had been. Never having a place or person she belonged to, how close she'd felt to belonging with Dean —how the core of the man she'd begun to fall for really was still there. Always there...

She was strong and resilient Sarah Overton, wasn't she? She could handle a little vulnerability—could handle unpredictability. She'd survived before. She'd survived tonight. But she wanted more from life now than just surviving. And when she separated Dean from his past, from the violence of this week, he'd given her more than she'd ever dreamed of.

"You know, if it weren't for the sheriff, and even my pain-in-the-ass ex being on your side, making me feel like maybe I wasn't totally out of my mind for caring about you..." She smiled, lifting her hands now and returning his embrace, her heart swelling, while his heat finally seeped into her cold and rattled bones. "I'd be more likely to run you over right now than say what I'm about to say..."

His pupils narrowed, an element of his enticing wickedness coming through. "And what's that?"

"First, that while you've been quick to point out how much you think I love you, you've given a bunch of apologies and not nearly enough claims of your own love for me." He moved to speak, but she shook her head, cutting him off. "Second, when I commit to trying something, it's impossible for me to be half-hearted about it. So, *if* I do say yes to *trying* to make a relationship with you work, you have zero chances to mess up again, got it? You better damn well not let me down, or I swear to the devil herself, I *will* run you over."

He let out a chuckle and caressed her face with an endearing level of firmness. "Shit, woman. I've had literal bullets flying at me tonight, and even those weren't half as scary as you are right now."

She tilted her chin down and stared up at him, holding back a chuckle while she warned him to let loose with the promises, or else…

"Dean…"

"Sarah…" A smile tugged at his lips, one he soon let run wild into a foolish grin. His dimples finally shone through, and that sweet expression caused her heart to do a quick double beat. "I love you."

Everything within her stilled. As much as she'd told him to say it, those words nevertheless floored her, the entire world seeming to disappear.

Those words spilled forward. Free and easy. As though he'd kept them safe his entire life just for her. And maybe he had, because right then, in that moment, her tears spilled again. Happy tears. And he leaned in and sealed his words with a kiss, one that devoured her with force and significance, his hands pulling her in and crushing any last speck of doubt.

He pulled away, his smile softened, and this time when he spoke, emotion seemed to turn his voice into a rough whisper. "Sarah Overton, I love you."

Epilogue

Epilogue: Two months later

Sarah smiled at Dean seated beside her in the bleachers at Memorial Stadium, a midseason baseball game playing out on the field. The Harlow Braves played the Marston Giants, and in light of recent events, her brother, Chip, had come home from Boston to reconnect with her and to not-so-secretly suss out Dean.

Chip, also a more-than-decent baseball player, stood at the plate. In her years away from the tennis court, he'd taken over as the family's overachiever, both in sports and through his software engineering major at MIT. Sarah wasn't all that surprised when he swung the bat and hit a home run.

The Harlow crowd roared and he threw the bat, bolting past the bases and back to the home plate in no time at all. Dean shuffled beside her for what seemed like the millionth time, his behavior generally unsettled all day.

She leaned into him and whispered through gritted teeth, "You okay?"

This was his first large-scale social event since that dramatic week where Blaine and Emilia had outed him as a former syndicate member, only for the syndicate itself to come looking for him. She could kind of understand his discomfort.

"I'm fine." He reached across and patted her knee. "Just have one of those feelings, you know?"

She peered up at him and raised a brow. "Ahh. No. I have no idea what 'feeling' you're talking about."

He kept his attention pinned ahead, posture still stiff and jaw equally rigid. "Never mind. Hard to explain. Just feel like something big is about to happen."

She chuckled to herself, shaking her head. What was with his staccato phrases?

He turned to her and smiled, a hard worker who hadn't let adversity stop him, yet still carrying the pressure to reinvent himself in the eyes of this entire town. Things hadn't been easy in the days after everyone found out he was staying.

Even as she'd learned of Ramos and his involvement in saving her life, there'd been little time to thank the man properly. He'd decided his presence would cause Dean more problems and promptly returned to LA with promises to visit Harlow when tensions died down. Given the deluge of side glares and painful silences that followed, he'd been right. Though no one was outwardly horrid to Dean, it was clear many wanted to keep their distance.

So, she'd come up with the idea of setting him up on a stool at the bar, and anyone who gave him time and a chance to explain, got a free drink. Of course, the idea horrified Dean, but bless Aggie, she'd been the first to throw her hand in the air and quite literally cuddle up to him.

The sheriff had been next, though without the cuddling. The mood at Maynard's truly changed when Blaine and Emilia went next. Emilia had shed tears, her full-circle moment clear to everyone when she threw her arms around Dean and parted with a smile. More and more people approached him after that.

The "redemption" stool remained at the bar for a full month, and one by one, Dean won most people over, all while he insisted on paying her and the bar back for each drink. Now he and Sarah fielded lunch invitations more than they did glares, even though a small minority of people still weren't convinced, Ally included.

Meanwhile, Dean's years of storing evidence proved invaluable to the case against Luciano Conti. Luciano's East Coast syndicate arm was fast falling apart, many of his cronies having bailed the day the sheriff arrested Luciano. Dean's corroboration meant he was able to negotiate a reopening of his military case.

A lot of his service peers had retired over the years and didn't have to fear professional repercussions, which meant new hope they might start talking about what they saw the night of Dean's altercation with his sergeant.

Sheriff Marlin had discussed maybe retiring in the coming years if Dean's case went well. His past charges were limited to misdemeanors that would be cleared if his case reopening went well. He'd be starting over with a clean record, and his military training, and even his experience with the inner workings of the syndicate, made him a good candidate to take over as sheriff if he wished.

Sarah stared down the row of seats to her right, her gaze catching with Blaine's. He gave her a gentle smile, his arm wrapped around Emilia, while Ally sat next to them busy watching the game. Sarah smiled back at Blaine, her hand over Dean's on her knee. Somehow things had worked out for her and her ex-fiancé.

She turned toward the field where play paused for a break, her brother running up the bleachers in her direction. Eventually, he puffed and stood before her, his hands on his hips, and his hazel eyes glinting. "Did you see that?"

"Sure did." She nodded and rose, instant joy taking up space in her chest while her brother wrapped her in a hug. "What did college do to my weaselly little Chip?"

He laughed and pulled away, adjusting the blue baseball cap crammed over his dark blond hair. "I do occasionally step away from my computer."

"Seeing as you moved into my house three days ago, and this is the first time anyone in town has seen you, I'm going to assume you're not joking when you say *occasionally*." She waited as he laughed again and ripped off his baseball cap to swipe sweat from his brow.

While Chip used her house to work on some special software project, she'd moved into Dean's—a win-win situation since she got more time with the man she loved. Well, between her shifts at the bar and him trying to establish things with work. She'd even started to genuinely consider applying for local funding to set up a tennis program in Harlow, so unlike her, residents of all ages wouldn't have to go out of town to learn or play.

Chip's smile faded a little, and she followed his gaze to Dean— firmly lost in his own world, his unfocused attention still pinned forward.

"Hey." She nudged him with her knee. He blinked and snapped his gaze to her, yet still said nothing.

"I think the man's seen better days." Chip maintained his cheeky grin.

She frowned at her brother before inspecting Dean again, his face lifted and his expression tight, as if he had something serious to say to her but couldn't bring himself to say it.

Oh no. Her heart sank and she shook her head, her mind running over the last couple of months and every horrible thing that had happened.

What now? What else could go wrong?

Chip had a goofy grin on his face, one he pointed at Dean, only adding to her confusion. "You better come out with it, man. She looks like she's about to curl up on the ground and cry."

She scowled at her brother, but Dean gave him a slow, resigned sort of nod, his hand disappearing into his pocket.

Despite what Chip had said about *her* going to the ground, Dean slid from his seat and onto one knee. The softened edge to his gaze had her backing away, the slight tick of his cheek through his sheepish smile turned her insides all weak and pained. She continued backing away, but Chip caught her at the shoulders. "You're gonna wanna stay for this, sis."

She gave a numb nod, her attention glued on Dean, for once in her life merely doing as she was told.

"Sarah Overton." A quick hush took over the hundred or so people around her, Dean's voice holding a low and raspy tone that still somehow made her feel like the only woman there. "This might seem a bit fast, but I can't imagine any other future or even a single day without you. So, please—if you need me to, I'll beg—but please, will you marry me?"

A pitchy laugh tumbled from her lips. One that made her sound momentarily manic, her hand flying to her mouth before her laugh turned into a strange sort of laugh-cry, and a swell of tears washed down her cheeks. "You're sure about this?"

He nodded, the tension on his cheeks slipping away in a look of empathy. "Never more sure."

Chip gestured to the world at large. "Hey, sis. A bunch of these people are going to fall straight outta their seats if you don't reply soon."

She peered about at all the gaping and wide-eyed faces staring back at her before scowling at her brother, that scowl holding no real malice. "You knew about this, didn't you?"

The stupid grin on his face grew even wider. "A good best man knows how to keep a secret."

Her jaw dropped open, and she turned to Dean, another incredulous laugh breaking passed her messy tears. "Best man? You're already making plans?"

"Plans…" Dean shrugged. "Dreams…" He produced a loose ring, with a thin, yellow gold band and a small blue sapphire edged with white diamonds, from his jeans pocket. "What I don't have is an answer."

He smiled now, and those stunning blue eyes of his glittered. She shook her head and laughed again, lighter this time, while she leaned down and cupped his face, pulling him up so he stood before her.

Much to everyone's apparent despair, she drew the waiting out a little longer, wanting to savor the hope on his face, this moment like a gasping breath at the end of a long dive.

Despite all the Harlow residents leaning in to hear what she would say, Dean was close enough that she could whisper her answer for him alone. "Yes, Mr. Holloway. Yes. Yes. And yes."

Instant relief spread through her body, releasing a strain that had been there for years. Dean swept her up, and her feet dangled as he unleashed a full-bodied kiss. A roar of cheers exploded all around her. Suddenly, and for the first time ever, everything about her life felt right.

He lowered her to the ground and opened his hand, the diamonds on her ring glinting in the sun atop his giant palm before he placed the ring on her finger.

She turned to Chip. "Happy with yourself now?"

He shook his head all too eagerly. "We're not finished."

Trumpets erupted around her—*literal trumpets*—and she startled and spun toward the field where Harlow High's marching band entered the pitch flanked by cheerleaders. She turned to her brother to say something, but he was busy gawping into the crowd—his line of sight leveled on Ally Egan, someone who'd meant so much to him, and someone he hadn't seen in ten years.

Chip marched off, ignoring the band, and Sarah laughed, slapping her palm playfully to the solid wall of Dean's chest. "For a rough, tough man of mystery, you sure are a dork. A really big dork."

"The best part is…" He nuzzled into her and pressed a kiss to the top corner of her forehead. "I don't have to pretend any more. I'm your dork, you love me, and you're stuck with me."

She tilted her head against his shoulder and watched the show ahead, happy tears still rolling down her cheeks because, despite all odds and assumptions, she and Dean had learned from each other. Not all stories were set in stone. At any moment, something or someone could come along and unlock a whole other future, one fuller and brighter than anyone could foresee.

"You bet I love you. And Dean Holloway, you're stuck with me, too."

THE END

JOIN TO GET A FREE NOVELLA AND EXCLUSIVE KATERINA SIMMS MATERIAL

Building relationships with my readers is one of the great joys of writing, it keeps me from turning into a robot! My newsletters are filled with information on new releases, cover reveals, sales, giveaways, and news relating to my series.

To claim your copy simply go to the "Free Book" page on my website.

www.katerinasimms.com

Also by Katerina Simms

The Love at Last Series:

The Last Heartbeat — Love at Last, Book 1

The Last Place You Look — Love at Last, Book 2

The Last in Line — Love at Last, Book 3

The Harlow Series:

Sapphires and Secrets — The Harlow Series, Book 1

Second Hand Secrets – The Harlow Series, Book 3

For latest releases, go to:

https://katerinasimms.com/books

Or QR code:

Katerina Simms is a contemporary romance author and RWA Emerald Award Finalist; originally born on a sunny Mediterranean island, only to move to the weather-challenged suburbs of Melbourne, Australia.

Tea addict, nature lover, and terrible gardener, Katerina's novels feature vivid modern settings and heart-stirring characters, punctuated with the occasional good laugh. Her romances skirt the edges of women's fiction, and her favorite tropes are opposites attract, slow burn, and heat with heart.

www.katerinasimms.com

How About A Review?

Authors love reviews, and good ones help us make a living, and thus write more books! If you've enjoyed this book, please consider leaving a review on Goodreads or your retailer of choice. Just a line or two would make a wonderful difference!

Eternally grateful,

Katerina Simms